I0571272

Library of Dreams

Edited by

Charlotte Ashley

LIBRARY OF DREAMS

Copyright © 2013 Charlotte Ashley

Compiled and edited by Charlotte Ashley

Cover art by Lisa Bagherpour

Cover design by Maya Starling

All rights reserved. The stories in this collection remain the copyrighted property of the individual authors, and no material in this book may be copied or reproduced in any form or by any means, including information storage-and-retrieval systems, without the express written consent of the author, except for brief quotations in critical articles and reviews.

These are works of fiction. All people, places, events, and organizations are the product of the authors' imaginations or are used fictitiously. Any resemblance to actual persons, living or dead, or to any places, events or organizations is purely coincidental.

ISBN: 0615934463
ISBN-13: 9780615934464

CONTENTS

ACKNOWLEDGMENTS

Thank you to everyone who helped make this anthology possible.

To Wattpad, who brought us together and gave us our first platform to express ourselves and share our stories.

To Lisa Bagherpour (http://fairiegoodmother.deviantart.com), for her beautiful cover art.

To Laura Perry and Sarah Courtney for their help editing and proofreading the final drafts.

To Andrej Škvorc, for the domain and hosting of our website.

And of course to all the members of the PSG for their encouragement, advice, conversation and support before, during, and after this undertaking. Keep up with us all at http://www.psgpublishing.com.

The Typewriter

JC McDowell

❦

There once was a man who was loved by all.

The smell of onions and garlic filtered through the young girl's senses upon entering the old 1950s bungalow. The hardwood floor creaked with each step as she tried to sneak up on her grandfather in order to tell him about her accomplishment in kindergarten that day. As she walked towards the back room, the smell of her grandmother's gumbo in the kitchen was overtaken by the scent of Old Spice and old papers.

His office was shaded from the late afternoon light, with only a lamp glowing on the corner of his vast desk. The young girl turned her head left and right when she entered the room, but her grandfather was nowhere in sight. She held her prize between her thumb and finger, being careful not to get it stuck on her blue-and-white plaid school uniform, and shuffled quietly to the work table in the middle of the room. Her eyes and nose barely reached over the top of the table as she tried to get a glimpse of what he had been doing that day.

Various shades of black and white photographs were scattered across the table with notes labeling each one.

The young girl slid a photograph from the table and gazed upon a man with a funny hat and a fat nose. The note that stuck to the photograph was typed. She couldn't read full sentences yet, but the first few letters were H-U-E-Y. Not knowing anything of this man, she shrugged her shoulders and placed the photograph back on the table.

Keeping a keen eye on her grandfather's work, she walked around the table, where another photograph caught her attention: an overhead view of a Mardi Gras parade. She could only imagine the vibrant colors that dotted the streets. Returning the photo to its rightful spot, she stood on her tip-toes and glanced at the rest of the labeled photographs. A photo of a train curving on a bridge had the same letters as the first picture, but this was typed directly onto the photo instead of a sticky note.

Her interest was piqued by the typed words and she grazed her fingers over the letters. She pivoted on the heel of her navy blue Mary Janes and noticed a black machine on the desk behind her. She stepped on the hardwood floor as softly as she could and stood in front of the typewriter. Each round button held a specific letter, and each button shined like it was brand new - except for one letter. She couldn't tell which letter it was because the circular button had fallen off. Above the keyboard was a blank sheet of crisp white paper.

She raised a finger to her chin and tapped it, deep in thought. With a hesitant shoulder shrug, she reached up her finger and gently pushed the button. A dulled, skinny silver bar rose slowly with the pressure of her finger on the button. She released it and watched the bar fall back down.

A small smile eased up her face. She touched the

button again with more pressure and watched it fly up, meeting the paper with a loud tap. The sound startled her, but peering closer at the paper, she saw the letter A. She lifted both her hands to tap on the keys, but she was hampered by the sticker she kept tightly between her finger and thumb. A thought sprang to her mind, and she grinned proudly as she placed the shapely red sticker dead center of the typewriter. She puffed out her chest and scooted up on the chair.

Since she knew where the A was now, her fingers hovered over the little round buttons and began pecking the alphabet on the typewriter. She found new buttons with numbers and another button that, when held down, could make big letters. She danced to her little pecking tune as she sat in her chair, not noticing anyone until a short glass of ice swimming in an amber liquid sat next to her. She jerked her hands back and tilted her head up. His warmth surrounded her when she saw his styled graying hair and his round frame. His reading glasses were nestled in the pocket of his short-sleeved, button-up shirt where they were always kept.

"Whatcha typing, Monk?" he said as the corners of his mustache quirked up.

She placed her hands on her lap, and with a gleaming smile, she answered, "I'm typing the alphabet, Pops!"

He peered down over her shoulder to study the paper, and the smell of Old Spice consumed her senses. "Well, gee whiz, you are! And you're doing such a good job!"

He squatted beside her, keeping an arm on the back of the chair. "You know, typewriters can tell a lot of stories, much like the photographs that I took." Her eyes grew with wonder as her grandfather grabbed a photo from the table and continued. "A picture is worth a thousand words, but a typewriter is worth millions."

Her jaw dropped as she looked down at her fingers, counting each one until she got to ten. She glanced back at him. "That's a lot." He nodded and smiled. She asked, "Pops, do you think I could write a million words?"

"Well, I don't see why not! You have a lifetime ahead of you. Keep pecking away, and one day, you'll get to a million." He stood up, grabbing his drink along the way, and took a sip, causing the ice to clang against the glass.

As he studied his pile of pictures, she said, "I'm just a little girl, Pops. I don't think I could type a million words."

He put down the photograph and glanced over at his granddaughter.

"Not only will you type a million words, but they will be put into many books. Everyone will want to own one of your books, if you put your mind to it. No one can tell you what you can't do. Only you can decide what you can and can't do. But if you're anything like your dear ole Pops, you'll be filling bookshelves across the world."

"Across the world?" He nodded at her question.

She shook her head before saying, "But Pops, I don't know all of those languages."

He cackled, and she beamed at him. "Come on, Monk. Maw-maw has the gumbo ready."

She hopped down from the chair and ran over to the door. She stopped before leaving the room. "Pops, I almost forgot!"

He looked down at her as she ran back to the typewriter. Her face rose into another proud smile as she pointed at the typewriter. "I got that in school today, and I wanted to give it to you."

Her grandfather crossed the hardwood floor and

peered at the bright red heart sticker placed in the center of his typewriter. He pulled her against his side, giving her a hug. She wrapped her arms around his belly and said, "I gave you my heart, Pops."

His eyes blurred with tears as he picked up his granddaughter. Carrying her out of the room, he said, "And you'll always have mine, Monk."

༄

Twenty-five years later, the young girl took on the daunting task of cleaning out her grandparents' house, but she couldn't bring herself to do the back room right away. The door had remained closed for years, so as to not disturb the memories. Now, knowing this was the last room, she stood in front of the closed door and took a deep breath. Her fingertips grazed over the old bronze knob, and finding the nerve she needed, she twisted and pushed the door open. The scent of Old Spice still lingered in the air with a hint of musty dust. Her eyes swept over the room, and her heart clenched with the memories of long ago.

A touch of red caught her eye, pulling her attention to the corner. Her heart lay on display for the memories that danced in this room. The floor creaked as she walked around his old work table, and she found herself peering over the typewriter, studying the missing letter. She ran her hands over the keys, and as her finger grazed the missing button, she pushed it down hard, hearing the tap on the paper. She studied the paper, and upon seeing the A, she remembered the day she had discovered the missing letter.

The chair scraped against the hardwood as she sat down. She hung her hands over the keys as her grandfather's words echoed in her ears. *"Only you can decide what you can and can't do..."*

The decision was made. The lingering presence of her grandfather gave her that last push. Her fingers pecked away, as the beginning of her story spoke through her fingers.

There once was a man who was loved by all.

ʚঙ

JC McDowell grew up chasing street cars around the city of New Orleans, Louisiana. She chased the love of her life to the foothills of the Blue Ridge Mountains where she discovered her dream to write. New Orleans beckoned her home again, where her dreams became a reality. Her evil twin, Jaycee Ford, is currently looking for homes for her romance stories while JC spends her days working in the city, continuing to chase street cars in her spare time. You can find JC online at https://www.facebook.com/AuthorJCMcDowell.

Dead Girl Walking

Kim Fry

∞

Myra found herself sitting at a bar listening to a group of enthusiastic drinkers at a nearby table. Despite the fact that she was painfully aware that at least two of the prescriptions in her bag were labeled with warnings against drinking alcohol, a beer sat before her.

Taking a sip, she turned slightly in her seat to watch people who were actually enjoying themselves. For a few moments, she envied the camaraderie they shared. She had entered the bar alone in her sleep deprived state.

A short time later, the bar was crowded and becoming rowdy. Myra had given up on watching the patrons, and instead watched the television recaps of whatever sports were currently in season. She wasn't really paying attention to that either. In a way, she was sleeping, staring at the flickering screen in a state that was calm and relaxed.

"Anyone sitting here?"

Blinking, the young woman made eye contact with a man with blazing green eyes. "Uh, no, you can take it."

Instead of carting it off as she had expected, he slid into it with a signal to the bartender.

She watched him from the corner of her eye as he ordered a beer and lit a cigarette. Carefully nursing her own drink, she felt a little uncomfortable. She could sense him staring, but she was too afraid to glance over.

"Can I buy you a drink?"

Myra finally looked over, finding a smile playing on his lips. She almost felt bad for him. Almost.

"I have a drink." She made a point of taking a sip. It was warm, but she managed not to make a face.

"Yeah, but it's almost empty. What's your name?"

"Not interested." In truth, it wasn't that she wasn't, it was that she'd given up on relationships. No one could deal with the sleep issues which had plagued her since childhood, so she wasn't willing to keep repeating that mistake.

The man's brow furrowed slightly, but he never lost his smile. "Is that spelled the same way it sounds?"

Myra fixed him with a pointed look, hoping he'd take the hint.

"Well, N.I., I'm Carson. *Now* can I buy you a drink?"

Maybe it was the smile, or the slight crinkle at the corners of his eyes, but she finally consented. He smiled triumphantly as he ordered her drink.

Two hours later, Myra felt herself pleasantly relaxed as they conversed. She switched to soda only, and Carson had rolled up his sleeves to show tattoos decorating both arms. This successfully kept her attention drifting back to the images and designs.

Something still weighed heavily on her mind. She knew that at some point, it would all end, and she would have to go back to her life. She would wake up, and it would all have been a dream. Kind of.

"Well, I have to be up early." Carson's tone belied

his disappointment.

With a chuckle, Myra nodded. "Yeah, me too." If only he knew how serious she was.

They exchanged phone numbers, but she knew she couldn't even consider attempting to start any sort of relationship with him. Technically, she wasn't even there. She couldn't properly explain it to people, but she was truly having an out-of-body experience.

As Myra made her way home, she reflected on her night. If she were a normal girl, she would have been elated at meeting such an exciting man, hoping he would call or text her. Instead, her sense of dread was nearly overwhelming, coupled with a sadness that could only be described as regret.

Climbing the steps to her apartment, she felt relieved to have made it home. She unlocked the door and wandered through the darkened rooms. In her bedroom, she flicked a light on and let out a heavy sigh.

Myra looked down at the sleeping form lying on top of the bedspread. The body lying in the bed was the true, living version of herself. Although the one standing at the end of the bed was true in physical feeling, it was just the restless form of someone who couldn't get a grip on sleep.

The pull was there - her sleeping body was pulling her back into herself like a magnet. Myra cleared her mind, imagining a calm beach on a sunny day. She found it helped ease herself back in. Once the two merged again, she was able to drift off into an uncomfortable sleep.

Only a few short hours later, the alarm was blaring, the sun was peeking through a gap in the curtains, and she forced herself to move out of bed. The taste of alcohol remained a dry reminder in her mouth, causing her to grab the bottle of water beside the bed and drink it down.

Myra already felt tired, though she couldn't remember a time when she'd actually felt like she'd gotten a good night's rest. She glanced at her Smartphone where a reminder had popped up. She had an appointment with her psychiatrist at nine.

She had already secured the time off, though the psychiatrist never really helped. He just prescribed amphetamines she couldn't take due to drug screenings at work. She had already explained this to him in depth, and had accepted a prescription for Valium and sleep aides instead, though they didn't work.

Myra had been diagnosed with a form of narcolepsy. The problem was that she didn't just nod off at random; she actually left her body and continued on in another form that was just as real to outsiders. She could be touched, could touch - she could carry on any activity in that form. The problem - aside from no doctor believing her - was that she didn't ever sleep. Whenever one body fell asleep, the other would hijack her consciousness and continue on. Which led her to bars late at night and conversations with men she could never have.

After a quick shower, Myra dressed in a business suit and brushed out her golden locks. She didn't do much else with the style, the loose waves already falling around her face. She didn't bother with makeup either; she had found long ago that she didn't really have anyone to impress.

Her phone beeped to signify a new text message. It was Carson - not a surprise - with a general 'Have a good day' message. She didn't bother responding. It was a waste of both their time if she fooled herself into thinking anything was possible between them, even as friends.

Myra made her way downtown, the steps so familiar, she could probably do it blindfolded. She had been using the same clinic since she was a child. Occasionally, the doctor would change, but it seemed the words they spoke never did.

When she entered the designated office, the receptionist looked up and smiled.

"Hey, Shirley. I have a nine o'clock with Dr. Sutherland," Myra said.

The older woman nodded, tapping the keyboard. "Okay, I have you all checked in. Have a seat. He should be out in just a few."

Nodding, Myra migrated to the waiting area and took a seat. There were a handful of others waiting as well. It only took a few moments before Dr. Sutherland - an aged man with a kind face - summoned her to follow him.

Once they'd reached his office, they took their respective places and the session began. "So, how do you feel?"

"Tired. Exhausted."

Nodding, he jotted notes down. "What about the medication I prescribed? How is that working for you?"

Myra shrugged. "I don't take it much. Most of that stuff turns up on drug tests, so they're hard to use. Even with a medical excuse, most places don't allow them to be in your system."

"How's the new job?"

"Well, I've been there two weeks and haven't gotten fired yet." She gave a wry chuckle. "Then again, I haven't fallen asleep on the job yet either."

More notes. "That's good. How are the dreams?"

She gave another shrug. It was a touchy subject with her because she knew they weren't really dreams.

Although she'd talked about them before, it was clear from the medication he had prescribed that he just assumed she was borderline schizophrenic. But if that were the case, and they were just dreams, how did she have a text message from last night?

"When was the last one?"

"I don't really dream anymore," she mumbled with little conviction.

Dr. Sutherland nodded, pausing in his writing for a moment. "I know we discussed the possibility of some hypnosis coupled with biofeedback therapy before, and I think now would be the perfect time to try it."

"Uh, I don't know, doctor."

He proffered a light smile. "I understand that you don't want to take the medication for your narcolepsy, but without some sort of active attempt to assist you, you'll be facing some bigger problems soon."

"Like what? I already fall asleep randomly. What's the worst that could happen?"

"Well, revocation of your driver's license, for one."

That sobering thought sunk in for several moments as they stared at one another in silence. "When do we start?"

Dr. Sutherland looked pleased. "Right now."

Myra took a calming breath, running a hand over her face. "Okay." Another breath. "Okay."

"You can do this, Myra. I think this could be the beginning of a new life for you. If we can get you to learn how to control your narcolepsy, you can effectively cure yourself."

Nodding, Myra didn't really feel as optimistic as he did. She wasn't sure she believed in all those metaphysical theories, but given the risk of losing her license, she couldn't afford to argue. That would make it more difficult to find a new job once she was inevitably fired from this one.

Dr. Sutherland dimmed the lights and called Shirley to request that she hold his calls. With a smile, he leaned forward slightly in his seat. "Are you ready?"

"Sure."

"Okay, close your eyes, and imagine a calm place. What do you see?"

Instinctively, Myra imagined her beach scene. She relayed that information to the doctor.

He continued to talk, to murmur things until she felt the pull of her inner self trying to escape. Fruitlessly, she tried to hold on, but she knew it would do no good. It was like a fresh breath of air when the two split. Myra was standing beside her seated self.

Dr. Sutherland launched back in his seat as he stared at what looked to be his patient's identical twin. He murmured some choice swear words beneath his breath.

"Well, doctor, either we're both crazy, or now you see what I have been talking about all these years. I am leaving my body."

The old man didn't say anything above a whisper, but she did hear the words "not possible" escape his lips.

"Yes, I know. Now, when I threw out the term 'Astral Projection' five years ago and you tried to send me to an institution, did you ever even think about what I was really talking about?"

Dr. Sutherland gained a little composure - and color to his paled face - and sat a little straighter. "This is phenomenal."

"*This* is a pain. *This* loses me jobs." Myra motioned to herself. "*This* leads to me wandering around town at night and never really sleeping. Can you help me control this?"

"Come here."

Myra did as instructed, passing by her sleeping form in the process. She reached her hand out and took the one the doctor had stretched out. He seemed shocked when they grasped hands just like two normal people. He examined her features closely, still looking as if he didn't believe that she could be both standing before him yet still asleep in the chair.

"Unbelievable."

"Yep. Can you fix it?"

"I - I don't really know." He grasped her hand again. "This, I've never heard of. I mean, I have heard of cases of purported metaphysical awareness - of out of body experiences. But never so literal."

"Well, it's literal now." Myra could feel rage boiling in the pit of her stomach. She had tried to explain everything five years ago, and no one would listen. Now that she was standing there, showing the doctor, he clearly had no idea how to proceed. "So, we've finally established that I'm not totally insane. What can we do about it?"

"Well, I'd like to consult with some colleagues, maybe have you do a demonstration."

"Uh, no. My name is not Sideshow Sally and I am not about to begin presenting this to anyone who will pay attention. Unless I'm charging admission - which I'm not. You can consult all you want, but I am not a hamster. I don't have a wheel to run in, and I'm not willing."

"It wouldn't be that. But I have to have some concrete proof, and what better way than to show them like you just showed me?"

Myra glanced down at her sleeping form. "Put me back and we can talk about it."

Dr. Sutherland nodded, though he hesitated for a moment. "Uh, I guess I'll go through the steps to wake a normally-hypnotized person."

"That might be a good place to start." Myra sat down beside herself, noting how odd it felt. Normally, she was able to feel the light tug of her own subconscious. Instead, she felt a strange sense of emptiness.

The doctor walked her through the steps that were supposed to pull her from the state of hypnosis. After a few long moments of silence, she opened her eyes to a perplexed look on the man's face.

"What?"

With a slight shake of his head, Dr. Sutherland offered only a weak smile at first. "Nothing. Close your eyes again please."

Doing as instructed, Myra went through the process a second time, again with the same results. She opened her eyes and looked at him expectantly. "What's wrong?"

An uneasy look crossed his features. "It's not working and I don't know why. I've never had an issue before."

Myra let out an exasperated sigh. "Great. What are we going to do now?"

Somehow, somewhere inside, she felt as if she'd been disconnected from her other half. She could no longer sense the presence of herself, and the most unnerving part was that her frustration was rooted more in the fact that the doctor couldn't fix it.

Dr. Sutherland began placing phone calls, leaving messages that grew more urgent with each new number he dialed.

"I hope you're not charging me for this," Myra grumbled as she waited next to herself. She stared at her features as she listened to his beseeching words.

The doctor only shook his head and called the receptionist. "Yes, please reschedule the rest of my appointments today. No, just reschedule. Thanks."

He was panicking and had finally given up the facade of being in control. Myra didn't know how to take that information. On one hand, at least she couldn't jump out of her body - she was already out. Yet, that didn't change the fact that she was stuck out.

Dr. Sutherland finally reached someone. He had a lengthy discussion, explaining the general facts of her case, though he was careful not to mention anything that might identify her. "Okay, but that's a temporary solution," he said. "Well, yes, it would work short term. Yes. Thank you, Dr. Richards."

When he hung up the phone, Myra noted that he looked more troubled. "The only thing I can do is research. There is no case of real astral projection that I know of."

"What am I supposed to do in the meantime?" She motioned to her other body.

"Well, I would like to put that one in the hospital."

Her brow immediately furrowed. "What?"

Dr. Sutherland let out a heavy sigh. "I need time to figure this out, and we can't just leave your body lying somewhere."

"Well, yes, I understand that part. Why can't I just take it home?"

"Your body? Don't be absurd. You've only ever jumped out for a few hours. What if it needs nourishment? We don't know anything about it. I don't want you to starve to death."

Myra scoffed. "Okay, but for how long? It's not like I can afford to be in the hospital - not even one of me. It's not like the other body is *doing* anything. It's just lying there."

"I will pay for it, but it may take a couple of weeks. And in the meantime, I need you to sign off on the treatment and any tests we do. The standard would be blood tests, but we would also want to monitor vitals and brain activity as well."

"Uh, okay. I guess it's not like I have much choice here."

Dr. Sutherland offered a well-practiced smile. "Very good." He showed her to the building's back exit and then had the secretary call a paramedic to come collect her sleeping form. He called later to assure her that she was well cared for and told her where she could find her body.

Myra found herself at home feeling more awake than she had in a long time. It felt as if she were actually rested. Instead of going to work right away, she sent a message to Carson and they met at a diner down the street for lunch.

"So, what made you decide to text me?" Carson asked.

With a smile, Myra gave a half-truth. "I have a sleeping disorder, but I'm trying a new treatment for a couple of weeks. I figured I'd go ahead and enjoy the next little while until my doctor screws me up again."

He offered a smile - the most genuine, heart-stopping smile she had ever seen. Somewhere inside of her, a feeling bloomed. What if she never jumped out of herself ever again? It may have been a false hope, but at that moment, she didn't care.

❧

Two weeks passed. Myra had learned to love sleep

again, and waking up feeling normal. She went offher medication completely, though something still nagged at her. What would happen when Dr. Sutherland put her back?

She was enjoying being normal. No more nodding off randomly, leaving her body behind, waking up unsure of what had happened. She grew more interested in Carson, though they were taking things slowly. She didn't want to get too attached, only to wind up having to walk away.

One evening, as Myra stood in Carson's apartment, her phone rang. She took a sip of her wine and grabbed for her phone. Not recognizing the number, she almost silenced it, but something nagged at her. She accepted the call and pressed the phone to her ear. "Hello?"

"Myra? It's Dr. Sutherland."

Her heart rate picked up immediately, hammering uncomfortably in her chest. She turned away from Carson and moved into the living room. "This is she."

There was a pause at the other end for a moment. "I wasn't sure if you would be there."

"What do you mean?"

"Do you feel strange at all?"

"No, why?"

Another pause. The discomfort grew exponentially. "Well, there's no easy way to say this. You died."

"What?" She half-shouted the words before remembering where she was and lowered her tone. "What are you talking about?"

He cleared his throat. "Well, no one is exactly sure what happened. Your... her heart just stopped. They're classifying it as heart failure, but we have another problem."

"What's that?"

"Well, you just died. I had to admit you under your name. They're going to call your next of kin and let them know that you passed away."

"Uh, what the hell does that mean? I'm still alive. I'm right here. How can I be dead?"

"It's complicated, but had I given out a Jane Doe description, they would have tried to locate your information anyway - and probably would have succeeded. I'm sorry, Myra, but there's nothing I can do to change this. There's no way we can explain that you are the girl they have a duplicate version of."

"Great, Doc. Thanks. Don't bother sending a bill." She disconnected the phone and headed into the kitchen.

Carson gave her a questioning look. "You all right?"

With a huff, she took a big drink of wine. "Apparently, I'm dead." She continued on, explaining from the beginning.

He took it much better than she had expected, but certainly didn't stop her when she said she needed to leave. She made her way home. She didn't know what she was going to do. Her family would come to clean out her personal things at some point - because they would think she was dead.

Myra packed a small bag and headed out her front door. She had no identity left. She had nowhere to go. She had been labeled as deceased and therefore stripped of her future. She needed to get out of town.

❧

Six months later, Myra sat at a table, looking at inkblot photos. The room was white, as were the scrubs she wore. A doctor sat before her, holding up each card and looking at her like she were a specimen. Really, she was. To the people in the facility, she was just a number - a lab rat without a life.

After leaving her apartment all those months ago, she had wandered for a while, but eventually returned to Dr. Sutherland, agreeing to meet his colleagues. The transition from there to the institute she sat in was short - so short, she barely noticed.

They ran her through a variety of tests, but could not determine how she had managed to project out of her body into another physical being, nor how she survived the death of what they referred to as her "host body."

Myra ached for her old life, even with all of its flaws. She wondered about the things she could have done and the future she no longer had. She was in the present, and was stuck there. She was just a carbon copy of who she was, because that other body had died.

She had overheard some discussion about a possible military contract - if they could get her to either project again or give details regarding how to do so. The problem was, she didn't have the problem anymore, and she didn't know how she had done it to start with.

Myra was alone, not really special or unique anymore, but she also didn't have a place. She missed her friends, the people who treated her like a human being. She even missed Carson, the little time she had spent with him. The resentment had become a large part of who she was. The doctors there didn't care that she had once lived outside of those walls; they simply wanted to know how she felt and if she had somehow miraculously rediscovered how to do something she had never learned how to control before.

As she was returned to her room, whispers followed her.

"There she is."

"That one? She doesn't look dead."

"No, she died, but she jumped out of her own body."

"She cheated death, that's why she's here."

"How did she jump out of it?"

"She died."

Myra took the words in, tears slowly beginning to brim over and spill down her cheeks. She glared at them in passing, wishing she could make them all shut up. The doors slammed shut behind her. She was no one, with no name. A dead girl who was still very much alive.

"Dead girl, walking!"

ೞ

Kim Fry is a wife, mother and writer who makes her life in Casper, Wyoming. Her work is currently posted on Wattpad at http://www.wattpad.com/user/KimFry. *Her horror/thriller Scream for Him won the 2012 Watty Award for 'On the Rise' in horror and made it to the second round of the Amazon Breakthrough Novel Award Contest. It has been read on Wattpad nearly 1.5 million times and will be published in 2014. Kim writes many genres, with numerous other fantasy, horror, thriller and paranormal stories in the works. You can find her at* https://www.facebook.com/AuthorKimFry.

Dream Job

Miloš Petrik

☙

She walks in front of a French window, straight into
the golden sheaf of sunbeams. Clive can barely see her
face in the bright sunlight, but her form is highlighted,
girt with amber, her sublime shape clearly outlined
beneath the light summer dress. Turning towards him,
she takes a few more steps and walks into the dimmer
light at the centre of the room. Suddenly, Clive can see
her face; her eyes of deepest, darkest, brown, her soft
lips, her every blemish, every wrinkle, each imperfection
of the skin woven into a harmonious visage fit for a
Baroque cameo. She raises her arms to her shoulders
and unclasps her dress. It falls on the rich, green Persian
rug at her fine feet, a heap of gossamer and golden
thread. She caresses her soft skin, her palms barely
touching her small, firm breasts, her thin waist, the curve
of her hips, before she turns around. Clive takes it all in:
the shapely calves, the V cleft into her lower back, the
soft downy hairs on the nape of her neck. She turns
halfway, casting a dreamy look at him over her pale
shoulder. Her lips part: "Like what you see?"

Clive awoke with a jolt. His mouth felt like sandpaper and his room smelt stale. He closed his eyes, sending his mind after the dregs of dream, even though he knew it was in vain. He took a deep breath, and felt his tumescence wane. The sour smell of Pink Oil still lingered, even though the well of the burner was dry. He got up and opened the window, letting the odour out and the chill in.

NEED MORE OIL. SAME SOURCE NO SUBS.

He texted Baxter as he brushed his teeth. He had maybe one more go of Pink Oil, and he craved more. The first vial Baxter had sent his way was fun enough; weird, black and white, and surreal, but the stuff he was on now was all about the dark-skinned girl. Whoever the dreams originally belonged to had been obsessed, and the obsession had started to rub off on Clive. He had wondered for a while, as he was working his way through the dose, whether the obsession was his, or whether it was carried in the Oil, piggybacking on the haunches of the dream like some bizarre parasite. He eventually decided it didn't matter. He could hardly imagine a night of sleep without the girl. And the vial was almost empty.

Baxter pulled the mask off the man's mouth as he blinked himself awake.

"Have a drink", she said, and disconnected the tube that fed the man's exhalations to a container not unlike a pressure horn, which she then sealed. He stretched and sat up. Mr. Clay was standing by the bedside, a plastic water bottle almost entirely hidden by the bulk of his huge hand.

"Feeling all right?" Baxter asked. The man heaved a heavy sigh and nodded. "What did you dream about, Stan?"

He furrowed his brow and rubbed his massive forehead. "Something about... flying. I think I was flying."

"Your two thousand quid is on a side table by the door."

He stood up and struggled into his jacket. "And that's it? Experiment all done?"

Baxter nodded. "That's all we need from you. The Camden Sleep Clinic thanks you for participating in this experiment. Mr. Clay will see you out."

"All right, then, um, Baxter? Baxter. Pleasure doing business with you."

Baxter's hulking bodyguard escorted Stan out, while she neatly labeled the container (Stan Brodsky, Nov. 23. 2013. Flight.) and slid it into a pigeonhole on the wall.

During Stan's collection session, her mobile had given out a couple of urgent buzzes. She answered it now, picked a canister from the bottom row of pigeonholes, and stepped into the adjacent room.

The tip of the ziggurat pierces the bright blue sky. They charge up the steps in the side, and the white brick crumbles at their feet, turning to dust at the slightest step, forcing them up and up. Breathless, they run and run, and the peak seems farther and farther away with every step. Finally, they reach a platform that they somehow know is half of the way to the top, and the massive structure burst in front of them, sending debris up into

the sky, suddenly dark and lit only by stars. They recoil just in time as snakes and scorpions and newts and frogs, dark, shiny, and slimy, burst out of the cracks; an aggregate of minuscule, dark movements. A pair of immense tentacles, jet black and veiny, pocked with spines and suckers, springs out of the top of the structure and flails madly. They sink into the living deluge of loathsome critters and it accepts them. Warm and wet, it writhes against their skin, feeling soft and smooth until even their faces are covered.

"That..." said David, gasping for air.

"...was just..." said Jodie, trembling.

"...wicked!" Awate finished, beaming.

They stood up from the mess of pillows they had strewn on the floor of David's room. The air was warm and heavy with their breathing. David opened the windows and the stuffiness eased a little. Awate stared at the shapes they had painted onto the walls of David's room that summer: curves and spirals of neon purple and yellow on black. He remembered thinking they were so edgy; like, the wickedest thing ever. Now they looked dull. Flat. 2D.

He shared a look with Jodie. Palms glistening with sweat, she caressed his face, and kissed him on the lips. He felt the heat of her face on his, and then he realized he was parched. Like he'd been chewing sawdust.

"Dave? Get us a drink, all right, mate?"

David nodded and swallowed, like he just realized he was thirsty, too. "Yeah, 'course. I think I got some cider in the fridge." He left the room.

Awate threw his arms around Jodie. She rested her head against his shoulder, and craned her neck to look into his eyes. Her lips twitched with a brief, uneasy smile he'd seen so many times. Jodie was his first real girlfriend, and that was the smile of firsts. The first time they got drunk together, their first – his first! – fumbling and awkward sexual experience, the first time they shared a spliff... and now this. Pink Oil. There was a happy glint in her eyes. He grinned widely. They kissed.

David came back with three tall glasses and half a bottle of Strongbow. They all drank greedily. The cider, fizzy and cold, soothed their scratchy throats.

"What is this stuff, anyway?" asked Jodie, holding the vial against the light.

David cleaned the burner. "Buggered if I know. New stuff, got it from this place in Camden. They say you can get all sorts. All sorts of dreams, I mean." He eyed the burner suspiciously. "I wonder what happens if you mix two together..."

Awate and Jodie shared an eager look. What could be the harm in trying?

ლ

Baxter turned off the electric heater and sealed the spout of her alembic. She then detached it from the cucurbit, and stopped the fresh vial of Pink Oil with a glass stopper printed with the image of Eros. She dripped the oil remaining in the distillation device into a silver burner for testing, and disposed of the metal canister.

One of her earliest clients, Clive, was badly hung up on an earlier batch of the stuff. She was all out, and the girl she had collected it from wasn't answering her phone. Not that Baxter would bother much with trying to locate her. She had all sorts coming in now, looking to get rid of whatever haunted them, or maybe earn a few bob. There was no shortage of dreams, no shortage of people who would share them. There was some variety, but one was pretty much the same at the other.

Clive knew she could give him no guarantees. Surely whatever subconscious erotica Baxter supplied him with would do him just fine. Noting that she should text Clive later that evening, she sat back in a comfortable chair and lit a tealight under her oil burner.

ص

The boat rocks; Clive plants his feet firmly onto the damp floorboards of the cabin. His fingers are dug into a hammock's rope netting. She brushes past him, playing with the soft curls of her hair, wearing nothing save a thin, ratty white t-shirt that barely conceals her nipples and covers maybe half her ample buttocks. Her skin glistens with sweat. She bites her lower lip seductively; brazenly sinks her nails into his inner thigh. "I'm going sunning. Come with?" Her voice rings like a silver chime, the weight of her breasts pressing against Clive's chest. She turns on the balls of her feet away from him to climb the short flight of steps out to the deck, Her t-shirt rides up, revealing...

Clive sprang awake in cold, panicky sweat. He felt angry and aroused at the same time. Baxter was cheating, and he felt - ridiculous as it was - like he was cheating, too. Cheating on the dark-skinned girl he'd only seen in his dreams. He walked up to the window to air the room, and took several deep, laboured breaths. With a shaky hand, he found his packet of fags and lit up. Acrid blue smoke mixed with the residual Pink Oil vapours. His mind wandered to the online articles he'd been reading, from serious academic works to New Age pseudophilosophy to paranoid ramblings of strung out insomniac junkies.

There's something about dreams and faces. Clive was hazy about the scientific reasons, and wary about ones less so, but the consensus seemed to be that you can't see an unfamiliar face in dreams. Therefore, the brown-skinned beauty he was so infatuated with must really exist somewhere. He'd spent nights surfing the web, looking at thousands of Facebook profiles, expecting reward and getting nothing but false alarms. And with each false alarm, a cold tug in his chest, and the bitter taste of disappointment. He realized he was obsessed and frustrated, but he couldn't help himself. He ground the remains of his fag into grits in his ashtray, and lit up another one. His dream girl must be real, and the person who dreamt about her must know her. The beginnings of a plan were taking shape in the dark recesses of his mind.

Awate's heart was beating. He held Jodie's hand in his sweaty palm, and squeezed, trying to reassure her. She blinked and half-smiled nervously. Her jaw was locked and she was gritting her teeth without knowing it. Awate could see it, could sense it, even though she was wrapped up in her scarf, the collar of her coat turned up against the wind.

"Is this the place?" she asked.

Awate shrugged. "This is the address Dave gave me."

She nodded and eyed the sign on the brick wall: 'Camden Sleep Clinic', it said in a clean, professional typeface. From the outside, the place looked every bit like a medical practice. It even had the snake-and-staff thing bolted onto the door. She shoved Awate towards the buzzer on the wall.

"Well, go on then. Do it." Jodie prompted.

Awate turned around, flashed her a smile of false confidence, and lifted his hand to touch the button, but the black door swung open before him. He froze. The doorway framed the largest man they had ever seen. And not only that: the giant's bizarre appearance contributed much to the shock. His skin was pale, with an odd grey tint, loose on the bones, but not wrinkled, and glowed with an unhealthy sheen. His eyes were dark, his lips a horizontal slit at the bottom of his face, and he had a bright yellow tattoo on his forehead - something in a script Awate didn't recognize. He wore a cheap suit, poorly fitted, and uncomfortably taut against his colossal frame. Awate was almost relieved. The man looked much more like what he'd been expecting.

"Can I help you?" the man asked. His voice was deep and powerful, his words slow and deliberate.

"Er... yes... um..." Awate was struggling.

Jodie stepped in. "We're looking for Baxter. We'd like to buy."

The giant's unblinking eyes shifted from one of them to the other, until he stepped to the side. "Come in."

Awate and Jodie exchanged an intense look. They spoke without words, and *No turning back now* was what passed between them. With some reluctance they entered the brick house, Awate first, Jodie following closely.

Baxter realized she'd always wondered what it would

be like to stare down the barrel of a gun. She was amazed at how calm and clear-headed she felt, how time almost seemed to slow down.

"Did you hear me, you worthless shit?" Clive shouted, gun shaking in his hand. "All the oil from the same source, in the bag, right the fuck now!"

Baxter glanced at the two wide-eyed youths who had come in minutes earlier, standing frozen in front of the big shelf chock full of vials. She knew it was up to her to try and diffuse the mad, gun-toting idiot that found his way to her rooms. She tried to sound as calm as she could manage.

"I can't help you, Clive. Look, there's no need for all of this. Here, let me show you what else I got..."

"Shut up! Shut up, shut up, shut up!" Clive spat as he screamed, shoving a duffle bag at her, and waving his gun arm around. "You won't stitch me up again, you rancid, sodding bucket of toss!"

Baxter took a step back, and felt her desk pressing against the small of her back. Her mouth suddenly felt dry.

"Well then, maybe Mr. Clay can help you."

Clive paused for a split second. It was enough for the golem, who'd snuck up behind him, to close his massive arms around him. It took a blink of an eye for Clive to collapse on the floor screaming with pain. That the gun had fired only registered with Baxter once she smelled the cordite that flooded the room. The girl screamed. Blood dripped from the boy's open mouth and onto his shirt.

The world is bathed in shining gold. Awate is carried

on the wings of angels, beautiful and terrifying, through cold starlight. The sound of trumpets fills the air; a single, haunting tone, extended into infinity, past and present, everywhere and everywhen. Suddenly, a green bolt of lightning tears the skies in twain, and he feels awed, naked and alone before the majesty of creation's motive force, in the lap of the Supreme Being, his very soul weighed and measured and judged. He hears Jodie's voice, her pleading tone, but he understands not a word. The cold grips his chest and he is plunged into darkness and all feeling goes...

"You have to help him, please, he can't die!" Jodie cried, tugging at the sleeves of the paramedic as they strapped Awate to a gurney.

"We'll do what we can, luv," said the paramedic, waving at a policewoman to hold her back.

A crowd of onlookers gathered in the street, as crowds are wont, drawn by the hypnotic lure of the bright lights on the emergency response vehicles. Clive was restrained as he was dragged to a police patrol car, struggling and kicking at the ground all the way. His jacket was drawn over his head, his face covered all the way; his identity protected from the baying hounds of the bloodthirsty yellow press, himself shielded from the sight of a beautiful South Asian woman standing just shy of the police perimeter, working her camera.

&

Miloš Petrik is a lawyer who, time permitting, also writes. He resides in his home town of Belgrade, Serbia (nowhere near Siberia), where he busies himself with his day job in public TV while making the best sandwiches in the world, with what dismally passes as a social life.

Library of Dreams

He goes by @miloshpetrik on Twitter and Wattpad, where he posts his stories after they have been rejected by the very best of the publishing world.

This Thing of Darkness
Yzabel Ginsberg

❧

They call it the Silent Train, and it weaves its path on a viaduct half-drowned in a quicksilver sea.

"Erebus Station," the conductor announces. He waves a tiny golden bell, its chimes dancing in the air around us. "Erebus. Please don't forget your belongings, for you'll never see them again."

His back is to me, only offering the sight of his gloved hands, crisp, gold-trimmed navy blue uniform, and large cap. Although his raspy voice sounds gleeful, he is quite serious. Whatever the passengers leave in the Silent Train, they can never get back. This does not concern me, since I never bring my staff with me when I use this means of travel—it is just too cumbersome. Besides, I do not need it here.

The engine lets out a long whisper, and the wheels emit only the faintest sigh when we slow down to stop in front of the platform. The wooden door at the front of the carriage is silent as it opens to let out a couple of Travellers wrapped in ivy-green cloaks. Here, there is no gleam of gaslight on shining metal, no hard wheels screeching as they come to a halt. The platform does not teem with ladies in straight-laced corsets and bustling dresses, nor men in waistcoats and top hats, with attendants standing at the ready to carry luggage.

Yes, my train is definitely silent, beautiful in its own way, its dark red carriages adorned with dancing golden arabesques. Its chimneys breathe out rolling clouds of white steam whose rounded shapes bask in the orange light of the sun setting on the horizon. The silence is pleasant. Peaceful. It is no wonder I have started using this road more and more often. Loud noises strain my ears and cause me too much pain nowadays—one of the reasons I had decided never to go South, and never to join my brother in the capital. *That would be too much of a change of pace,* he would say, *for you who will never change.* He didn't want me to change, didn't want me to meet him in any other place than those I could truly call my own.

"Such a strange weather tonight, Mr. Ezekiel, wouldn't you say?" the conductor muses as he walks past me.

I look out of the window to see what has prompted this odd comment. The moon has taken its rightful place in the sky, following the trail of the dying sun in a perfect ballet, but I do not need more than a glimpse to realise something is wrong.

Fear stings my innards and seizes my heart within an iron vice. The silver crescent I expected to see is not there—or, should I say, its colour is now a dirty red that soon shall cast an eerie light on the sea. By the time the train reaches the next station, even the lamps inside the cars will not suffice to hide the bloody hue spreading from the horizon.

A warning. It must be. This ghastly travesty of a moon exerts a call, a pull, like I have seldom felt. I cannot tell why: I just *know* I must take action, and fast.

"Sir?"

I don't listen, and dart towards the exit, passing by the bemused conductor, his yellow eyes shining from within the shadow of his cap's visor. The closing door almost catches the hem of my iridescent cloak as I land on the platform's birch planks. While I did not intend to come here at first, it does not matter anymore. I shall be able to find my way back again, whether I follow the rails or go another direction. This path is just one among others. Right now, it is of the utmost importance that I keep an eye on the abnormal moon.

Perhaps I was mistaken. Perhaps I do need my staff, after all.

The engine whistles and starts again in a whiff of greying smoke. The Silent Train is leaving. I catch sight of the two Travellers who disembarked before me, the taller holding the smaller one by the hand. Their feet carry them towards the narrow obsidian arch on which an unknown hand once engraved the name *Erebus.* Soon, they will be gone, and it is for the best. At least whatever is going to happen shall be my concern only, and no one else's. With the train now gliding towards its next stop, I can focus on the sky.

I spin on my heels, ready to face the unnatural phenomenon. The slim crescent's colour has deepened and rays of moonlight cast odd shadows and reflections on my clothes. Above the usual smell of the sea, on the other side of the railroad, wafts the faint stench of blood, and for a second, I picture my brother's face, his eyes the same steel-blue as mine, his dark-brown hair floating down his shoulders in light curls, his confident smile hiding the darkness lurking inside him. My father used to say we looked alike, even though we were only half-brothers, so much so that it was impossible to mistake us for anything else.

For as long as can I remember, blood has always been Aidan's element. Blood of the battlefield. Blood of duels. Blood of our sire. Blood of Elsa Maria, the creature who poisoned his soul, although she never managed to sever our bond. Blood, like the heavy droplets forming at the moon's surface, dripping one after the other into the sea, and in spite of the distance, the sound of their tainting the waters pierce my heart like so many ghostly arrows.

Time goes by and nothing changes.

I still feel the moon calling me, causing my whole self to scream in horror. There is such an inhuman quality to that call that deep inside, I know I should not heed it. If I were to, something terrible would happen. I cast a glance at the arch, at the platform now devoid of any presence other than mine. Was I mistaken? What should I do now? Remain here, waiting for the bloody, mysterious moon to send me a sign? Or leave it be, in the hopes that, like so many things in this world, it will simply fade away?

The Silent Train is long gone. The obsidian stone beckons. Tonight, perhaps it may be best to walk another path. Erebus is just as good as Tramontana, the Windy Plains, or Ráth Breasail. After all, as far as I am concerned, every road ends up leading to the City of Twilight, and I am in no hurry to get there, am I?

I manage to tear my eyes from the moon for good, and turn my attention to the portal, walking towards its mirror-door with as much calm as I can muster. I place my hands on the warm, liquid surface, allowing the watery currents to wrap around my fingers, blurring my reflection. Every time I see that pale, haunted face of mine, I am reminded of my brother's warnings. *Inappropriate. Stranger. Unable to conform to what proper society dictates.* Of course, there would not be any place for me in the South. The woad tattoos spiralling on my arms, cheeks and forehead are so foreign to the new age our world has entered into, that only here can I still find peace.

The portal's waters grant me passage. In the blink of an eye, I find myself on the other side of the arch, stepping onto the hard, dusty ground of Erebus, under its countless stars that hang in an eternally indigo sky. The path at my feet stretches onward, meandering between small hills. Further down, the bright green of the Travellers' cloaks swirls in and out of sight with each turn of the road, the soft wind carrying fragments of conversation and laughter as they make their way at a casual pace towards the forest. Mossy stones interspersed with tall ferns dot the side of the *Via Noctis*, granting places of rest to the weak and weary, but most of those who come here do so because they like to take a leisurely stroll in a quiet, resilient realm, one that is not fraught with promises of danger.

Yet my instinct tells me to look up, which I do.

My throat narrows down to a pinhole. Anguish constrains my chest. Erebus is a safe land, one of night, its only light that of the twinkling stars. So how come the red crescent is also suspended in its sky, now?

A drop of blood splatters on my shoulder, reeking of iron and rot, leaving a trail of rust. Another one falls on my hand, and with a muffled yelp, I wipe its sting with my sleeve. *It burns! It burns, and it should not, because blood does not burn, does it? Blood should not*—Blood should not be falling from the sky directly above me, since the moon itself is still far away on the horizon.

I crane my neck, and this is when I first see it. The crack in the night. The rift in the very fabric of the firmament. A black line stretching from one horizon to the other, an ichor-rimmed, bleeding wound inflicted upon Erebus. From the deep, utter obscurity behind it, darker than anything I have ever seen in this landscape, an eye opens, then another, and another. Soon, instead of stars, I am staring back at just as many eyes, perhaps more, observing, peering, scrutinising, all filled with hunger. Whatever those eyes belong to, they are on the prowl, seeking their quarry. I am afraid I might be the one.

A Nightmare. A Nightmare the likes of which I have never seen.

Yes, I definitely need my staff.

All eyes are on me now. I try not to blink, not to avert my gaze for even a split second, for that one moment may be my demise. My fingers twitch, ready to invoke my weapon. My hand still hurts where the blood hit it— not the blood of the moon, but that of the firmament being torn by a darkness whose hands keep on grabbing at the gaping wound, pulling, pushing, widening the gap. *How strong it must be, to create such a large opening into this place!*

All the while, those steel-blue eyes remain fixed on me, waiting for something.

It dawns on me at last: steel-blue eyes, like mine.

At this mutual recognition, dozens of long, black arms spring out of the wound. Now strong enough, their long, serpentine fingers dive for the world around me. One hand reaches for a tree, rips it from the soil, crushes its very essence. Another grabs at the portal's structure, tearing off a whole block, causing the water-door to scream in wordless, convoluted ripples. A third one wipes off a cluster of stars. All around me, they are tearing Erebus into shreds, leaving only holes with ragged, bleeding edges. The one thing they do not seem to target is the moon itself.

Down the road, so far, yet still too close, the Travellers have stopped and raised their heads, bearing witness to the impending doom. The small one is pointing at the dark gash in the night. This time, a new, sudden gale brings the sound of a young boy's voice to me, all too clearly. "Look, Mama, the sky's all red! And bleeding!" The hands are rushing right towards them.

Now I understand.

I was not the prey. I was the guide, the clueless hook that *thing* needed, although I do not know why. Was it my power? My eyes? Did it feel a connection—for few we are, indeed, who are born with such an unusual eye colour? I do not know; yet, fool that I am, I led it right into one of the largest, most stable realms!

There is no more time, as fleeting a concept as *time* is here. The portal is already crumbling under the relentless assaults of those deadly claws. If the mother and child who came in before me depend on mirror-doors to leave, they will need to reach the next one.

I raise my arm, willing my staff into my hand, distorting reality in a reflex etched in me by years of practice. My fingers close on the icy-cold, but comforting, shaft. At my mental command, the metal half-disc at its heavier end immediately deploys five silver branches, an irregular sun to wield off the assault of the bloody moon's minions. *Razor-sharp*, I decide, right before taking a leap of faith into the air to slash at the most threatening arms. I am not a natural fighter, but one cannot go on for as long as I have without learning a few useful moves.

Every realm is governed by its own laws, by which regular Travellers must abide. Erebus is for peace and contemplation—for walking, not for flying. I am not a regular, though. I am a true Dreamer, one who contemplated many mad sunsets, danced with the kelpies in the waters of Loch Cailleach, waded through the marshes of Sylva Suspiriorum, journeyed on the Silent Train, found my way alone to the City of Twilight, and leapt head-first into more Hell Rides than I could keep track of. I built the Twilight Tower. I placed every single stone in it, carved every constellation in its rotunda, opened its many doors to other realms. Although the process leaves me drained and weakened, when I choose to do so, I am able to bend the laws to my will. Right now, I can be the fastest flying creature in Erebus if I wish to be so.

And I do. I do so much.

My silver sun flares its magic around me as I rush towards the unfortunate pair. I do not pause to see how many hands and arms I am slicing, and clench my teeth to resist the painful, vibrating roar of anger now echoing throughout the realm. The mother is already on the run, dragging her son by his frail, tiny wrist. Now that I am getting closer, I notice the elegant, curved horns protruding from their foreheads, their fiery hair freed from their cloak's hoods, their furry white legs, and their light-brown hooves clattering on the flat stones paving the road. Satyrs, creatures of merriment, born from dreams full of desire and lust, but also from hope and wishes. They would not stand a chance against the Nightmare possessing the sky.

I can take a guess as to where they are headed: the second obsidian portal, standing on the other side of the hills, past the large forest. Alas, it is too far away. They will never make it in time. The laws of Erebus bind them, slowing their pace. The child stumbles and falls flat on his stomach, scraping the palms of his hands as he tries to catch himself. More arms spring from the gash in the sky. Wild slashes from my razor-bladed sun manage to cut their assault short, but how long will I be able to keep the threat at bay?

Down below, the Satyr woman has scooped her child up in her arms, galloping for the sake of both their lives. She cannot make it, not without help. Gathering my willpower again, I force my cloak to extend into iridescent wings, and let myself fall into a fast dive, hacking, again and again, into what is turning into a living sea of darkness. The mother's panicked screams allow me to pinpoint her position. I reach for her, slide my right arm around her narrow waist, and we take off right before several hands come tearing at the cobblestones that had lain under our feet a mere second ago.

She does not know me, I do not know her; nevertheless, as our gazes meet, a new connection is forged. She clasps a trembling arm around my shoulders, holding her son with the other. Strong sobs rake the boy's chest. So young. So fragile. A long time ago, I was just the same, just as powerless, begging and praying for someone to come and save me. Their wide, emerald eyes are brimming with tears, like mine used to be; silent, yet pleading for help.

We fly above the road, above the hills, between the towering fir trees; so many obstacles to leave in the Nightmare's way. The blood-dripping moon bathes us in the sick light of its mocking grin. A thousand gleaming steel eyes glare at me, filled with a fury I can barely stand, their strong hatred turning the air into poison, violating the laws like I never did. *Faster, faster*—there it is, in sight at last, beyond a river: the water-door that shall free my wards, or so I hope. If I can drop them right in front of it, they may stand a chance.

Thank God for my staff, the one I forged from the very stuff of dreams in the City of Twilight's highest tower. The rays of my sun whirl around us, forcing the darkness to retreat for a short while, enough for my ethereal wings to carry us downwards. The second portal is still standing, all shiny white marble, a perfect counterpoint to its now-defunct twin. The letters adorning its arch read *Phasia*, the Realm of Crossings. Even though the Satyrs may lose their way for a time there, at least they will be safe on its large quartz bridges. "Go through the portal," I tell the shaken mother. "Go, and don't look back!"

Or come back, for that matter, but there is no need for me to add this part. With a few words of gratitude, stammered in an almost inaudible voice, she turns her big eyes to me, before brushing her lips with mine—a traditional goodbye among Satyrs, albeit the one for strangers, not for kin. Her little boy only looks up and gives a serious nod—too serious for such a youngling.

The hands of darkness are upon us, catching up much too fast. No more time for exchanges, not even of brief glances. I give a push, sending mother and son tumbling into the mirror-water. The last I see of them, as they glide through the quicksilver surface, is flame and green, hair and cloaks, and sad ripples of loss and longing. Black fingers dive past me, fingers I can barely keep at bay. They reach for the stones, to tear them apart like they did with the obsidian ones.

I do what I never thought I'd do: I will my sun rays into longer, more lethal blades, and send them crashing against the arch's pillars, hastening the latter's fall. The

Nightmare shall not follow me into yet another realm. I shall not make the same mistake twice.

Just like that, the portal is destroyed.

For a moment I find myself hovering mid-air, staring at what I tried to push into a corner of my mind in order to blind myself and forget. *Steel-blue.* The colour is the key, the one I unwillingly share with that thing. If only I could find out what it means, what those eyes now turning back to me are trying to convey, beyond hate and hunger.

But I cannot think about this. The next thing I know, black fingers wrap around the shaft of my staff, almost ripping it out of my hands, and I tumble towards the ground. All around me Erebus is crumbling, patches of sky and grass and forest dissolving into nothing. The whole place is collapsing fast and I cannot do anything to prevent it. That battle is doomed to failure. I am not so strong. I am not my brother.

Aidan. I do not need to close my eyes to picture him, the brother who always protected me. There on his battlefield, standing atop the mountain of corpses, he would keep battling day after night after day, drenched in the light of that realm's black sun. Were he with me now, surely he would fight blood with blood, fire with fire, like his name fated him to. He would unsheathe his mortuary sword and stand up to face the threat, a grin on his lips, death in his hand, blood pooling at his feet.

A part of me wishes for him to be here. I silence it in haste, for I have no right to do so, not after what he went through because of me. I am the only one left now.

No. Though I am not my brother, should I let myself be defeated without a fight, I would never be able to face him again, whether in dreams or in death.

I will another sky, another moon, another road—close

in colours, with just the slightest hint of a difference—and use them as the first step into a Hell Ride.

Downwards we both go, the Nightmare and I, falling through layer after layer of sky, earth and sea, tearing through one dream after another. I do not like travelling this way for it is the most violent, the one that wakes up many sleepers in gasps and causes many others to toss and turn in fitful sleep. Hell Rides create ripples that turn into crushing waves, making the Oneiros itself scream in anger, and summon nightmares in their wake. How cruel and ironic, really: weaving bad dreams to escape an even worse one. Yet what other choice is there? I cannot fight that thing of darkness if I also have to protect whole realms.

Downwards, upwards, backwards—there is neither rhyme nor reason to such travels. One sky turns into another. One cluster of stars takes the guise of a slightly different sibling. One reflection vanishes, leaving room for more mirrors. Still, the darkness keeps following me. At least this means it is not interested in the dreams we crash our way through.

I might be losing ground, though, for its fingers crawl over my staff all the more, over my hand, my arm, my shoulder—and then it comes, the moment of close contact, the one I had so wanted to avoid. The darkness wraps around me, tries to find its way into me, pouring down my throat, invading my eyes. My mind screams like never before, as I try to wave it away, rip it away from my sight.

Like me, it whispers. *Like me. The eyes. Like me!*

The Nightmare *I* could have become, if my brother hadn't put his life on the line for me.

This is when I see it, my chance, my only chance. In their attempting to possess my body, the hands have let go of my staff. With the last spark of my will, I manage to strengthen my grip on it, to turn it into another weapon. The silver sun erupts in a hundred chaotic blades, extending from all sides, piercing through the Nightmare; through its eyes, through my own body, even. I do not care how much blood I may shed, nor about the terrible wail of pain and fury storming everywhere around me. I must stop its course, at least, lose it somewhere in the depths of the Oneiros, from where it may never come back. This is what matters.

The twisting, rolling tentacles let me go for that one precious second and I keep falling, falling, imagining my own blood as transparent droplets. *Rain, just rain, innocent rain, falling, falling, towards a soil that could not be tainted by darkness; towards safety, the high marble arches of my Tower—no, not there, not the Twilight Sea, I cannot afford to bring that thing there, I must find another place, another part of the Oneiros, one I wouldn't endanger, one I wouldn't—* "Wake up..."

I open my eyes at the sound of that voice. Blink several times. Unable to see anything. The darkness. It's still here. *Still here! It hasn't left me! Let me go, let me go, I thought I had escaped it, it can't be, it can't be...* "I can't see! Oh God, God, I can't see!"

A large, warm hand on my shoulder. A smaller one on my brow, light and soft.

"Papa, wake up," the voice says again—a young woman's, as full of tenderness as the hand now caressing my hair. "Come back. Come back, please."

"I can't see..."

"But that's normal." Another voice, male, vibrant—the strong hand. "Remember? You told us so. You can only see in your dreams."

"You and your legendary tact," the woman sighs.

"Papa, it's alright. You're home. You're safe here."

I scramble around in my own mind to grasp at fleeting memories. I know these voices, these fingers, the soft ones and the callused ones, the warmth seeping out of these people. I know their names. I know the home they're speaking of. My home. The cottage. My home. My family. My children?

"Lily? Douglas?" I manage to whisper, raising my own hands to touch them, to feel their faces. I have never seen them—not in the human world—but I know they have their mother's eyes and hair, grey-blue and light blonde, and that Douglas is a tall, sturdy, happy soul, and Lily calm, determined and hiding the tattoo on her own temple with her braid, and that—

"Papa, your arms! You're bleeding! What have you been doing there?"

Lily's tone is both worried and reproachful, carrying one last, unspoken word: *again*. I do not mind. I cannot mind her. She knows. They know. They're only light Dreamers, but they understand. "A Nightmare." My voice sounds alien to me, strange; the voice of another man, older than the one I am in the Oneiros. "It was... dark. And powerful."

She lets out a sigh and mutters something to her brother, something about staying with me while she goes down to the kitchen to fetch her herbs and take care of my wounds. Then the sound of her footsteps retreating from the room that used to be my own father's, footsteps as light as her touch. I am not even surprised. Wounds suffered in such potent Dreams have a tendency to leave their marks on me once I wake up.

Has it always been like this?

My thoughts are already escaping me, never as clear in this place as they are when I am Travelling. I close my

46

eyes again, my eyes that cannot see in the real world—unless the Oneiros is the only real world for me, and what surrounds me here is but another dream? Sometimes, I cannot tell anymore. All I have to anchor myself to are my children, this cottage, and the shadow I call my brother.

You. Like me. Mine, a voice in the depths of my heart suddenly stirs and whispers, and in a reflex, my fingers grasp Douglas's, making sure I am indeed on his side of reality. It is too late. I already know. Despite my efforts, I brought the Nightmare back, and the Nightmare, my Nightmare, isn't going to let me forget.

No, it is not over. Which means I cannot give up.

In the human world, I am but a blind man.

In the Oneiros, I am king of countless dreams. I am going to protect them as well as I can.

Even from myself.

ଔ

Once upon a time, Yzabel Ginsberg made a deal with the God of Dreams, whom she might have swindled out of a few extra seeds of wild imagination. From her current home somewhere on the road to Paris, this strange French woman always clad in black weaves many webs of stories, whether on paper or through the delicate art of online storytelling. Rumour has it that she will only stop when Death comes to claim her, but even that is less than certain.

In the meantime, you can follow her at http://www.facebook.com/yzabelginsberg *or as @yzabelginsberg on Twitter.*

Emotions

Dee Drin

ॐ

The very first thing Gemma always did after making herself a large cup of black coffee was log in to her favorite social media account, ChatMe. All of her best friends were there and they always seemed to take away some of her emptiness, at least for a while, until she had to get ready for work.

Among the friends who meant so much to her, there was one in particular whom she adored above all others. He resonated with her perfectly. They had known each other since elementary school, and had been through a lot together.

She loved the fact that every time she turned on her computer, his message was there to greet her. What's more, he was so fine-tuned to her emotions, that if she wasn't well, he wouldn't beat about the bush with the regular 'good morning' messages, but would get straight to the point.

People had asked why she wasn't in a relationship with him, since they knew each other so well and seemed to be compatible in most things. Truth be told, she did think of it a few times, especially because it looked to her like he was open to that idea as well, but she was terrified of the prospect of losing her best friend if it didn't work out. She could never risk it. She loved him too much.

Their relationship had always been based on mutual trust, confiding in each other things that nobody else knew about them. He knew all about her problems with her parents, and she knew of his head-over-heels crush on Danielle, a girl from his gym, where he worked as a trainer.

Gemma was the one who pushed him to go and talk to her, to build a connection with her and ask her out. A few months later Gemma was in on almost every detail of their relationship, and she was amused at their quarrels and passions.

How are you doing? he messaged her this morning. She looked at it and smiled, but then she got serious. If there was someone she couldn't fool into believing that she was fine, it was Michael. If she so much as tried to convince him there was nothing wrong, he would scold her like a child and insist she tell him what was going on.

She sighed and quickly messaged him back. *I want to kill myself. That's how.*

She deliberated over whether or not to send it, knowing it betrayed her deepest despair. Then she did it anyway. She knew he was online when she wrote it, and that he saw it immediately, but there was no reply for a good few minutes. Maybe he had gone to eat something, and that's why he was so silent? After ten more minutes she turned off the computer and went to prepare for a photo shoot. He was probably too busy with other things, but that was all right. Ten minutes later she started feeling bad about what she had written, so she logged in again and wrote:

Michael, I didn't mean to write it the way I did. I hope you understand that.

A few more minutes of silence, then she tried again:

Oh, come on, Michael, please! Just because I wrote it doesn't mean I'm actually going to do it! I'm too big a coward for that, anyway... Michael? Mike, where the hell are you?

Nothing. It looked like he wasn't even online. Why was she surprised? He had his own life, and he couldn't be there for her 24/7, nor did she expect him to.

She was just about to go and make herself a big breakfast when she heard a buzz at the door. She hadn't expected any visitors at this early hour, so she carefully approached the door and peeked through the spyhole.

"What the... Michael?"

She quickly unlocked the door and let him in. He didn't pay any attention to her. Instead, he strolled past her into the kitchen, stopping in front of the stove. Then he turned back and crossed his arms, staring at her almost wildly.

"Can I offer you something?" she asked.

"Yeah, sure. How about an explanation for your message?"

"Well, if you had read *all* my messages, you would have seen that I didn't mean it that way," she said testily.

"Oh, but you did, Gemma. I know you almost too well, so you better give me a good explanation for why you want to end your life! Which, by the way, I won't let you do, so you might as well stop thinking about it right now."

"And how are you going to do that?"

"It really doesn't matter, but I will find a way. Now speak!"

"How dare you!" she said, wanting to throw

something at him. He was frustrating her with his calm stance. He raised a brow, obviously not disturbed by her hissy fit.

"Hey, I'm not leaving here until I find out what's going on."

"I'm fine. It was just an expression."

"You've known me for ten years, Gemma. Do you really think I'd fall for something like that? Take your time and think about how you want to say what's on your mind and I'll make us some eggs, okay?"

She gave him the dirtiest look she could muster, which he only answered with a smile. She remained dead silent as he went to the fridge to get the eggs.

"You're not helping yourself here, you know?" he continued. "You and I are so much alike. Always so persistent in trying to convince people that we're fine, inside and out. We're not, and I'm surprised you would keep something like that a secret from me."

"Oh, stop it, Michael!"

He stopped beating the eggs and looked at her, this time with calm determination in his eyes. That didn't make her feel any better. She felt like he was scanning her soul. If he wasn't her best friend, she would have kept insisting that she was only joking. But with him it was impossible. Even though she was ashamed of her current emotional state, she sighed and said, "I know you think I'm being melodramatic, but I am really not in a good place right now. That's why I sent you that message."

"I know, and that's why I'm here. But I don't know why you want to do it. Are things really that bad?" he asked her and she broke down, crying. He immediately came to her and pulled out a stool, helping her sit down. Then he knelt down and tried to meet her gaze.

"I hate this so much, Mike."

"Hate what?"

"This emptiness that is eating me up from inside! I can't stand it! I don't want to stand it! I want this to be over."

"What are you talking about, Gemma? Emptiness caused by what?"

It took her a good minute before she could force the words through her lips. She couldn't imagine telling him all that had been bothering her for the past ten years. Not even her parents knew the way she felt, because she always put up a brave face and pretended she didn't need anything more than her job and her family. But now that the tears were falling and she couldn't stop them, she decided to bare her soul in front of him. At least he would understand her and probably wouldn't judge her too harshly.

"Caused by the fact that I'm all alone."

"That's not true, you have me. You know I'll always be there for you."

"But that's not it, Michael!" she snapped at him. He was only trying to be supportive and to calm her down, but it annoyed her that he was trying to downplay the seriousness of her feelings. "It's totally different. Yes, you are always here for me, but that doesn't change the fact that you're in a relationship with Danielle. She is your soulmate, and I am really happy for you, you already know that. But that doesn't change my situation. I'm all alone."

He looked like he wanted to say something but she cut him off. She didn't want to hear any words of consolation. They would only hurt more, and now that the gates had been opened, she didn't want to hold herself back. "You can't tell me I'll be fine. You can't tell me there is someone out there for me, just because you've found that special person. You got lucky; I haven't. Don't repeat the stuff I've been hearing for the most of my life, about how I only need to wait a little more. And don't you dare give me some religious crap about God keeping me for someone special. I've been waiting fourteen years with no boyfriend in sight, while the rest of the world is out there enjoying themselves, having sex and cuddling, and walking hand in hand! I'm not looking for happily ever after. Hell, I'm not even looking for marriage, just sex and a bit of romance. Is that too much to ask?"

She broke in gushes of tears, and the suffocating pressure in her lungs wasn't helping either. Her throat was swollen and she could barely speak.

"Oh...Gemma..."

"Don't 'oh, Gemma' me!" The flame of fury lit up once again. "You don't get to say anything here, because you've done everything right in your love life. I don't care how close to perfect it is or isn't, but you've found someone worth fighting for, and living for. Someone who adores you and who you adore equally. Don't you dare tell me there is someone like that waiting for me, because there isn't, Michael."

"Please, don't do this to yourself..."

"What am I doing to myself?"

"Tormenting yourself with these thoughts that..."

"That's because they *are* tormenting me, and they are real! I can't avoid them! You don't know what it's like to wake up every day, alone in your bed, with no one to kiss good morning, or to lie down at night and see that there is no one you can curl up to, nobody who could warm your back when you're cold! You don't know what it's like to go to a party and be the only single person, and you most certainly are not the one who has never been hit on. Not once."

She took a deep breath, trying to calm down. He pulled her to his chest and helped her to the living room. Then they sat down on the couch and he embraced her, running his fingers through her hair.

"It's all right, baby. Vent it out."

"Venting won't bring me anything good. It won't change reality!"

He didn't say anything. He just kissed her hair. She didn't know what to do. One part of her just wanted to relax into his hug, and another part wanted to kick him and scream at him because he was being so compassionate.

"I'm just so sick and tired of this," she whispered, with tears flowing so stubbornly she didn't even bother to wipe them. They had already left big stains on his shirt.

"Of what?"

"Being left out. Being the last option, the one who is only good enough if everything else fails. Being just a friend, not a girlfriend. Being told by other people that the right guy just hasn't come along yet, but that he will. I know he won't."

"How do you know that? I didn't know..."

"Don't you dare go there! You and I are totally different! Girls all swoon at the very mention of you. You don't even have to try. But I've been waiting for so long. I've put myself out there. Drama school, photography lessons, multiple dance classes. At first I thought that I was doing something wrong, so I tried to change my ways and be someone I'm not, but no matter what I do, the result is always the same." She paused. "Mind you, I did meet an asshole who actually told me on our second date that he was the best option I'll ever have, so I should just give in join him in his bed. If he's the best I can do, I must be really disgusting to the normal ones."

"I wish you would stop saying that."

"I'm only saying it because it's the truth. What is it about me that repels men so much?"

She moved away and looked at him. He obviously wanted to say something, but she wouldn't let him.

"Can I ask you something?"

"Whatever you want."

"I want you to be completely honest with me."

"Gemma, when was the last time I wasn't honest with you?"

"There's always a first time. I want you to answer me one simple question. You've been my best friend for so long, and I trust that you will tell me the absolute truth: am I really that disgusting? That appalling?"

"What? Gemma!"

"I mean it, Michael! Am I really so disgusting that no normal guy would ever dream of touching me?"

"Where in hell did you get that idea from?"

"Have you not been listening to anything I have been saying?"

"Yes, I have, but I also can't believe that this is what you really believe! It is ridiculous to think that there aren't normal guys out there who would be interested in you."

"It's not ridiculous. I might as well join a nunnery, since celibacy is the lifestyle that's obviously waiting for me."

"Stop that!"

"No! You insisted on me telling you the truth, so you're not backing away now!" She wanted to tell him so many things. So many more things that were piling up in her heart, that needed to be said, but he didn't give her the chance. He cupped her face and kissed her lips. It happened so fast. She tried to move her head to get a better look at him, but he wouldn't let her. Her face was so firmly and so gently settled in his palms, all she could do was wait for his next move.

He kissed her again, teasing her lips with his. Two instincts battled inside of her. One that wanted to push him away, because she knew Danielle was waiting for him at home, and the other that wanted to cling to him almost desperately, to melt into his kisses. When he was done, he slowly moved his head away, and she looked at him with her brows tightly knit.

"What are you doing?"

He looked at her and smiled. "Well, what does it look like I'm doing?"

"Kissing me."

"Precisely. You just made it my personal business to make sure that no such hideous thoughts cross your beautiful mind ever again. I will be your boyfriend today."

She moved away and tried to protest, but he sealed her lips with one move of his finger. "No. No more words from you, babe. You've had your rant, and now I'll have mine. I don't care what Danielle's thoughts are on this, because she won't find out. Whatever happens between us is nobody's business."

"What...?"

"Hey, I thought I said no talking? Today and tonight I'm your boyfriend, all right? Which means that I will do all the boyfriend stuff with you."

"Boyfriend stuff?"

"Yeah. I mean the full package here, from making you breakfast to walking down the street with you holding your hand, to sleeping with you and all the things in between. That's right, you heard me. We'll go as far as you want to go. I will make sure you remember very well how appealing you are."

She mouthed something, but no reasonable words came out. She figured it would be better if she just shut up and let him do it his way. She nodded and looked at him in astonishment as he took her hand and entwined their fingers.

The sensation of his hard skin pressed against her own sent a wave of heat all over her body. She felt exhilarated. Someone so dear to her was touching her in such a loving way. She knew it was a relatively small gesture, but to her it meant a whole new world was opening up to her.

He led her to the kitchen and told her to sit down. Then he got down to making her a big breakfast. When he was done, he sat beside her and held up the spoon.

"I can eat by myself, thank you."

"But where's the fun in that? You're seem to be forgetting that I'm your boyfriend today. Now, open your mouth, please."

She could have said no, and that would have been the end of it. She had been given the perfect opportunity to feel loved for a whole day and she couldn't give up on it. She opened her mouth and looked at him as he fed her. "Wow, you're so good at pretending that-"

"I don't need to pretend about anything. I don't have to imagine anyone else because I'm looking at you, Gemma. You are my girlfriend. Please try to remember that."

She smiled and allowed him to continue. As the food slowly vanished from the plate, she took a wild risk and grabbed the spoon from his hands, deciding to feed him.

She wanted to see if he was really into it, because if she was going to go the whole way with him, she needed to make sure he was okay with her taking the initiative.

He didn't let her down. They kept feeding each other until there was no food left.

"Do you want to take a walk outside, or do you want to stay here?"

She hummed. As much as the idea of staying inside and cuddling with him on the couch or bed seemed inviting, she had always wanted to know what it would feel like to walk outside, embraced by her boyfriend.

He wrapped his arm around her waist and pulled her tightly to him as soon as they were outside. She risked an even closer snuggle and felt butterflies in her stomach when he smiled and kissed her lips. He kept kissing her until she was short of breath.

Her body was in flames from the closeness and happiness. So *that's* what it meant to have someone wrap their arms so protectively around her.

They walked quietly for two hours, just enjoying the closeness and heat their bodies radiated. She felt as if his energy was finding its way into her, and her heart filled with gratitude. They were there for each other, and that made it perfect. Along their way they bought Thai takeout and her heart almost exploded with delight when he insisted that they eat from the same box.

"What?" he asked after she gave him another one of her astounded looks.

"Nothing. I just didn't think it would be so easy... being with someone. I thought other people were just exaggerating, trying to comfort me by saying that when I meet the man of my life, it will have been worth all the wait and tears."

"Well, it's true."

He took off her coat when they got back home, and pressed her back against his chest. His free hand removed the hair from her neck and his lips made their way to the soft spot right behind her ears. She began hyperventilating. She enjoyed the feeling of his body warming her back, just the way she had always dreamed.

"Yes... that's.... just...."

"Mhm...I know what you need, and I will make sure you get it. I suggest we go and take a hot shower, all right?"

"I think I'd prefer a cold one, but I get your point."

After a throaty laugh he led them both to the bathroom. Once there, he allowed her to turn around. The way he looked at her made her melt into a puddle. In that moment, the two of them were all that mattered. She took the initiative and took off his sweater. She thought she would be more nervous when it came to undressing him completely, but she felt no shame. In fact, she enjoyed the look of him.

Then she began taking her own clothes off, but he stopped her and started to remove them by himself. Now she was shuddering again, because for the first time in her life someone was looking at the very core of who she was. Just when she thought she was completely lost, he turned on the shower and pulled her back to his chest. That's where she belonged, she realized.

The closeness of their naked bodies, the way they gently brushed each other, and the warmth of his beautifully sculpted chest pressed against her brought all sorts of tingling feelings alive within her. She focused on kissing his lips, because she wasn't ready to do anything else. He understood that, and didn't press on. He took the soap and started washing her. She kept her eyes closed, afraid they would reveal the intensity of her emotions.

A man was playing with her body in the gentlest of ways. Her dreams had come true, and she didn't even care it was only for a day. Today, Michael belonged to her, and she belonged to him. That was everything that she needed to know, and it made her happy. When they were done showering, he helped her dry because she was almost completely immobile from the intensity of pleasure that the whole experience had brought her.

She turned around to take her clothes and get dressed, but he had other ideas. He took her in his arms and led her straight to bed. All the while he was kissing her lips, and she clung to him as if her life depended on it.

He put her down on the bed and lay beside her, continuing to play with her lips, ears and waist. She moaned and managed to pull away from his lips just long enough to breathe, "I can't go all the way with you. It wouldn't be right."

"All right. But you have to know I don't have a problem with it."

She smiled and caressed his cheek. "I know. But this is so amazing I really don't need anything else. Only... I would like for you stay with me like this for the night. That's really the only thing I need right now."

And he did. He warmed her back and kissed her neck a little more, until they both relaxed. She enjoyed feeling his chest lightly pushing against her back. She slipped her hand beneath the covers and grabbed his. He entwined their fingers.

After making sure he wasn't going to go anywhere, she finally found the courage to close her eyes and fall asleep. She let herself slip into sleep once more, and for the first time in her life enjoyed a beautiful dream, full of hope and happiness.

She couldn't tell how long she slept, but when she woke up in the morning, he was gone. She still felt so comfortable and happy she couldn't bring herself to feel bad that he had gone without saying goodbye. Still, deciding it would be weird if she sent him an instant message after the day they had just experienced, she took the phone and called him. It didn't take him long to pick it up.

"Hey, kid! What's up?"

"Hey, I just wanted to thank you for last night."

"Okay...I guess..."

"Wait a minute, what's with that tone?"

"It's a tone that says 'I have no idea what the hell are you talking about'. We didn't see each other yesterday."

"What do you mean? You came over and-"

"I was away, visiting Danielle's parents, you know that."

"Huh?"

"Gemma... are you all right?"

"Yeah. Um, I guess I am. Um...can I ask you something?"

"Sure."

"If I told you that I wanted to kill myself, what would you do?"

"I'd come over with a bunch of DVDs, and make you confide in me while we ate Chinese takeout. I'd probably stop by the pharmacy and pick up a drug test, as well. Do I need to do that now?"

She giggled. "You're so sweet. No, thank you. I was just wondering."

"Well, we are best friends, right? I always take care of my best friend."

"I know you do, Mike. Thank you. I'll talk to you

later."

She sat on the bed and held the phone in her hand, staring absently. So... it was all a dream? It couldn't be. She knew the way his cheeks felt under her fingertips. His scent was still in her nostrils, and his hands on her waist had surely left a mark. She looked down, seeing herself for the very first time. She wasn't naked, as she had been last night. She was fully dressed with her socks on her feet.

So why had it felt so real? Why did she feel him so intensely? He hadn't been blurry in her dream, like people usually are. He had been crystal clear. She sighed and got up.

She decided to head to town and stop by her studio. She didn't have any clients scheduled for today, so she was flabbergasted when she saw a man leaning on the door, obviously waiting for her. She knew the neighbors were out at that time of day, and they weren't that friendly anyway.

"Excuse me, but I'm afraid we don't-"

He turned to her and she stopped dead in her tracks. Her legs went weak. Those eyes... those same blue eyes that had looked at her so lovingly last night were here, looking at her. He was about her height with dark brown hair neatly cut so the locks didn't fall into his eyes.

She looked at him curiously, knowing she was seeing him for the first time in her life, but the underlying familiarity was unavoidable.

"Do I... know you?" she stammered.

"I'm trying to find out the same thing. You look strangely familiar." He shook her hand.

"Likewise. Erm... I don't think we have an appointment. I'm Gemma, by the way."

"Matthew, pleased to meet you. You're right, we don't

have an appointment, but I thought I would take the chance anyway. You see, my niece's birthday is coming up and I heard some good things about your work. I got intrigued."

"All right. Why don't we go inside and I'll see what I can do."

"That is all I'm asking. Are you sure we haven't seen each other before? Anywhere?"

"I think I would have remembered you. The combination of blue eyes and dark hair is not something I usually come across."

"If I had a penny for every time someone told me that..."

They both laughed. The familiarity she felt with him in that instant was enough for her to know she would have to see this man again.

She would make sure that she would. Something told her that this man was exactly who she had been so desperately looking for most of her life.

∞

Dee Drin is a young writer who flirts with different genres and moods in her stories. She is all about magic, and she finds her daily dose of it in reading and writing her stories, as well as cooking. She writes to make herself happy and hopefully in the process will make someone else happy as well. You can find her writing at http://www.wattpad.com/user/DorChi.

Finding Marty

Katherine A. Ganzel

ത

Marty lay perfectly still, drenched in his own sweat, while he listened to the loud buzzing of cicadas. He watched the faded blue curtains above his bed lit by the morning sun, hoping for a breath of air that would cool him, but they didn't move.

What I wouldn't give for an electric fan, he thought with a sigh as he rolled away from the window, but he knew that was stupid. Even if he did have a fan, it's not like he'd be able to use it. The old man hadn't bothered to pay the electric bill in over a year. Unable to take the hot, humid air of his bedroom and aware of how long he'd been lying awake, he decided he'd better get up.

After taking a quick bath in blissfully cold water as quietly as he could so as not to wake the old man, he quickly dressed in a t-shirt and battered jeans, finishing by lacing up his worn brown leather boots. Already sweating, he ran his fingers through his still-damp dark hair, then reached under his bed and pulled out a small brown paper sack.

Aware of how late it was getting, he went to the

kitchen and made three peanut butter and jelly sandwiches as quickly and quietly as he could. Once he'd wrapped them in large squares of wax paper, he put them in the paper bag on top of items he'd purchased at the grocery store and left, easing the back door closed.

The heat wave had been relentless but had provided him with great opportunities. He'd spent the last few days in town, knocking on doors looking for work. It had been grueling out in the hot sun, but he felt a deep satisfaction. There wasn't a house he'd missed with an owner willing to pay a teenaged boy a few bits to mow the lawn, weed flower beds, or any other chore outside in the stifling heat. At the end of each day, he'd made his purchases and hid the goods under his bed. It wasn't wise to make a habit of bringing home money, not even if he hid it in his room. If the old man got wind of it, he'd be sure to make his life even more difficult.

Walking across the weed-filled yard, past the rusting pick-up truck, he finally felt like he could breathe. He'd made it out before the old man woke up. Even in the oppressive heat with the already-hot sun beating down on him, he felt happy. He turned down the dirt road, surrounded by the near-deafening sound of cicadas in the trees. Dust rose up with each step, coating his boots and the cuffs of his jeans.

When he reached the end of the dirt road five miles from his house, he stopped and wiped the sweat off his face. Stretching for miles in either direction was the highway - the main road leading to town. Directly across stood a high iron fence with spikes at the top, and clusters of large trees on either side. He pushed his hair out of his eyes and looked up and down the highway, but there wasn't a car in sight.

He crossed the road and went to the fence. Holding

the paper bag in his teeth, he pulled himself up the bars of the fence until he reached the top. Grabbing onto one of the low branches of a tree, he navigated the spikes to reach the other side, then slid down the bars to the ground. Smiling as he took the paper bag out of his teeth, he headed into the dark woods, enjoying the feel of the slightly cooler air enveloping him.

He'd begun sneaking onto the property two years earlier when he was a bored twelve-year-old. He knew better than to let anyone know he'd found a way over the fence since it would get him into all kinds of trouble. This was the estate of the richest man in the county, Jonathon Blackwell. He owned the iron mine, the newspaper, and the largest grocery store in town. There were other residents who did pretty well: the two doctors, some lawyers, and a few of the other store owners; but old man Blackwell was practically the king of the community. If he ever found out Marty was trespassing on his property, Marty had no doubt he'd be locked up and Blackwell would personally throw away the key.

After a few minutes, he reached a clearing and stopped as he surveyed his final destination. It was a small, one-story cabin with a wood-shingled roof and a chimney made of river stones. Window boxes in front of the two front windows had orange and yellow marigolds growing in them. Not long after he'd started climbing over the iron fence, he'd found this place while exploring the woods.

☙

As soon as Marty stumbled into the clearing and saw the little cabin, he jumped behind a large tree to hide, terrified he'd already been spotted by whoever was living there. With his heart pounding in his chest and alarm bells ringing in his head, he knew he should run, but he'd been wandering aimlessly for over an hour and wasn't sure which way he needed to go to get back to the fence.

While he looked at the sun almost directly above him, trying to decide which direction he was facing, he listened hard for approaching foot steps. Hearing only the sounds of the usual forest creatures around him, he decided to chance a peek around the tree. There were weeds growing between the steps leading up to the front door. The flower boxes under the two front windows were empty, and fallen branches from the surrounding trees littered the clearing. The place looked deserted.

Plucking up his courage, he slowly walked up to the nearest window, keeping his ears and eyes alert to any signs of occupants. Through the dirty pane of glass, he saw two large wooden chairs and a small table arranged haphazardly. Magazines and newspapers littered the floor. He breathed a sigh of relief, knowing with certainty no one was living there.

Feeling emboldened, he tried the door handle and it opened, the hinges groaning loudly from disuse. He wasn't surprised the door was unlocked. After all, the cabin was in the middle of a private estate. He stepped into a small parlor with a large stone fireplace. The air was musty but heavy with the perfume from the pine wood planks of the floor. He walked through to a small kitchen, noticing a thick layer of dust coating everything. The back door was a little harder to open, but after a few hard tugs on the handle, he managed it, letting in more light and fresh air.

When he opened the cupboard doors and drawers,

he found a few mismatched dishes and silverware, but most were empty. There was a pump that supplied water to the wash basin and when he pumped the handle, a steady stream of rusty water came out. There was a small table with two stools under it and an old, battered tea kettle sitting on top of a small, cast-iron cook stove.

Walking back into the parlor, he saw his boot prints in the dust covering the floor. It was clear he was the first person who'd been in there in years. Marty's heart sped up as a bold thought filled his mind. If no one was using the cabin, then why couldn't he? It almost seemed like a dream come true. He would make this his special place. A place where he could come and hang out, doing whatever he wanted without anyone bothering him. Later that afternoon when the light began to fade as the sun sank, he turned around for one last look just before he left the clearing. That little cabin was his, he thought with satisfaction.

᪐

From that moment on, he'd snuck onto the estate whenever he could, spending hours at the cabin. At first he'd thrown himself into the task of cleaning, attacking the years' accumulation of cobwebs and dust and washing the grime off the windows. He even cleaned up the clearing, pulling up weeds and planting flower seeds in the window boxes. Instead of spending the money he'd made doing odd jobs around town on Saturday morning movies, he'd spent it on things for the cabin and small amounts of food.

Marty entered the cabin, leaving the front door open. The air was hotter inside and stuffy, but he breathed deeply, taking in the smell of the pine floors. He set the paper bag down on the table by the fireplace and went around opening the windows, noting the glass was overdue for a good washing. Then he went to the kitchen, taking his bag with him. Once he had the back door open, he wiped the sweat off his face with his shirt sleeve, thinking how thirsty he was. He could make his own version of iced tea, but it was far too hot to make a fire in the wood-burning stove. He'd make a fire in the fire pit outside, he decided, reaching for the tea kettle.

His hand froze halfway to the handle and all the hairs on the back of his neck stood on end. He'd always put the tea kettle on the rear right side of the stove, but now it was sitting on the left side, close to the front. Looking around, he listened hard while his heart pounded in his chest. Someone had been in the cabin. They knew he'd been using it. He couldn't afford to get caught, he thought desperately. He had to get the hell out of there.

Terrified it was already too late, he turned and ran to the front door. He jumped down the steps then skidded to a stop on the grass. In front of him was a young girl looking just as startled to see him as he was to see her.

"Oh! Hi!" she said with surprise, her voice high and strong, while he looked at her with shock.

He hadn't thought about the possibility of being caught for years, but when he had, he'd always imagined old man Blackwell would be the one to find him. If not him, though, it would most likely have been the groundskeeper, or maybe even Blackwell's son, Douglas, who was a year older than Marty. But all the times he'd pictured it, he'd never in his wildest dreams imagined he'd be caught by some kid he'd never seen before.

She was thin, and shorter than him by a good foot with short brown hair. She wore a pale blue, short-sleeved dress that hung on her skinny frame, and Mary

Jane shoes with white ankle socks. It felt like minutes were passing as she stared at him with wide brown eyes, like she was waiting for him to say something, but he stayed silent as he frantically tried to think what he should do.

"You don't live here," she said, and the tension inside him snapped.

"Are you going to rat me out?" he blurted out angrily before he could stop himself.

"What?" she asked. "To who?"

"To your daddy!" he spat, and she flinched.

"You mean my uncle?" she asked quietly.

Oh, shit, he thought with a terrible realization. Was her uncle old man Blackwell? He could feel the walls of a jail cell closing in around him.

"To whoever!" he shouted, waving his arms as he lost control. "You said it, didn't you? I don't live here! This is *your* property!" he sneered. He was surprised when he saw anger flash in her eyes.

"This isn't *my* property!" she yelled as she took a step towards him, her hands balling into fists.

It wasn't very often someone was willing to stand up to him. He had a reputation in town of being someone who didn't back down from a fight, and he couldn't help being impressed, seeing her unafraid and ready to take him on. The little squirt had some fight in her.

"So *you* don't live here either," he challenged. She slumped as if his words had wounded her.

"I guess, I do - now," she muttered.

His stomach sank. If she lived here, she'd soon be running her mouth about him. He felt a pain in his chest as he realized it was over. He'd lost it. The one thing he cared about in the world was gone.

"I'm out of here!" he growled angrily, and brushed

Katherine A. Ganzel

past her as he stalked away.

"Wait! Please don't go!" she cried out, but he kept walking. "I don't care if you're not supposed to be here! I won't tell!" He slowed and then stopped. "I promise!" He slowly turned to face her. He searched her eyes, trying to decide if he should trust her. He knew he was making a huge mistake even considering it. He'd learned long ago there wasn't anyone he could trust. Even his own brothers had betrayed him, taking off as soon as they were old enough to escape, leaving him alone and at the mercy of his old man.

The oldest, D.J., had enlisted in the army on his eighteenth birthday. His middle brother, Stevie, hadn't even lasted that long. One bad night after he'd gotten into a fist fight with the old man, he'd run off, swearing he'd never come back. He'd been good to his word and they'd never heard from him again. He had been fourteen then, the age Marty was now. How he'd managed to survive on his own, Marty didn't know, nor did he care. Both brothers knew what the old man was like after he hit the bottle, and yet they'd left Marty behind. They hadn't bothered to come back once over the last five years to see if he was all right.

"Why should I trust you?" Marty demanded.

"Because - because you can," she said hesitantly, almost making it sound like a question. He snorted and turned to leave.

"Wait! I swear on my mother's grave I won't tell!" she shouted. He stopped in his tracks.

The image of his own mother came into his mind, her body wasted away from the cancer that had taken hold of her. Once the symptoms had shown themselves, it was only a few months before she was so sick she could do little more than lie in bed. Marty knew it was bad when she couldn't even read to him anymore. She'd died, leaving him the week after he'd turned six and his life had never been the same. With his brothers reeling from the loss, there was no one he could turn to. The only way he could deal with it was to force himself not to think about her. And he hadn't for the last several years, at least not until now.

He carefully composed his face before he turned around. Her brown eyes steadily held his gaze, and while he searched them, he recognized something he'd seen many times in his own eyes. She'd been masking it well, but it was there, the pain just beneath the surface.

"Oh-kay," he said slowly, and her face lit up.

"Great!" she exclaimed happily. "I'm Jessica Blackwell, but you can call me Jess," she said confidently, closing the few feet between them and holding her hand out to him.

He looked at her hand while his stomach sank. She *was* old man Blackwell's niece. He took it, knowing he didn't have any other choice. He'd sealed his fate with her. All he could do was hope she'd meant it when she'd sworn to keep her mouth shut.

"I'm Martin, but you can call me Marty," he said, barely able to keep the mocking tone out of his voice. He'd keep his last name to himself - not that it would keep him from getting caught if she blabbed.

"Pleased to meet you, Marty," she said, pumping his arm with a surprisingly firm grip. In spite of himself, he couldn't help thinking it was funny. He had to give her credit. The squirt had moxie.

She stood there, continuing to grin at him until it became awkward. He didn't usually talk to people, especially not girls he didn't know. After a minute, he couldn't take it anymore. "Well, I have things to do," he said firmly, and turned to walk back towards the cabin, hoping she'd take the hint.

"Like what?" she asked cheerfully, catching up. His shoulders drooped as he realized she wasn't going to be so easy to get rid of.

"Uh," he said, stalling while he tried to think. Leaving was out of the question. It would be hours before the old man had drunk himself into a stupor and it was safe to return to his house. Going into town wasn't a possibility either, since teen boys weren't allowed to hang around with nothing to do. He remembered the windows needed washing, but he wasn't about to let this girl see him cleaning. "I'm, uh - gathering firewood," he said, veering towards the trees.

"Really? That's neat!" she chirped happily.

He decided to ignore her, and walked several feet into the woods before starting to pick up small branches. To his annoyance, she stood there watching him.

"*So,*" she said, drawing it out, "do you come here often?"

"No!" he barked, and glared at her. He didn't need her gathering information about him. She already knew too much. He turned his back to her, picking up more pieces of wood.

"Oh, that's interesting. I've been here almost every day for the past week. But this is the first time I've seen you so I figured maybe you don't come here that often."

He was astounded. Somehow he'd managed to miss seeing her both times he'd been there.

"Don't you just love that cabin? When I saw it, I thought it was so pretty! It's like a little play house, like the house from Hansel and Gretel - only it's not made of candy - and without the creepy witch. I wish I'd found it a long time ago. When I first came here, I was too scared to go in the woods. It's so *dark* in here - and there's all these creepy *noises!*" she said, shivering dramatically.

Did she *ever* shut up, he wondered angrily as he walked further away from her.

"I didn't want to go in there but I just got so bored walking in the yard. All you can do is go *around* and *around.* Then last week, I saw this path behind the garage and I decided to take a chance and see where it went to."

He knew exactly which path she was referring to. He'd used it occasionally to sneak up to Blackwell's mansion. The entrance to the path was hidden from view by the large garage, but he'd skirted around the edge of the woods to get a look at the big house. He'd spied on them a few times but it was hardly worth it. He never saw anyone outside except for the groundskeeper. Even Douglas never came out, but then maybe rich people's homes were so nice they never felt the need to go outside.

"I'm so glad I decided to go down that path," she continued chattily. "Now I love the woods! I guess it's time I got used to them since I've been here for three months." He turned to look at her.

"You've lived here for three *months?*" he asked astonishment.

"Yeah. Why?"

"I, uh - haven't seen you around town before." It wasn't a very large town. Visitors always stuck out like a sore thumb. And it was the kind of place where everyone knew everybody else's business. He was surprised he hadn't heard Blackwell had a niece, nor that she'd moved in with him.

"Oh," she said, looking away. "I haven't been - out

much." Then she turned her back to him and started picking up twigs. He expected her to keep talking, but for once, she was quiet.

As he resumed gathering wood, he couldn't stop thinking about her mother's death, and wondered if it had something to do with her moving in with her uncle. Then he heard a faint rustling noise in the trees, growing louder as it came closer to them. Both of them straightened and turned just as a strong breeze made the trees overhead start swaying. The heat and humidity vanished as a cool burst of air hit them.

"Oh! Doesn't that feel great!" she exclaimed, grinning at him. It did feel good.

By the way the wind was picking up, he could tell a storm was approaching. He started back towards the cabin without saying anything, but he glanced over his shoulder to make sure she was following him. He went to the back door and threw the wood he'd gathered into the old soap crate just inside the kitchen. When he stepped away, she came forward and threw in the twigs she had in her hands.

Thunder boomed loud and long, making the floor of the cabin shake as it rolled across the forest. She looked at him with wide eyes. A gust of wind blew through the cabin and the front door slammed shut with a loud bang, making both of them jump. He closed the back door, then quickly went around closing the windows before the rain started. When he returned to the kitchen he was surprised to see the girl hugging herself, her body shaking. Goose bumps covered her skinny arms.

"Are you cold?" he asked, and she nodded. It figures, he thought. The temperature was a lot cooler and the squirt had hardly any meat on her bones.

"Here," he said taking one of the stools out from the

table and putting it near the cook stove. "Have a seat."

She sat, still hugging herself, and he put some of the twigs into the stove's fire box along with crumpled newspaper. He struck a match and she leaned forward to watch the flames take hold. Soon he had a small fire going and he fed it, putting in wood a piece at a time just as rain began drumming on the roof. Once the fire was established, he was going to close the fire box door when he looked at her. Her body was still trembling as she leaned close to the stove, watching the flames with fascination. He decided to leave it open.

"Do you want some tea?" he asked, and she looked startled.

"But you'll have to go out there to get the water!" she exclaimed.

"No, I won't. There's a pump right there," he said, shocked he had to point out the obvious at the washbasin.

"That's broken," she said with certainty.

"What?" He took the kettle over to it and began pumping the handle. When water began pouring out, she looked at him like he'd just performed a miracle.

"How did you do that?" she asked.

"You just pump the handle. Don't you know you have to prime the pump?"

"No."

He couldn't believe it. He thought everyone knew how pumps worked. "Where are you from anyway?"

"Manhattan."

"You mean - New York City?" When she nodded, he let out a low whistle. "That's a big city," he said, shaking his head. He'd seen it in the movies. He couldn't even imagine what it must be like to live in a city that big, but it was starting to make sense. She was a city girl. He looked at the rain hitting the windows while he filled the kettle and then he suddenly felt sick as a thought occurred to him. "Aren't they going to be worried you're out in the rain and come looking for you?" he asked her.

"No one knows I'm out." When she saw the look on his face, she added, "No one's at home. It's the housekeeper's day off and Uncle Jonathon is at work. He won't be home until late tonight."

"What about - your cousin," he asked, not wanting to say his name. He saw a look cross her face before she turned to look at the fire.

"He's in France for the month," she muttered. She hated him too, Marty thought, but he wasn't surprised. Douglas Blackwell was an arrogant asshole.

He put the kettle on the stove then got two mugs ready with tea bags. With nothing left to do, he pulled up a stool and sat beside her. He noticed her body had stopped shaking and she no longer had goose bumps. When her stomach grumbled loudly, she hugged herself while he pretended not to notice. A moment later it grumbled again and he remembered his sandwiches in the paper bag.

"Are you hungry?" he asked as he stood up, fetching the bag.

"No," she said, but her stomach grumbled again. "Not really," she clarified, looking embarrassed.

He fished out a sandwich and held it out to her. "Here." She looked at it, but didn't move.

"Go on," he encouraged, "It's peanut butter and jelly."

"I - I don't want to eat your food. I mean, it's your sandwich," she said, looking worried.

"I have two more, see?" he said, taking them out to show her.

"Are you sure?" she asked, looking torn.

"Of course," he said, smiling to reassure her.

"Well, okay," she said, smiling back at him with relief as she took it. "Thank you, Marty."

"It's nothing," he said as he sat on his stool, and began unwrapping a sandwich. He didn't want her thinking he didn't get enough to eat, even if it was sometimes true. He didn't need her pity. He got enough of that in town. It was no secret his old man was a drunk and he'd sometimes catch people, mostly women, looking at him like he was a lost puppy. He *hated* that.

"Oh, it's so good! It's the best sandwich I've had in a long time!" she exclaimed after she'd taken a bite. He looked over at her, skeptical she would get so excited over a simple sandwich.

"We don't have peanut butter in the house. Uncle Jonathon doesn't like it," she explained when she saw his expression. "I've *missed* it," she added with a dramatic sigh.

He turned his attention back to his sandwich to hide his expression. He thought rich kids got to eat whatever they wanted. The water started boiling and he stood up to pour it into their mugs. To his surprise, she stood up too and moved their stools over to the table. Then she sat down with her sandwich in front of her on the square of wax paper. She smiled at him with her goofy grin when he set the mugs on the table.

"It's okay if we eat here, right?" she asked hopefully.

"Uh, yeah, sure," he said, but it felt weird.

He'd never expected he'd be eating a meal with someone at this table. But then, he didn't know the last time he'd sat at a table to share a meal with anyone. He didn't even eat with the other kids at school. Long ago he'd made a point of eating outside by himself. It kept the other kids from seeing how little he had, or from noticing the days he had nothing.

"Neat!" she exclaimed. "I thought this would be easier than holding everything on our laps," she added, as if he needed an explanation. He kept quiet and hunched over his sandwiches. When she sipped the tea, she exclaimed, "I never had tea without milk and sugar before but this is really good! Thanks for making this for me!" He didn't meet her eyes as he drank his own tea. He'd never had it *with* milk and sugar. After they'd finished, Marty stood up and reached for her mug.

"Oh, let me wash them. It's the least I can do after you shared your lunch with me," she said cheerfully.

Before he could say anything, she'd taken both mugs to the washbasin and opened the cupboard where he kept the dish soap. He was amazed she knew where it was, but then he remembered she'd been coming to the cabin for a week. He damped down the stove to kill the fire and opened the back door while she pumped the handle to get water for washing.

A clean, cool breeze came into the warm kitchen and he leaned against the door frame. The storm had passed and the sun was shining. Water droplets sparkled as they dripped off the eave of the roof and surrounding trees, and the grass in the clearing glittered.

"It's so beautiful," she said with wonder in her voice, and he realized she was standing next to him, wiping her hands on a dish towel. "It's not like this in the city," she said, looking up at him with a smile, and then he caught a flash of sadness in her eyes before she turned to hang the towel on a hook over the washbasin. "I should probably go," she said when she turned around, her voice sounding strong and the pain in her eyes masked again. "I don't want anyone to know I've been out. I never told my uncle I found the cabin. I was afraid he'd forbid me to come here. He - doesn't like me to be away from the house." He didn't quite know what to say to that. It seemed so odd, but it explained why she hadn't been to town yet. She stuck her hand out. "Good bye, Marty." He looked at it and then up into her brown eyes.

"C'mon, squirt. I'll walk with you," he said, pushing off the door frame. She looked startled for a moment, then her face lit up and she smiled her goofy grin at him.

"Okay!"

He was grateful she didn't talk his ear off during the walk on the path. Instead, she seemed absorbed with the view, looking all around at the wet forest with the dappled sunlight making everything sparkle. He stopped just before the curve that would bring the back of the garage into view.

"Good bye, Marty. I hope it's okay if I visit you again," she said, sticking her hand out. He couldn't help thinking it was funny she was asking for permission and smiled back at her.

"Sure, squirt," he replied while she pumped his arm with her firm grip.

"Great!" she said happily, smiling her goofy grin.

Then she turned and disappeared around the curve. Marty watched the spot for a moment before he shoved his hands in the pockets of his jeans. As he walked back to the cabin, he thought about the windows that needed washing.

ଔ

Katherine A. Ganzel began writing late in life, starting her first novel when her kids were nearly grown. Her suspenseful romance, Stolen Hearts, *appears on* Wattpad *under the username*

Katherine A. Ganzel

KatherineArlene, where it has become a beloved favorite for many readers. The sequel, Love You Forever, *soon followed and both books together have been read over 1,200,000 times. Her new romance featuring the characters from 'Finding Marty' will begin uploading in December 2013. She currently resides in Ann Arbor, Michigan with her husband, two daughters, three cats, and two dogs.*

You can follow Katherine at http://www.facebook.com/AuthorKatherineGanzel.

Eternal Dreams

Emerald Delmara

⁂

Blinking tears from my eyes, I focused on the road as I whipped around the corners I knew so well. The beautiful scenery I had always loved was a blur, the trees and mountains just a myriad of colors amidst a darkening sky in my peripheral vision.

I needed someone to talk to. I desperately needed it. There was only one person who would understand what was really going on. I was in fight or flight mode, and I had clearly chosen flight.

I spotted the side road I needed to take and whipped onto it, albeit a little dangerously. I didn't care at the moment. Wind beat furiously at the trees and my car. A storm was coming, and that suited my mood just fine.

My car began to shake as the road turned from asphalt to dirt. My heart surged in my chest. I was close to my destination, and I couldn't get there fast enough.

The landscape passed by unnoticed as I traveled deep into the woods, finally spotting the grove I was looking for. Coming to a screeching halt, I jumped out and ran as fast as I could into the trees. I let myself be swallowed up by the forest, my heart pounding more and more with each step I took.

At last, the huge laurel tree that was my safe place came into view. I slowed down to catch my breath. The smells of the forest permeated my senses, invoking a feeling and remembrance of home. Damp earth, rich loam, moss, and a heavy scent of oncoming rain seeped into my nostrils, comforting me more than any hug could.

A bubbling sound drew my attention to the small creek flowing about twenty yards from the laurel. Walking over, I bent down and washed the tear tracks off my face, taking a deep breath before filling the small flask I always carried with me.

I thanked the creek for its gift and walked back to the looming tree. I took a sip of the cold, crisp water then poured the rest of the contents of the flask on the tree before placing my hand upon it. Instead of being cool like the water, the tree bark was warm and thumped under my hand, like a heartbeat. A simultaneous thump resounded on my chest, where my pentagram of sterling silver and moonstone lay. I wasn't taken aback - this was what I had come here for.

Letting my mind fill with precious memories of this tree and the person I wanted most to see, I breathed words into the suddenly silent air.

"Daphne, I release you. Come to me. I really need a friend."

The laurel tree shivered mightily, but when the woman I needed the most slipped out of the now oily bark, I grabbed her hand and she threw her arms around me.

"I am so sorry I wasn't there for you earlier. It's going to be alright, Alexandra," she whispered in to my ear, and a sighing, broken sob burst from my chest. As I hugged her tightly, my knees buckled and I fell to the forest floor, burying my face in her stomach as I cried.

Her hands caressed my head lovingly as pain, anguish, and betrayal poured from me in violent torrents of repressed emotion. At that moment the storm broke, pouring down upon us just as ferociously as my tears, enveloping me in a wet but welcome embrace.

As my sobs subsided, the emptiness of emotional numbness took over and I shakily got to my feet.

"Are you feeling better?" Daphne spoke softly to me.

"A bit." Despite my curt tone, she graced me with a reassuring smile.

Daphne and I had a strange relationship. My mother had died when I was very young and my father never remarried. Like most people in true love, he retreated deeply into his pain and never resurfaced. As a child, I would take long walks and explore the forest away from prying and pitying eyes. One day, after a particularly exhausting expedition, even with a child's nearly limitless energy, I stumbled upon this sacred grove.

Hot and sweaty, I wandered over to the small stream. Shrugging off my backpack, I noisily gulped as much water as my stomach could comfortably hold before splashing it on myself to cool off.

I walked over to the tree and braced my back upon it as I withdrew my lunch of peanut butter and jelly sandwiches, chips, and a banana. Setting the pack beside me, I heard a tinkling clunk from within. Curious, I reached my hand in.

It was my mother's necklace, one that I hadn't seen since she died. I only remembered it disappearing because my father had flown into a rage looking for it, convinced I had stolen it.

Stunned, I dangled it in front of me as it glistened in

the sunlight. It was the most beautifully crafted piece of jewelry I had ever seen, and the most unusual.

It was a delicate silver five-pointed star within a circle, with swirling vines laced between the outer edges of the star. In the middle, there was a white stone, both cloudy and yet almost transparent in appearance, softly glowing in the daylight. Alternating dark blue sapphires and clear, calming aquamarines graced the tips of each point of the star, glittering as the sun hit them. The chain felt warm and strangely alive in my hand, and I held it to my chest.

Loneliness engulfed me as I sat against the tree, drenched from the stream and trying to stay strong, as I was expected to do, but I began to feel sad and angry at the same time. In an unusual moment of weakness, I spoke aloud.

"I wish I wasn't so alone. I wish I had someone to talk to." Closing my eyes, I leaned my head back only to find there was a warmth against my back that hadn't been there before, and something pulsed strongly enough to jar my entire body.

Jerking myself forward, I spun around to see the shimmering figure of a woman stepping from within a black, watery portal. The world stood still as I froze in shock.

After an hour of trying to calm me down with sweet words - and only partially succeeding - the beautiful woman had introduced herself to me as Daphne. She explained that the mixture of the water, my words, and my mother's mysterious necklace had released her from her imprisonment in the laurel tree. She was a Dryad, or a tree nymph, as well as a Naiad, or a water nymph, bridging two worlds.

Over time she became a mother, sister, confidant,

and best friend all rolled into one. When I needed her, she was there, though it took more of my energy to call her if I wasn't by water or a laurel tree.

She eventually explained to me that my mother wasn't mortal. She was a Naiad as well, descended from Daphne's own bloodline, who had wandered from her river and fallen in love with a Druid - my father - who was himself the offspring of a Dryad who had a dalliance with his father.

My mother had chosen her love for my father and me over her own life. Living away from her river with only small sources of water around our house had weakened her over time. While my father had known there was something magical about her, she never revealed the truth of her background, and that directly led to her death.

The necklace, a symbol of her ties to the moon and the water, vanished the day she died because she willed it to be so. However, the day my powers started to awaken, it reappeared. It was my birthright. While it isn't a life my mother would have chosen for me, even with my strange family tree, I have no regrets. Magic, even with its downsides, is an essential part of who I am. It has given me many irreplaceable gifts, like Daphne, the Dryads and Naiads who are my friends, and even Ian.

Ian. Just thinking about him brought me back to my misery.

"Alexandra, you must snap out of this." Daphne's patient and loving voice brought me back to the present as forcefully as a slap to the face.

Goddess, I really am out of it. This shock-y feeling is starting to be a pain in the ass! I internally shook myself as Daphne began to giggle, her ocean-colored, knee-length hair falling over her face when she snorted into her palm.

"If you can think thoughts like that, I know you'll be fine." Her golden eyes sparkled with mirth.

"Says the Goddess who just snorted into her palm like a schoolgirl." I couldn't help but giggle a little myself.

"I knew something was very wrong when I felt a storm pop up out of nowhere and head this way, but I had no idea it was something like this until your thoughts screamed out to me as you arrived. You were so out of your mind with emotion you couldn't even hear me trying to soothe you," Daphne sighed, slumping her willowy shoulders. "What happened exactly? It isn't like you to let your emotions overwhelm you so much. Even your power over the weather was about to get out of control."

"It's Ian," I told her, "he's back." My voice broke and I coughed into my hand to cover it.

"What happened?" She spoke carefully, and I knew she was afraid of making a bad situation worse. As much as I wanted to avoid reliving it, she had a right to know.

"He showed up out of nowhere while I was at the bookstore. I was perusing the shelves, looking for a new book, when I felt something strange. My shoulders tightened, and when he spoke, I shuddered because I knew it was him." I took a deep breath.

"I asked him what he was doing there, though I wanted to just scream at him. He said he had come to fulfill our promise. After all these years, instead of acting apologetic he was indulgent and amused! That set my temper off.

"Without meaning to, I stepped toward him and slapped him across the face so hard every bone in my hand vibrated." My voice quaked. I had scared myself a little, because while I was appalled at my behavior, my subconscious was laughing sadistically in glee. It had just felt *so* good to vent my anger on the one who deserved it. I could barely keep myself in check. Daphne rubbed my back comfortingly.

"I screamed questions at him but then I realized I was about to cry, and I refused to do that in front of him. I ran out of there as if hellhounds were on my heels, jumped into my car and sped off, just leaving him there while he yelled my name.

"That might have been a bit childish, but it was better than the alternative. Part of me wanted to just run back to him, throw myself into his arms and cry out years' worth of pain and anguish before I beat the shit out of him." Daphne's hand shook, her barely concealed chuckles prompting me to turn my swollen, dark blue glare on her.

"I know that might have been too violent of an impulse. But you know Ian has always had a way about him that pushes me to extremes." I dropped my voice to a whisper, trying to mask the agony it contained. "Apparently, time hasn't changed that."

A contemplative but hesitant look crossed Daphne's delicate features as she kissed the top of my head, making me dread what she might ask.

"What exactly happened with Ian all those years ago? When you came to me the night he disappeared, you were worse off than you are now, and you wouldn't say a word. I couldn't even get a detail from your mind. It was blank, without even a thought. Just soul-shattering emotion. I was terrified you would break from the strain of it. I understand if you don't want to talk about it, but if you are all right with it, I wouldn't mind hearing it now."

Pain pierced my heart at her words, but I knew she

was right. It was time to lay it out for her.

"Well, shall I start at the beginning?" I sighed as she nodded. As close as we were, Ian had always been a sore topic. "Then let's get comfortable."

The rain subsided as dusk faded, leaving the stars twinkling merrily in the night sky. I made a blanket appear on the ground, thick enough to be comfortable but magical enough to resist rain soaking into it. I sat down, stretching my legs out as Daphne settled into some pillows she conjured for us. With a snap of her fingers, a cozy campfire appeared near us, soothing me with its flickering flames.

Knowing how painful this was going to be, I did what any self-respecting twenty-three year old woman would do. I snapped my fingers and a goblet appeared in my hand, filled with a chilled, dark-red wine. Two seconds later, Daphne had her own goblet in her hand, filled with her favorite white. We both drank and she looked pointedly at me, making me grimace.

"...All right. When I was in sixth grade, Ian transferred into my school. I fell for him the first time I laid eyes on him, even at twelve years old. He was handsome and had the most captivating golden-brown eyes I had ever seen, like a glass of aged whiskey. His black hair had natural blue and purple highlights in the sun, like a raven's wings. I also loved his height, because he was the first boy I had met who was taller than I was at that age. At first, it was just a crush and I couldn't even look him in the eyes. His serious exterior made it even harder. I avoided him whenever I could, too embarrassed to even make friends with him. I just buried myself in books and spent time with you in the forest." A fond smile slipped across my face as I began to become lost in my memories.

"In the seventh grade, we were grouped together at the beginning of the year to do a project for our History class. I was so nervous my hands would shake when I sat next to him, and I was worried about how the project was going to progress, especially if I wasn't going to be able to make eye contact with him. One day he cornered me in the library, scaring me out of my skin. He demanded to know what he had done to make me hate him, and I was so shocked that I blurted out that his presence was frightening. Realizing my mistake, I clapped my hand over my mouth and my eyes flew to his face without thought. The hurt I saw there made me regret what I had done, and I apologized profusely. After stuttering out that I just wasn't good with people, he softened and said he would forgive me, but only if I became his best friend. That's when I fell in love with him. As you already know, I immediately agreed, and we were very close to each other up until prom night.

"After years of seeing him with other girls, I was at my limit. Carrying around a heartbreaking, unrequited love had taken its toll, and I was determined to make a move. The week before, his girlfriend had dumped him and he was depressed, so I asked him to be my date, as a friend, so that we could go out after the dance. I wanted to celebrate his birthday with him, which was the next day, the day before mine. He said it sounded like a good plan, and I was overjoyed." I leaned back to look at the moon rising in the sky before continuing.

"I spent hours dolling myself up like any normal girl going to prom, hoping he would notice my efforts. He must have, because when he came to pick me up he took one look at me and blushed, stuttering as he tried to give me a compliment. It was the first time I had seen his stern, blunt exterior crack a bit and I found it enchanting. It was adorable." I rolled my eyes and Daphne laughed.

"The night was incredible. We went to the dance and had a blast, spending all of our time laughing as we danced like fools out in the crowd. I had more hope than ever that he liked me back because he didn't take his eyes off me the entire night, so I flirted my ass off. To my surprise, he seriously flirted back.

"Finally, in the early morning hours we stopped at a pancake shop to grab some breakfast, and then went to my tree house in my back yard to drink some wine one of his friends had given us. The wine seemed like a wonderfully forbidden way to end a perfect night.

"We drank ourselves tipsy, and that's when disaster struck. The alcohol had torn away my inhibitions and I found myself in his lap, hugging him with all of my might. He asked me what was wrong and I couldn't stop myself from spilling my secret. I told him that over time I had fallen in love with him and I couldn't take seeing him with other girls any longer." My tone turned pensive as Daphne grabbed my hand in a show of support. I wanted to hug her for comfort but I knew I needed to continue.

"After I finished speaking he made me look at him, and with a tender expression, he kissed me. It was my first kiss, and the most wonderful thing I had ever experienced. I told him so and he turned pink, which made me kiss him again.

"We made out until the sun came up and I left the tree house a virgin. He hadn't even pressed me for sex and that made me giddily happy. I was looking at the world through rose-colored glasses. He had been so gentle with me and seemed to return my feelings. Everything was falling into place. He told me I had given him the best birthday present he could have hoped for, *my love*, and this time *I* blushed, which made him laugh.

"We both went home, and I was a regular seventeen year old girl in love with a boy who happened to be her best friend. However, I was a seventeen year old fool." I gulped as much wine as I could and forced the words out of my mouth. "That was the last time I saw him, before today."

"What!" Daphne, who had been listening intently, voiced her indignation. I raised my eyebrow at her and laughed bitterly.

"Yep, you heard me correctly. After that night, he disappeared. He didn't come back to school, didn't attend graduation, and didn't call me. As you saw, I was destroyed. I thought something had happened to him but his family wouldn't tell me a thing. They didn't seem worried at all. Instead, they seemed annoyed with me, which was unusual because I had been close to them for years. I even went as far as calling the cops, but they didn't even really look into it. They said I was being a melodramatic teenager. All of these years I've wondered if he was dead, lying in a ditch somewhere because I couldn't believe he would just leave me without saying anything. It was so suspicious. Yet I couldn't shake the feeling he was alive, though I hid that feeling behind fear and anguish. I was certain if he *was* alive, he would have come back to me. And now, he shows up to fulfill a decade-year-old promise without a care in the world." I chugged my wine, trying to drown the hurt. "Yet today, I'd had a feeling something was coming my way, something big... but I never imagined this."

"You poor thing. But I do have to say, maybe it was a good thing he left when he did..." Daphne trailed off when the wind whipped fiercely around us and I sat straight up, shaking with anger. She had touched an agonizingly painful nerve.

"What do you mean it might have been a good thing?" I yelled in outrage. Sparks crackled off my skin from the heat of my fury, my long, brunette hair swirling around me from the gale I created.

"Darling, I simply meant you will stop aging on your next birthday. You are immortal. You knew this was going to happen. Once those of our bloodline reach a certain stage of development, we freeze in time. What would happen to your relationship if you two were still together now and he began to notice?" Daphne's calm words penetrated the haze of my anger and I slumped backwards, feeling the will to fight leave my body as the wind died down.

"You're right." My whispered words made me ache and for the first time in my life, I wished for a split second that I were normal. I scoffed at the thought and scowled. My heritage was something I was proud of and being mortal wouldn't change a thing.

"Alexandra, what is the promise you spoke of? It must be pretty important for him to have come back for it now." Daphne's golden eyes glittered in the light of the fire as they searched mine. With a sardonic laugh, I emptied my goblet and snapped my fingers to make it disappear.

"At the end of seventh grade, the first year of our friendship, we both buried time capsules in the farthest field from my father's house, under a big oak tree. We promised we would dig them up when we were twenty-three, which was about ten years later, and show them to one another. The Dryads still assure me each year that they are buried there, waiting to be dug up. But, Daphne, I don't think I can do it. I don't think I have the strength to face him." Burying my face in my hands for a moment, I sighed and got up.

Walking over to the creek, I jumped in, reveling in the feel of the water over my skin. Daphne sat on the edge, dangling her feet in the water.

"I remember when you freed me for the first time and this creek, only a stream then, grew into something more beautiful and powerful. You were so amazed you believed everything I had told you was true and you truly embraced your heritage. You also made me a promise to keep your powers a secret, and that is a secret you have truly kept." Her tone was thoughtful, and I turned suspiciously to look at her.

"Your point?"

"You always keep your promises, even if you think you can't handle them."

I stared at her, paling as the truth of her words hit me, and I dreaded what I was going to have to do.

"Alexandra, just go home and sleep on it. All of these problems will still be here tomorrow. You have had enough to deal with for one day. Just remember, you deserve to be happy too, not miserable all of the time."

"Okay." We shared a loving hug, then I watched her slip back into her tree. I walked back to my car and drove home with my mind whirling from the day's events.

Arriving at my tiny cottage, I placed my purse on a table after locking up and trudged off to my room. I had been through the emotional wringer today and felt worn out.

Throwing myself on the bed, I snuggled under the covers and let sleep drag me under.

៩

Opening my eyes, I was relieved to see that tonight's dream was a romantic veranda overlooking a Hawaiian beach and the ocean, and I was curled up in an exquisitely comfortable chair. The salty smell of the surf was pleasant and candles stood everywhere, their flames dancing in the warm night. The stars and the moon were shining brightly, gracing the terrace with an iridescent glow as the breeze flitted softly over my skin, tugging at my buttery-smooth silver gown and my free-flowing hair.

With a thought, a small table appeared near me with a bottle of red wine and a crystal goblet. Sighing in happiness and relief, I poured a glass and sat back, fully intending to relax until something popped up in the corner of my eye.

Entering dreamland had always been a mostly pleasant experience for me, and was usually my escape from the world. Since my powers blossomed on my eighteenth birthday, I had been able to control my dreams except for one little thing...

"Ian!" I screeched at the tall, dark, devastatingly handsome and yet loathsome man who had plagued my dreams at least once a night for five years. My subconscious loved to terrorize me with dreams of him, and though I had often tried to change them, it hardly ever worked.

"Hello, Alexandra. Took you long enough." A slow smile spread across his lips and I shivered. No one should ever look that good, especially not him.

"Fuck you!" I spat the words at him as I gulped the wine and placed a ring of candles around him with a flick of my wrist, their flames shooting up more than seven feet in the air, effectively imprisoning him. Goddess, it felt good to do that!

"Alexandra, stop being childish. We need to talk." Ian's stern tone almost made me obey him out of habit but instead I shook my head, even as his eyes flashed dangerously at me. He crossed his arms over his form-fitting black t-shirt, which hid a tightly muscled chest. I barely stopped myself from drooling. Each time he appeared, he looked even more delicious than I remembered.

"I don't think so, Ian. This is not childish. What's childish is my subconscious tormenting me with dreams of you, or you running away and leaving me hanging for five years - don't you think?" I snapped at him.

Oh, great, I was taunting Dream Ian again. You'd think I'd learn, but I guess not.

The candles around him went out with a whoosh as he strode determinedly to my chair and picked me up, silencing my shrieks and protests with a kiss.

I whimpered against his mouth as his tongue invaded, seeking mine. I wrapped my arms tightly around him. This was the only benefit of having this asshole in my dreams: because he made me feel like no other could, even when we clashed. Although it was just a dream, I melted like butter when his hot flesh touched mine.

I had fought jumping his dreamy bones for five years, but today had made me weak. While I was not a virgin anymore, I had not let Ian touch me much, even while I dreamt. It was just too painful to be constantly reminded that no man could ever replace him.

Remembering myself at the last second, I tore myself away from his mouth with a sob. I hid my face in the crook of his neck, just like the night he left me, and was deeply ashamed as tears poured like rain from my eyes. I was so tired of the difficulties that came with the memory of Ian, even if this was only a dream.

You know it only hurts this much because you still love him! My inner voice screamed at me, and I lost the will to keep fighting the truth.

"Alexandra, my love, why must you persist in hating me? I have often told you I left you for a reason, but you refuse to believe me," Ian spoke softly close to my ear and I sobbed harder.

"Because this is nothing but a dream! You are not real and when I wake up, like always, you will be gone again! I can't take this much longer..." I trailed off as my sobs grew in strength. Ian clutched me tighter while caressing my hair.

"I came back for you, did I not? I told you I would and I have. Now if you could just trust me again, we could be happy. I will dedicate my life to making you happy, I swear it."

"But you're mortal and I'm not! I would never be able to watch you grow old and die without going crazy with grief and hatred of my own unchanging shape." I clutched his neck tightly when he forced my chin upwards.

"And why is that, my darling?" His words were urging me, pushing me toward something I swore I would never say again, but it was too late for anything but honesty.

Looking deeply into his strangely bright eyes, I said, "Because I love you. I will never love another as I love you. I have yearned and burned for you for years, and some part of me knows I don't really want to escape you. I just want you back, Ian-" My words were cut off as he kissed me with a raw look in his eyes that struck me to my core.

I kissed him back fiercely, putting everything I felt for him into it, and grasped him tightly, never wanting to let him go.

He moaned into my mouth and walked over to the bedroom, setting me gently on the large bed. I cried out as he pulled back, my arms reaching out to him, unable to handle even the slightest distance.

"Shhh, Alexandra, it's alright. I just want to show you something." Caressing my cheek, he kissed me quickly and stood up.

Looming over me, he stripped his shirt off to reveal a smooth, muscular chest that I intensely desired to lick. I reached up to trail my fingers over his skin but he stepped back and spoke.

"Watch."

His face tensed, almost twisting in pain, and I heard a swish of air before two large, midnight-black wings swept out of his back. I stared at him. It was the most magnificent thing I had ever seen.

"You - you aren't human?" I rasped as he tensed, looking scared and unsure, yet undeniably powerful.

"No, Alexandra, I'm not. Do you despise me now?"

His words made my heart tug painfully in my chest, and I shook my head at him. "No, I don't. I think you are the most beautiful man I have ever seen, or will ever see." *Looks like I'm going for absolute honesty tonight.* Too bad this was just a dream and not reality.

With a shout of joy, he launched himself at me, gathering me up in his arms as he kissed me fiercely. I wrapped my arms around him and his skin was so warm it scorched mine, as if he was branding his essence on me. I wanted *more*, right now. I wished his clothes away and he chuckled as I gasped from the pleasure of feeling him fully against me.

"Impatient, are you? Don't worry, I am too." His breath tickled over my neck as his lips and hands traveled down my body to my breasts.

My back arched against him as my hands caressed his wings, soft and fragile, but amazingly strong. The contrast made my body tighten with pangs of intense desire.

In a haze of yearning, I leaned up and bit his shoulder lightly as I rubbed myself against him shamelessly. "I want you, Ian. No more waiting."

"This is our first time. I want to take it slowly." His tone was breathy with longing and I could tell he was close to losing control.

"First of all, you should never say no to a naked lady in your arms. Second, forget slowly, I want to feel you inside of me so badly I cannot stand it. We've had five years to take it slowly. *Capice?*" Gazing into his eyes, I was delightedly satisfied to see them darken with a fierce desire that mirrored my own.

"Yes, ma'am." He grinned at me.

"Well, darling, if you complete my request, we might be able to go slower on round two. Sound good?" I giggled up at him as he smiled and nipped at my breast.

"As my lady wishes, so shall it be. Now, no more talking," he growled as he captured my mouth with another mind-blowing kiss.

He rubbed himself against me, teasing me with his hardness as he skillfully plucked alternating moans and screams from my body with his fingers, as if I were a musical instrument meant only for him. I reached out and grabbed his ass, grinding him against me.

"Goddess, Ian, please!" I shouted, out of my mind with pleasure, and he finally obliged.

Grasping my hips, he thrust into me with all the delicious forcefulness I had fantasized about. He tried to set a steady pace, but I was having none of that. I wanted him to lose control *immediately.*

Wrapping my arms around him, I met him thrust for thrust, consumed with the sensations my body was experiencing. I felt like I was on fire but I embraced the flames joyfully. My eyes fluttered closed as my back arched, but Ian yanked me up to him.

"No, open your eyes, Alexandra..." His breathy tone turned me on even more, if that was even possible.

My eyes snapped open only to be caught in his glowing gaze and I couldn't stop myself from saying, "I love you, Ian."

He laughed and grabbed my wrists, pinning them above my head as his thrusts became harder inside of me. "That's my line, Alexandra. I love you so much I just can't stay away from you any longer."

"Then don't." I kissed him and glanced down to see him sliding in and out of my body. It was so sexy I felt an orgasm building within me just from the sight. "I'm close," I whimpered.

"I know, love, me too." Ian let loose a powerful, triumphant shout and I felt the world burst apart in a glorious explosion of color and sensation. As my body shuddered, I heard Ian yell out my name in panic. I reached up to him and my hand went through his body. I screamed in anguish.

My scream woke me from my sleep and I looked around, confused, before I realized the dream was over. An agonized cry flew from my throat and I curled my body around a pillow, praying for sleep to return.

My dreams had finally fulfilled my deepest, truest wishes. I didn't want to stay in reality if it meant being alone again, without Ian. Burning tears poured down my face as I clutched my pillow tighter.

A tickling sensation brushed my cheek as I realized my hair had stuck to my face. Wiping it away, I caught something in my hand. Uncurling my fingers, my body jolted as if I had been shocked with electricity.

There was a black feather in my palm, shimmering with magic.

Bounding from the bed, I haphazardly threw on jeans and a t-shirt, grabbing my shoes and purse as I raced out of the house. I slipped into my shoes and jumped in the car.

I knew Ian was waiting for me, and I knew where.

I flew past my father's house, heading straight for the field with the time capsules. I pulled up and parked, jumping out and slamming the door before freezing with fear.

Doubts assailed me like a tornado but I knew I had to find out the truth. One foot in front of the other, I made my way slowly to the great oak at the back of the field.

Tall grass swayed in the breeze, glimmering like diamonds in the moonlight. The smell of damp earth made me feel more comfortable, while chirping crickets kept me company. I walked into the clearing where the tree I was looking for stood guard over all the others. I looked around for Ian.

He wasn't there.

Tired of crying, I repressed my tears and flung my arms around the great oak, hugging it with all my might.

"Ian, where are you?" I whispered.

The oak tree shuddered in response and I could feel the Dryad within consoling me warmly.

"Alexandra, I'm here. Right behind you," Ian spoke carefully, though longing was apparent in his tone.

Startled, I turned and stared at him. His beautiful,

golden-brown eyes were glowing slightly, like the candles in my dream, and he was wearing the same clothes he had on before. There was no trace of his wings but I felt the heaviness of his magic in the air, keeping them contained. I desperately wanted to throw myself into his arms and erase the unsure shadow in his eyes but I was scared of getting hurt again.

"So, my dreams aren't really dreams, are they?" I eyed him suspiciously.

"No, they aren't."

"Then why would you let me believe you were dead?" The question burst from me. I needed an explanation before I could fulfill my yearning and hold him.

"That's a long story."

"Well, we have time! Spit it out!" I snapped at him. He sighed, pausing a moment before speaking.

"Have you ever heard of the legend of the Goddess Athena's Crow?"

Racking my brain, I vaguely remembered a tale about how Athena's familiar, a snow-white crow, had somehow angered the Goddess and she turned his feathers black before banishing him from her presence for all time. I nodded to him and he continued.

"I was that crow. Now, before, you ask any questions, hear me out. I made a mistake long ago when I bore false tales that made me lose the love of my Goddess, my home, and my place in this world. After I was cast out I roamed the world for centuries, lonely and reclusive, until Morpheus, God of Dreams, found me and took pity on me. He owed me a favor so he gave me a place to stay. But I was still lonely. I decided to become a mortal for a set number of years, erasing my memories and beginning life anew, if only for a short time.

"The night we spent together is one of my most cherished memories. I didn't run from you, I ran from myself. After I left you that morning, my crow memories returned along with my power, as was supposed to happen on my eighteenth birthday. My mind was so jumbled and confused that I kept turning into my winged form for months at a time." A pained look shot across his face and I ached to comfort him.

"My only respite was when I saw you in dreams. Morpheus had bestowed me with the power to dream-walk but I was never truly grateful for it until then. Learning you weren't human and we could live out eternity together was my greatest joy. But when I realized you might never forgive me for leaving, I knew I had to gain control of myself once and for all before I could come back to you. It took a long time, but I tried to be with you, even though it was physically impossible for me to do so.

"Learning you had slept with another man almost killed me but I know why you did it. You were as lonely as I was and I cannot apologize enough for that. I meant what I said earlier tonight, Alexandra. I love you, and I never want to leave you again." Ian whispered his last words, and I knew of only one thing to do.

"Swear to me on my mother's necklace you aren't lying and I am yours forever."

Ian blinked at me, shocked, but walked forward and grasped the pentagram in his hand. "I swear to you, and to the moon, that I am not lying and I meant every word I said. I love you, and once I have you back, I will never let go of you again."

The chain began to feel tingly and warm around my neck and I knew he was telling the truth. I placed my hand on his chest and looked shyly up at him. "What's five years next to an eternity? You aren't getting away from me again, Ian. I love you, too."

My heart sang with ecstasy as his lips captured mine and his wings appeared again, unfurling and ripping through his shirt in response to his joy. Shimmering black feathers floated around us and I felt like I was finally where I was meant to be. Through our eternal dreams in his arms, I found my home.

03

Emerald Delmara is a writer, college student, and avid collector of books who loves to work with herbal remedies. Growing up on a farm in the Ouachita Mountains, she spent her days reading every book she could get her hands on, dreaming of fictional characters, and roaming the countryside with her beloved pets. Most of her writing inspiration comes from mythology. She believes magic is essential to her stories, which she hopes to have in bookstores one day. She currently resides in Oklahoma with her family and her dog. You can read more of her works on Wattpad at http://www.wattpad.com/user/GoddessSirena.

The Light

Josh Vitalie

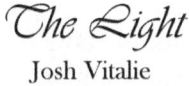

Warm, pinkish light from beyond the black silently called to him. Standing alone, he tried to thrust his hands into his pockets, but there were no pockets to hide his calloused fingers. Only skin. His nervous habit did him no good in this place.

One step. Then another. And another.

The pink grew, its intensity overbearing. He shielded his eyes from its rays, strong enough to warm his skin, but not strong enough to push back the darkness. There was nothing powerful enough to dispel this isolation. He was alone. He knew he was alone and he accepted it, just as he had accepted everything else that had brought him to this place.

Breathe. Focus.

He repeated the mantra silently, yet his internal voice boomed through the lifeless chamber as if he were shouting into a great chasm, echoed back by ghostly voices. The shadows caught his words and twisted them into new ones.

Run. Awaken.

The pink light reached for him with skeletal fingers,

trying to take hold and pull him towards beauty. The darkness held firm, hugging his waist and refusing to let him go. The war of choices raged within his soul, marring the landscape and leaving blood trails along his psyche. He struggled to take that next step. It felt as if he was mired in quicksand, pulling his will the same way it pulled his limbs. His were heavy. He was trapped.

"Jim."

The voice was distant and far away, an alien sound which caused the beautiful light to dim.

"Jim."

That voice again. It kept repeating that name. He should have recognized it, but he didn't. Whoever Jim was, it wasn't him. Not here. Not in this place. He had no name here. He had no identity. All that he was vanished the moment he looked into the pink.

"Goddammit, Jim. Wake up! You're late for work!"

As Jim's eyes fluttered open, that alien voice suddenly became sickeningly familiar. Feminine and hostile, a tone of voice he had grown so accustomed to over the last fifteen years. A hand fell on his shoulder and he felt himself being shaken to consciousness. All he could do was blink and stare blurry-eyed up at the stucco ceiling, desperately wishing he could return to that place, wishing he could return to the light.

As with all things in his life, Jim rarely got what he wanted. He worked a job he hated, married a woman he could hardly stand to be around, and spent all of his time doing everything the world expected of him. Mortgages, Taco Tuesdays, town meetings, and Saturdays spent roaming the aisles of Ikea wishing he could burn the Temple of Yuppie Tastemakers to the ground. This was the life that had claimed him, forming a stranglehold around his throat like a vicious anaconda, choking the life out of him little by little, day by day.

Emily stood at the foot of the bed with her arms crossed and a disapproving look in her eye. He never blamed her for it, though. Hell, *he* didn't approve of who he was at this stage in his life, why should she be expected to?

He rolled out of bed. Groggy and stumbling, he made his way to the master bathroom. Hovering over the sink, he stared at his own reflection and barely recognized himself. A splash of cold water to the face could not wash away the stranger he saw staring back at him. He commenced the daily routine and pulled his clothes on, like an actor putting on a costume and falling into character. It was the role of a lifetime. More accurately, he would play the role for the rest of his life.

Riding the train to work was always such a droll affair. The clatter of the vibrating windows and seats, the incessant, mundane conversations barely overheard, the callous air of the strangers about him, their conceit and discontent seeping from them in waves as they traveled along their dimly lit lives. Jim hunkered down in the crevice between the seat and the window for a twenty-minute snooze. He knew that once he reached the downtown area, he would not get another chance to revisit his inner world.

He was surprised to find how easy it was to slip back into the realm of dreams. The sounds of the living world faded and left him in the empty void of his mind. Jim stood in the black once again, disembodied, yet completely present.

The feeling of quicksand swallowing his feet had disappeared and this time it felt as if he was actually standing on solid ground, able to move freely of his own accord – to walk towards that which called to him from the endless night. The voice cried for him to come every time he slept, beckoning him to the warmth. It wasn't the first time, nor the hundredth. Countless sleeps Jim had spent trying to approach that which lured him, but it always remained aloof, just out of reach, just beyond the realm of reality.

Luminescent pink blinked like a distant star. It was further away this time, further than he could ever remember it being. He watched it flicker, hypnotically lost in its color. Muffled voices filtered in and out of the ether, unintelligible and frantic. The longer he focused, the harder it became to do so. It seemed as if some force was trying to tear through the fabric of his realty, to whisk him into the fray.

"It's not time for you yet." A small boy appeared, uttering the words as he took shape between Jim and his destination. His skin seemed to be made of canvas, his eyes buttons of black marble, and his mouth nothing but a series of stitches curved up into a smile. It reminded him of the doll his Nana had made him when he was a toddler.

The boy pressed his palm to his stitched lips, planted a kiss, and blew it towards Jim.

Jim's eyes popped open and he realized the train had reached his stop. He scrambled to his feet, briefcase in hand. Throngs of people bustled about as he stood on the subway platform, and Jim caught more than a few elbows and foul remarks for blocking the paths of the busy folks. Soon, he joined the swollen rush. He did not have to think, he only had to move. Inevitably, his legs would carry him to the place where he had spent the last thirteen years of his life: Pilgrim Financial.

His day was filled with the same soul-sucking monotony that every day spent in a cubicle offered. He put on his game face and did what he had to do. Despite the growing detachment eating away inside of him, Jim Gardner was a man who got things done. Yet, his mind was elsewhere, transfixed on his dream obsession. That pink glow was so powerful he could scarcely focus on much else these days; his wandering mind always found a way to return to that sacred inner oasis. It fed him. It nourished him. It consumed him.

That night at dinner, Jim barely spoke. He could feel Emily watching him, could feel her worry seeping through her pores and into his conscious mind. Afterwards, they sat together in the living room, watching some inane television. Jim didn't even wait to see the end before he snuck away under the guise of having to use the washroom when his true intent was to pop an Ambien. Tonight, he decided, he would touch the light and bathe in its brilliance. He did not wish to be interrupted.

Minutes later, he was lying in bed, feeling the onset of drug-induced sleepiness. He closed his eyes and drifted off.

Everything was different this time. The black had evolved into swirls of midnight blue and deep violet. Jim was alone, much to his relief. Ahead of him, the light beckoned, as it always did. Jim did not hesitate, yet his legs refused to move as quickly as he would have liked. A hundred years seemed to pass between each step and a restlessness settled over his subconscious, a hurried panic that he could not control. He only wanted to be closer - close enough to touch it and to feel it on his skin.

Why?

It wasn't a voice, but a thought that kept gnawing at him. Why did he want it so badly? He had no answers, but with the certainty of dreams, he knew it was the only thing that mattered, the only thing that held any true importance. Reaching the pink light meant everything and if he failed . . . No, he refused to think that way. Jim was not a failure. He had never been one and he refused to start now – not when his desire to succeed was so strong.

Desire. There was no other way to describe it. He couldn't say if it was the light he yearned for or whatever lay beyond it. All he knew was that he needed it. He needed it more than he had needed anything. The fires of craving burned within his gut, coursing through his veins and seeping into muscle tissue. Every fiber of his being wanted to feel the light.

He barely noticed the world about him changing, the blues and violets swirling and spiraling like a hurricane on a meteorologist's map. Towards the center, all the color eddied into a vibrant white, illuminating the ethereal landscape. For the first time, he could actually see where he was.

Around him lay a brightly glowing field with grass of neon green and daffodils that stood nearly seven feet high. They bent slightly to look down on him with the botanical eye lodged inside the corona. No matter where he stepped, the eye of the daffodils seemed to follow him, like one of those spooky paintings in the Halloween haunted houses he used to visit as a child. Through the vast floral forest, Jim could barely make out the blinking light in the distance. He began to walk forward with complete disregard for the looming flowers all around him. Slowly, one by one, they vanished, as if the simple act of ignoring them nullified their existence.

Soon, he was alone in the now-desolate vortex, walking with fierce determination through the scorched desert world that had replaced the daffodil fields. The pinkish light blinked and flickered but never vanished. It remained always visible, always tangible, and always so close, yet just out of reach.

He couldn't remember when the singing began. It was as if it had always been there, filling his ears with its soothing melody. The rhythm drove his steps, each foot falling like a metronome's click as the song's eerie harmonies intensified the swirling color of his dream world. He stopped and closed his eyes for a second – only a second – and felt his body humming along with the spectral song, every molecule in his being vibrating with the beautiful melody that had no name.

Shadows burn and shadows fall
The Shadow comes to hold us all
A piercing beam shall mark the Gate
For you to enter where we await

His eyes opened and everything changed.

He stood on a vaguely familiar shoreline, probably one he had been to in his younger days, when he still had time for such idle foolishness. The waves broke and crashed against the beach, sending black sea water washing over Jim's bare feet. The water was cold, much colder than he had ever thought an ocean could be, and as the gooseflesh crawled up every inch of his body, he realized he was naked. He shivered spasmodically.

The sky above was rust and blood, creating the darkest red Jim had ever seen. The moon – possibly the sun? Who could really tell in this place? – was blotted out of the sky, a black dot looming ominously overhead. Despite the darkness, Jim found he could see across the ocean. Off in the distance, there was a small speck on the horizon.

Is it coming to me? Or sailing away?

He hoped the former. There was anxiety in his soul now, the first he had experienced in this reality. It was exacerbated here, like a growing tumor. The black speck closing in worsened his tremors. The tides shifted, raising the water just above his knees.

The speck became a clear outline. A cloaked figure stood in a rickety vessel, using a long oar to steer as the tides carried it closer. Water splashed around his naked legs, cold droplets tickling his skin.

He craned his neck, twisting this way and that as his eyes shifted back and forth, searching. The light was nowhere to be seen. There was only fear.

I will die on this shore. I will never see it. I will never see my beloved.

His body shook violently, that same fear urging him to flee. Yet it was as if some invisible force had hold of him and refused to let go. Paralyzed in place, all Jim could do was watch and wait. Somewhere, an alarm sounded, so invasive it shattered the crimson sky, cracking the crimson horizon as if it were some piece of fragile china. His dream rushed out and the world rushed in as he woke abruptly, his body soaked in a clammy sweat. Emily lay half-awake beside him, face filled with quizzical concern. On the dresser across the room, the small digital alarm clock buzzed frantically.

"You were crying in your sleep," Emily said, sitting up and placing a maternal hand to his forehead. "You're burning up. Are you okay?"

"I'm fine!" He pulled away from her, the feeling of skin on skin causing his muscles to contract painfully. He pushed the comforter off and stumbled out of bed, straight for the master bathroom. He spent the next half hour staring at his thinning, pallid face. Dark circles formed a crescent beneath his eyelids despite the generous amounts of sleep he'd been getting. He could hear his wife pacing outside the door, awaiting his emergence. He ran the tap and silently cried, though he could not have said why.

Sadness lingered with him for the remainder of the day, neither good nor bad, a neutral cloud that shaded everything he saw. He was unable to catnap on the train ride this time, forced awake by an overweight man reeking of Old Spice and a night spent emptying a wine box of its contents. His suit was worn and wrinkled, and he elbowed Jim in the ribs every time the train gave an unexpected shudder. Perhaps it was best. Jim had no desire to return to the sea, to look upon the face of the traveler. He hoped that when sleep did finally come, he would find the pink light once more. Everything would be all right if he could only return to that divine glow.

That night, as he watched Emily undress for bed, he felt something animalistic inside of him. There was a glow to her skin, bright and intoxicating. He told her how beautiful she looked. She smiled and thanked him, but he sensed her worry beneath the surface. Stepping up behind her, he wrapped his arms around her naked waist and pulled her into him, whispering a reminder of how beautiful she was. She responded with a smile and an inviting tilt of her head. Jim's urges overcame him. He spun her around by the shoulders, kissing her deeply the way he used to back when their love was fresh and new. That night, passion burned like napalm in his heart, singeing his skin and sending rushes of blood to his loins in a whirlwind of carnality. He had not felt this present in days, tending to her every need and craving, bringing the heavenly song from her mouth, the erotic chants to the gods of orgasm. It felt like a true reconnection to the real world as they both tapped into the lustful animals that possessed their bodies for the next twenty-seven minutes.

When their lovemaking had run its course and both Jim and Emily had spent themselves completely, Emily rushed into the bathroom to clean herself. Jim could not be bothered. He knew the time had come at last. Rolling onto his side, he submitted himself to slumber.

He found himself on the beach once more, standing face to face with the dark figure in a hooded cloak, weathered and gray. The shadows of the hood hid its face from view so that Jim could not determine its gender, but the idea that it was a sexless creature sent to take him away from his paradisiacal light felt like the truth.

"Abandon your search," the cloaked figure warned cryptically, its voice a raspy shriek that caused Jim to cringe. "Your ignorance shall be your undoing. Across the sea is where you must go. Your world awaits you." A sweeping gesture brought Jim's attention to a small vessel, floating in place despite the turbulent state of the black sea. "You must come. There, you shall find the answers you seek. Your family and your life await you on the other side. You must return to where you belong. I have navigated these waters for an eternity, and shall continue to do so for another eternity. You will be safe with me."

The figure's bony, skinless hand stretched out, palm up in offering. Jim stared, tempted to reach out and place his hand in its grasp. The figure's words carried neither deceit nor mischief and Jim felt neither fear nor despair, only an instinctive knowledge that accepting the offer was the right thing to do. Still, he could not bring himself to take the hand. Something was holding him back, a rhythmic throbbing in the pit of his stomach that reverberated up his spine, musical, precise, and familiar.

"I'm sorry," Jim whispered with lips firmly pressed together.

The figure emitted a booming laugh, filled with demonic malevolence. "The pink light cannot save you. I will make this offer only once more. Abandon your foolish quest. This is not your world. You do not understand the way of things."

"I understand things well enough," Jim said, swelling with confidence. "After all, this is *my* dream."

More laughter came, causing Jim to deflate a little. The laughter continued as the shadowy figure climbed into the vessel, using the oar to push off into the tide's embrace.

Jim stood on the edge of the world where water met earth and watched the departure. Cackling wails of amusement rang out, slowly growing fainter and fainter as the small vessel and its creepy passenger became little more than a speck on the horizon.

Having no idea what to do next, Jim walked north along the beach. The sky above had lost its ominous feel, appearing now as a perfectly normal night sky, littered with sparkling stars and a full, silver moon that shimmered off the surface of the black waters. On and on he walked. The beach seemed infinite, yet Jim's legs never grew tired. He felt as if he could walk forever.

Truly, he had never felt this good in his entire life. Never in the real world had he been afforded such a majestic feeling. It certainly dwarfed any sense of pride and accomplishment he'd ever felt about receiving a promotion or a prestigious company award. He could feel the world humming in his ears, talking to him, telling him he was a king amongst men.

He was perfection.

More than human.

A living god.

His speed increased, and Jim could swear he was being carried by the ocean breeze, pushing him onward to his final destination. He closed his eyes and let his feet take control. The air against his naked skin rejuvenated him. Nothing could hurt him in this state. There was nothing to fear. The whistles of the wind and the humming of his soul launched the familiar dream song, hypnotic and enchanting. Jim moved freely, his bare feet covered in wet sand, and he listened until he could effortlessly sing along.

Pain shot up through his foot as something pierced the skin, pressing up into the tender muscle tissue beneath. Jim opened his eyes as he hopped on one leg, cursing and shouting at the top of his lungs. He fell to the ground, pulling his foot up to inspect the injury. A thorn about eight inches long had lodged itself completely through the bottom of his foot, its bloody point emerging between the top of his foot's twitching tendons. He struggled to pull it out, emitting a blood-curdling scream when he finally felt it slide from the wound. Warm, red plasma covered his foot, running down his fingers and hands. As he stared at the wound, he felt his freedom replaced by despair.

The beach disappeared and the sound of crashing waves vanished as well. Barren, skeletal trees rose up all around him, their crooked branches reaching out for him but never quite touching. The forest floor was a blanket of dead leaves, soft and wet. The musical hum of the dream song now replaced by the buzzing of crickets, growing louder until the sound rattled through Jim's skull.

"Such a sad little boy. So wounded and scared."

Her voice was soothing, a sweet melody that Jim could listen to forever. She appeared before him, skin like ivory with eyes of gold and fiery hair draped over her shoulders. She did not hide her naked body from his gaping stare. He gazed upon her exposed breasts, firm and supple; his eyes trailed down the flat of her stomach, locking on the essence of womanhood between her long, slender legs. As he looked upon the thing that all men feared, he did not feel the stirring of sexual desire. Rather, there was a complacent peace, as if her mere presence caused all the pain in his mind, body, and soul to evaporate. She reminded him of his mother; she reminded him of Emily; she reminded him of every woman he had ever met. Yet she was none of them.

When she spoke again, her voice was gentle and matronly. "You're lost."

Jim wanted to protest that he was not lost, simply misplaced, and that he would find his way through the trees so long as he followed the moon, but when he tried to speak, no words came out, only a rush of warm air and a choking gasp as saltwater spewed from his mouth and dribbled down his chin. She drew closer, looking upon him with her golden eyes, compassionate and nurturing. Jim felt safe with her and believed that she might wrap him up in her long, hairless arms to hold him until the end of time. She didn't. She simply looked him over with a curious fascination, as a scientist might look over a new specimen.

"Don't speak," she whispered, placing a soft hand against his heart. Her palm was softer than velveteen against his bare skin. "I know what you seek. I have come to guide you. You must follow me or you must turn back. There is no other way."

"But I can't. I can't walk." The words came easily from his mouth this time. "I'm injured." He rubbed his impaled foot. A sharp sting ran through his leg at the touch.

The golden-eyed goddess only gave a half smile. "Then you must crawl."

Like a child.

Those unspoken words hung in the air, lingering between them, heavy and mutually understood. She leaned close and placed a light kiss upon the crown of his head. With elegant grace, she stood and glided slowly between the trees, the sweeping of her hair in the breeze beckoning him to follow.

Feeling peace with his decision, he followed behind on hands and knees. At first, it wasn't so bad. The fallen leaves created a soft cushion that provided a certain level of comfort in an otherwise uncomfortable situation. The deeper into the barren forest they ventured, the rougher the trail became. Rocks, fallen branches, and prickly weeds cropped up until that was all there was. Jim groaned and occasionally cried out that he must stop to nurse his sores. The woman ignored him. Jim clenched down hard and crawled after her. The ground's relentless attempt to break him continued as the dry skin of his knees split and bled and cuts formed along the blackened palms of his hands, open wounds becoming rapidly contaminated by infection.

I can't. The phrase played in a loop inside of him. He knew he would never reach the light this way. It was becoming harder to stay up on all fours. He ached all over and collapsing on his face became a common occurrence. All he wanted to do was lie down, to rest, to give his aching, weary body time to recover - even if only for a minute.

That, of course, wasn't an option. He knew what was expected of him, yet he didn't know if he could do it. There was only one way to find out.

He pushed himself to his knees first, then brought one foot firmly up on the rugged ground. Just his luck, it was the foot with the hole through it. The guttural roar of an animal rose up in his throat and erupted from his mouth. His jaw clenched, teeth grinding painfully as he pushed to his feet. The struggle was great, but the strength he found was invigorating, sending waves of adrenaline coursing through his veins.

He stood – off-balance and shaky, but standing. Trails of drying blood created a jigsaw effect on his legs. Panting, he focused on the patterns until he felt steady. Looking up, he saw the woman with the golden eyes staring back at him, beaming with what Jim could only interpret as pride. He took a step, faltered, but managed to maintain his stability. After a moment, he took another step... and then another, until he was walking normally.

The trees began to thin, and soon Jim stepped out of the forest. He stood silently beside his goddess, staring out over a vast, frozen tundra. Wind blew violently and large snowdrifts gathered here and there. The sky above was clear and bright, though there was no sun. Some kind of magical light brightened the white waste before his eyes.

His disappointment and fear vanished at once. Across the tundra, a range of purple mountains stretched across the horizon. Ahead of him, set into the base of the grand range like some kind of mountain gateway, he saw the sparkling pink light he had thought lost forever. Joy swelled up inside of him, manifesting itself as tears streamed down his face, stinging his cheeks, and blurring his vision.

"The rest you must go alone." The goddess watched him. Jim could sense her sadness despite her unwavering words. "Only you may enter the White."

"What's out there?" Jim's voice trembled. Fear befell him again suddenly, like a blanket thrown over his head. It darkened his view of the world, and the sky darkened in kind.

"Your final test," she replied. "There you will find the Beast and you will be challenged. Kill or be killed, there is no other way. If you do not slay the Beast, it will certainly kill you. Then you will never reach the Gate and learn your true fate."

"How am I going to kill a Beast?" Jim concentrated on breathing, as it seemed to quell his fears. "I'm unarmed. I'm unprotected. I'm nothing but a naked man with a destination."

She took his hands in hers, and looked at him directly, her golden eyes piercing through him, as if able to see into the darkest recesses of his mind. She saw his fear, he knew.

"You have my protection," she said softly. The woman leaned forward and kissed him with an open mouth. Jim was shocked but non-resistant. Her lips tasted of ripened strawberries and she smelled like freshly fallen rain.

He felt energy transmitting between them; an electric spark that slid down his throat and warmed him from the inside out. She broke off her kiss, gave him one final smile, and bid him farewell. Then she was gone, leaving only a mist of ice particles that quickly blew away.

The ice crunched beneath his feet, sending cold shocks up through his soles and into his belly. He shivered, wrapping his arms tightly around himself to huddle against the cold. He walked, losing all sense of direction save for the light glowing brightly in the distance. His teeth chattered and his skin burned and chapped against the elements, but he would not give up. He was already halfway there.

Suddenly, his foot sank beneath the surface of the snow. He tried to pull it free, but the snow held him firmly, as if he were caught in a hunting trap. So where was the Hunter? He looked around frantically, straining to see against the rising winds that threatened to become a blizzard at any moment.

If you do not slay the Beast, it will certainly kill you.

The words echoed through his mind, each repetition increasing the violence of the winds. The sky darkened. The world fell into the shadow of twilight. Standing between him and the light, the silhouette of a figure approached. Its long strides would bring it close within a matter of minutes. Jim dug at the ice around his foot, yet it remained firmly cemented in place. He would not escape. This had all been for nothing.

The silhouette closed in on him, and he could distinctly see that atop its massive, barrel-chested torso were three heads: a man's, bearded and decorated by the scars of battle; a woman's, with delicate features framed by long, silver hair; and the head of an infant, wide-eyed and genderless. In place of hands, it had claws, and its legs were long, sinewy and blackened with frostbite.

Bending over, Jim managed to break off a large chunk of ice. He threw it at the Beast's heads. He didn't care which one he hit, so long as it bought him another moment of life. His aim was off and the ice chunk soared high over the Beast. The three heads appeared confused by this, looking between themselves and then back down at him, as if trying to decide what to do next.

For a brief moment, Jim believed he had nothing to fear.

The heads all leaned in and began to meld together, their flesh adhering until three became one. The shoulders narrowed as the Beast let out a growl that sliced the crisp air like a blade through fabric. Was the Beast shrinking? Jim had to blink a few times just to be sure. The once enormous three-headed monster had taken the size and shape of a normal man.

Jim gasped. He was looking at his own face, his own naked body; a bestial replica of himself with claws. His heart raced and his body shook, but all he could do was stare.

The wind carried the distant howls of wild dogs to Jim's ears. He knew they could smell his fear; worse, they could smell his blood. The replica began to circle him with predatory intent. He tried to follow its movement, but the harder he tried, the quicker the replica moved – always keeping just out his line of sight.

The replica lunged.

A bony shoulder slammed into Jim's back while muscular arms wrapped tightly around him. Jim let out a pained shriek as razor-sharp claws tore at his skin, leaving red slits in their wake. His howls of pain were swept away by gusts of wind, carried off into the white to be forgotten. The weight of his enemy's body crushed him and an overwhelming hopelessness swallowed him. Still, he could not bring himself to give up. The world seemed to be set on spin cycle as Jim looked up at the sky one moment, then down at himself the next, then back up at the sky, pinioned between the snowy ground and the Beast's straddle.

If you do not slay the Beast...

His foot had been freed of the ice trap, he realized suddenly. As confidence returned, Jim reached up to grab his opponent by the face with the intention of gouging those glossy blue eyes from their sockets. The Beast howled and tried to break free, but adrenaline gave Jim the strength gain the upper hand. Pushing up with all his strength, he managed to knock the Beast onto its back in the snow. A split second was all it bought him, but it was enough time for him to get to his feet. There was no time to compose himself. The Beast tackled Jim to the ground and pinned him once more, two naked bodies wrestling in the snow. The Beast gnashed its teeth and howled what could only be interpreted as a victory call.

...it will most certainly kill you...

Then he felt energy expanding in the pit of his stomach; a sense of courage he had never felt before. The goddess' last gift to him swelled until he felt hot blood coursing up through his body and into his mind.

Like hell it will!

Jim brought a fist up and slammed it square into his replica's face. The crunching of cartilage followed. The Beast fell back, disoriented. Unleashing three more vicious blows, Jim managed to gain the upper hand, rolling the Beast onto its back as he sat victoriously on top. The Beast was strong, though, hissing and twisting with such inhuman strength that it took everything Jim had left inside of him to maintain his advantage. Desperation to survive was all he had.

Rage warmed his naked skin. A primal scream shook the arctic tundra and Jim lost himself to his instincts. His next blow made contact with his replica's face, crushing the already-broken nose once again. He continued to pummel that familiar face until it was little more than a bloody mass of skin and tissue. The crack of bone and a sharp smack marked the moment the Beast's face caved in, sending trails of spattered red across the pure white ground. Jim felt the body of the Beast twitch and convulse beneath him, the final dance of death.

His heart pumping like a piston, Jim got to his feet. He could feel the warmth of the blood on his hands coalescing at his fingertips and dripping down into the snow. His ego swelled along with his manhood and he stood erect with arms outstretched and face towards the dark sky, letting out a roar of victory.

The world faded out until Jim found himself standing alone in the black void once again. In the distance, the pink flight blinked invitingly, its enchanted voice calling him home.

He floated effortlessly across the black, closer and closer to the light. Somewhere in the dark, he could hear a voice calling out for him, sad and disparate. Ignoring it, he pressed forward until he felt the rays of light wash over him, pulling him into its pink embrace. The warmth boiled his blood and burned his skin, his memories, his secrets, his hopes and goals - all purged by the invisible flame that engulfed him. Jim stared into the source, mesmerized by what he saw.

Nothing.

He moved closer, wanting to be inside of it, wishing to lose himself in its empty beauty. He reached out, the tips of his still-bloody fingers connecting with one of its lancing beams. Stillness settled over his soul.

A bestial growl came from somewhere, a horrifying sound that seemed to come from all around him. His breath caught in his throat, but Jim could not turn away from the light, drawn like a moth to the flame. There was safety in its brightness, he knew. Nothing could hurt him so long as he remained wrapped in its brilliant arms.

A black shape appeared before him, cloaked in the

bright light into which he stared. Slowly, it crept towards him until he could identify it: a wild dog with eyes as yellow as the sun and fur as black as deep space, dirty and matted. Two more appeared just behind the Alpha, eclipsing the brilliance of his desire as they awaited a cue. Jim had little time to react.

The Alpha dog lunged first, emerging from the light as if tearing through a dimensional fabric into this reality. Jim fell back with the Alpha atop him. With sharp, glistening fangs, the dog hungrily tore off a strip of salty skin from Jim's torso. It gave an inviting howl and the rest of the pack followed suit. With ravenous hunger and vicious intent, the dogs feasted on Jim's body. He was torn limb from limb, flesh and muscle peeled away in bloody chunks.

Jim did not fight. He did not scream.

As they devoured him, he could only lie there with a smile of acceptance as he stared into that light, if only for a minute. Soon, the world faded away for the last time. He knew it was the last time. He knew that this time, he would not wake up to the world he'd left behind. Yet, he didn't care. He had finally found the source of his longing and it was as beautiful as he had always imagined it would be. Nothing else mattered.

ঙ

A minstrel, a ruffian, and a roustabout, the creature known as Josh Vitalie (Joshuas Vitalius) grew up in the sweltering deserts of California before migrating into the forests of the Pacific Northwest. This nomadic creature emerged from the woods frequently to roam the countryside, inflicting the infectious beat of his War Drum upon an unsuspecting populace for years before traveling further north to plant his seed in one of the locals. With an heir in his care, his wanderings have been reduced to splitting time between the Wilds

of the Northwest and the Snows of Canada.
You can catch him on Wattpad at
http://www.wattpad.com/user/TheRake.

Between The Sun and The Moon

Maya Starling

ଔ

Talia yawned. The time on her laptop read 01:57 am. *Time to get some sleep.* She saved the document and turned off the laptop. The room was enveloped in darkness, and streetlamps shed dim light through lacy white curtains. When her eyes adjusted to the dimness, she laid the notebook beside her bed and then pulled the blanket up to her chin, snuggling in to the warm body sharing her bed. A small, loving smile tugged at Talia's lips as soft snores coming from beside her breached the silence. Soon, sleep claimed her as well.

A steady beeping noise penetrated Talia's sleeping mind. She wondered whether Eleanore had forgotten to take the cellphone with her to work, and if now the snoozing alarm had broken through Talia's deep slumber. A groan escaped her at the thought of having to get up just so that she could turn off the blasted annoyance.

"Talia?"

She furrowed her brows at the sound of a man's voice. When she opened her mouth to speak, she only managed a croak.

"Oh, honey, you're awake. Wait, don't speak. Let me get you some water."

She wanted to object to being called 'honey' by this stranger, but her throat was as dry as if she had eaten a pound of sand. Footsteps shuffled about, followed by the murmur of water being poured into a glass. The scent of antiseptic mixed with stuffiness confused her further, but the bed's warmth enveloping her eased her trepidation.

"Here..."

The cool, smooth edge of a glass pressed against her lips and she welcomed the fresh water washing away the sand in her throat. When no more water flowed, she licked the last drops off her lips, eager for more.

"Thank God you're finally awake, sweetie! The doctor's on his way."

A warm hand brushed her cheek.

"Don't... don't touch me," she mumbled while fighting the daze clouding her mind. She struggled to open her eyes because the rest of her body was just too heavy to move. The beeping continued, following the rhythm of her galloping heartbeat.

"It's okay, sweetie. Everything will be okay, just stay awake."

Talia's eyes fluttered open, then squinted at the sudden onslaught of light.

"The light..." she said, her voice still a bit raspy.

"Right." The man moved away again, and the light dimmed.

Her head spun once she fully opened her eyes. She was disoriented by her surroundings. The beeping noise came from the machine to her left, and above it hung an

IV bag connected by a tube to her wrist. An empty chair sat by the side of her bed and a couch rested under the curtained window, a blanket and pillow stacked neatly on top of it. A TV was mounted on the wall in the left corner, facing her bed and the couch. But the walls were all wrong; they were white, instead of the usual hospital yellow. And the whole room... everything had an unearthly glow about it.

"Who are you?" Talia said as her eyes settled on the stranger standing at the foot of her bed. He looked familiar. He ran his hand over short-cropped, peppered hair. His light blue eyes were sunken and crinkled with dark circles around them, and his eyebrows scrunched with worry.

"You don't remember who I am?"

"No. Where's Eleanore?"

"Who's Eleanore?"

"My girlfriend... where is she? What happened? I—"

The door opened and a man dressed in a white coat entered, followed by a nurse and three more people dressed in scrubs, a year or two older than Talia - two women and a man.

"Hello, Talia. It's nice to see you awake again. How are you feeling? This has been your longest episode yet," the doctor said as he walked up to the side of her bed.

Talia's eyelids were heavy but she fought against the tantalizing promise of comforting sleep. She needed to know what had happened. The doctor, too, claimed to know her, but she certainly didn't remember him, all ginger, freckly and round as he was.

"She doesn't remember," the man at the foot of the bed spoke up.

"Oh. Well, I'm Doctor Hubert, Talia. Do you know where you are?"

She looked around the room again. "In a hospital?"

"Good. What is the last thing you remember?" He opened a chart and scribbled in it.

"Falling asleep at home next to my girlfriend and waking up here." The doctor glanced at the other man who shook his head 'no' in return.

"Do you remember the date?"

"Ummm... no... not really. I never was good with dates, but I remember it being Monday."

The doctor scribbled some more, but his features remained neutral, easing some of Talia's worries. "Let me just check your vitals and I'll explain to you what's going on."

❧

"All right, everything is normal. Well, considering you've been asleep for a while now." He turned to the nurse and said, "Let him back in."

The doctor tucked away his pen, and the interns scrambled back, listening intently. The pepper-haired man had had to wait outside. When a nurse let him back in, he quickly moved to her side and sat down on the chair. She watched the struggle in his eyes, and the twitch of his hand as he forced himself not to reach out for her own.

Her gaze drifted lazily back to the doctor. "How long was I asleep? What happened? Was there an accident? Why is my head so... heavy?"

"Talia..." the doctor sighed, "This might not be easy for you to understand, but you're suffering from Kleine-Levin Syndrome, also known as Sleeping Beauty Syndrome. Your latest episode lasted for four weeks. You had us worried there for a while."

"What's Klein Le... Le—"

"Levin Syndrome. It's a neurological disorder that makes you sleep a lot. You've had a few episodes before, but not like this one. You've been asleep for the last four weeks with only a few, short waking moments each day."

"But I don't remember... and who are you?" Her gaze shifted to the man at her side again.

"That is your father, Talia."

"No. I don't know that man." She yawned, and her belly rumbled.

"Talia..." said the man claiming to be her father.

"Please, sir. You're making me uncomfortable." She turned to face the doctor again, her eyebrows drawn down. "That's not my father, doctor. I don't have a family, I only have Eleanore. I want her here."

"No, Talia. Stefan here is your father. He brought you in when he couldn't wake you up to make you eat. There is no Eleanore."

"No, no..." Talia shook her head. "I don't remember him."

The doctor frowned. "We'll figure it out. You should remember next time you wake up fully. It's one of the more complicated symptoms. Now, stay awake, Talia. We need you to stay awake longer this time."

"I'm hungry. And I need to pee."

"I'll get her some food," the man, Stefan, said as he stood from the chair. "I'll bring you your favorite." He walked out, shoulders slumped in defeat.

"The nurse here will help you to get cleaned up, and to walk around a bit. You'll probably feel very weak, but don't let that frighten you. Your muscles have been neglected for the last few weeks. Once you've settled back and eaten, I'll return and answer all your questions. You might even remember more by then."

Talia nodded, and the doctor, along with the interns, left the room.

ى

When the man who claimed to be her father returned with a tray of food, she was standing by the window, gazing outside. The nurse kept a watchful eye on her slow movements as Talia reached out and touched the glass.

"Everything is so strange. So wrong," Talia said.

"What do you mean 'wrong'?" Stefan set the tray on the sliding table over the bed and motioned to the nurse that he would take over.

"The grass is green and the sky is blue instead of the other way around. And the walls are white. Everything has this... glow. It doesn't make sense. I think I'm dreaming."

Stefan approached Talia and stood by her side, watching her face while his own was laden with worry. "No, Talia, you're finally awake." He raised his hand, but thought better of it, letting it fall by his side again. He sighed.

"I don't like this." She yawned. "I'm sleepy and I'm hungry. Can I eat now?"

"Yes. I've brought you food. Here. Let me help you get back to bed," Stefan said as he gently took Talia by her elbow. With the other hand, he wheeled along her IV stand.

She didn't protest. She just wanted to eat and then go back to sleep. She hoped everything would go back to normal once she woke up again.

"I didn't know what you were in the mood for, but the doctor said something light, so I got you a bit of

everything," Stefan explained as he helped Talia settle in the bed, and slide the table over her lap.

"Thank you," she mumbled as she grabbed the spoon and started slurping down the food. It didn't take her long to eat everything on the tray: the two bowls of soup, cooked meat and vegetables, toasted bread. When she reached for the pudding, Stefan stopped her.

"I think you've had enough to eat. I don't want you to get sick."

"But I'm so hungry," she said, pleading with her sleepy blue eyes. When the man's features didn't soften fast enough, she jerked her hand back. "I will eat!" She grabbed the pudding and glared at him.

Stefan sighed, but let her eat. He sat down on his chair and observed her, his eyes tired and glistening with unshed tears.

"You really don't remember?"

Talia shook her head as she finished licking the last bits of pudding from the cup. She burped, and then sighed contentedly. Her chin inched lower toward her chest as her eyes drifted shut.

"No, no, no, sweetie. The doctor will be back soon to explain everything. Maybe try a new medicine. So stay awake for that, all right?"

"My eyes sting, and I'm so tired. And everything is just... so, so confusing." She yawned, and slid lower under the covers.

"Stay awake now, Talia." Hands gripped her chin, forcing her head up.

"No. Let me sleep," she slurred, "Go away. Don't touch me." She swatted at the hand. "Why won't you let me sleep? What's wrong with you?" she yelled as Stefan fought to capture her flailing arms.

"Calm down, baby girl. I don't want to hurt you.

Please calm down. I just called for the doctor. He'll be here soon."

"No!" Talia protested as she wrenched her hands free. Her eyes snapped open and she slapped the man.

A stunned silence ensued. Stefan put his palm against his burning cheek.

"The doctor won't let me sleep either," Talia pouted. "Go away." Closing her lids, she heaved a weary sigh.

"Sweetie, listen to me. Just for a moment, please." The man grabbed her shoulders and she groaned, tugged back from the verge of sleep.

"Sleep..." she mumbled.

"Yes, sleep," the man said and Talia smiled, "as soon as the doctor comes." Her smile transformed into a frown, but her eyes were too heavy to open again.

"Come on, Talia... my little princess. Stay awake for Papa," Stefan said.

His familiar words brought her comfort and a feeling of safety, so she let herself sink deeper into the darkness.

"No, Talia. Be a good girl and stay awake."

"Sorry, Papa..." She pushed his hands away. Darkness came up to meet her, sounds drifting away, her breathing slowing...

"Stay awake!" The distorted, screeching tone of his voice hurt her ears.

Talia jerked back and scowled at him. Fury at being tugged back to awareness again consumed her. It was really annoying. She just wanted to rest a bit, and the man wouldn't let her.

"Let. Me. Sleep." She glared at him. "Get out of my room, old man!" She pointed at the door.

"That's enough!" Stefan argued. "I'm your father, whether you like it at this moment or not, and I say you need to stay awake until the doctor returns." He crossed

his arms over his chest and glowered down at his daughter.

Talia glared back, eyes narrowing, nostrils flaring. She ripped the needle from the back of her wrist. Stefan gasped in surprise. Before he could react, she snatched away the covers and swung her legs over the side of the bed. The adrenalin pumping through her body kept her steady on her feet as she lunged at Stefan, pushing him back by the shoulders.

"Get out!"

Stefan struggled to catch Talia's hands, but she just continued her assault, forcing him closer and closer to the door.

"Shhh... calm down Talia."

"Get out of my room! Get out of my head!"

She clenched her fists and pounded at Stefan's chest. He never fought back. He only protected his face against the onslaught, tears of hopelessness streaming down his cheeks. The doctor and nurses ran inside, restraining Talia as she kicked and flailed. It took four people to restrain her enough for a nurse to plunge a syringe into her thigh. The sedative took effect and she slumped to the floor. Voices distorted and became distant, faces blurred and swirled. A burly male nurse picked her up, and tucked her back into the bed.

"Sleep..." Talia murmured, and she succumbed to slumber once more. A man's sobs drew nearer and a warm hand grasped her own.

ॐ

Talia woke up with a gasp.

She bolted upright and held a hand to her chest. Her heart beat wildly under her palm as she took quick, shallow breaths.

"Honey?" a soft voice said in a sleepy tone. "It's okay. You only had a bad dream."

Talia closed her eyes and took a few deep calming breaths. A warm hand caressing her back soothed her further.

"Elle?" Talia asked in a soft, unsure voice. She looked over her shoulder, her eyes adjusting to the darkness as she struggled to make out Eleanore's features.

"Come here."

Talia lay back, sinking into the soft embrace of the warm bed and her girlfriend's arms. The sound of Eleanore's steady heartbeat helped ease her distress, and tender fingers trailing up and down her spine unwound her coiled muscles.

"Better now?" Eleanore said as she kissed the top of Talia's head.

"Mmmhmmm."

Talia tucked a dark curl behind her ear, yawning, and then placed her hand on Eleanore's waist, absentmindedly tracing the hem of her purple top.

"Want to talk about it?"

Talia sighed. She lifted her head off Eleanore's chest and settled on her own pillow.

"It was so creepy."

Eleanore caressed her cheek. "Tell me, if it'll help you get back to sleep. It's..." Eleanore glanced at the red numbers displayed over the bedside table. "It's only 4:37 am."

"It was one of those dreams where you wake up and you aren't sure whether it's all real or not. I mean... when I woke up in the dream, everything was a bit hazy and I was tired, but when I looked out the window, the colors were all wrong. The grass was green and the sky was blue. Imagine that."

"What happened that got you so upset?"

Talia grasped Eleanore's hand and kissed her palm before placing it on the pillow. "I woke up in a hospital, and they - the doctor and a man saying he was my father - kept telling me I was finally awake, that I had some sort of a disorder and they wouldn't let me go back to sleep. It just... it *felt* so real, but seemed wrong, you know?" She shrugged. "It was confusing as heck. I just wanted to get back to you."

"It was just a dream," Eleanore murmured. She leaned forward and pressed her lips against Talia's in a soft, loving kiss. "Think you can go back to sleep?"

"I don't know. I'm still a bit shook up."

"I can help with that," Eleanore said. "I can make you forget." She rolled over on top of Talia with a mischievous smile on her face.

Talia moistened her lips before quirking them into a smile. "I'd like that very much," she said as she buried her fingers in Eleanore's hair and pulled her in for another kiss, this one scorching and branding.

Eleanore ceased her ardent declarations of love to trace her lips down Talia's neck, leaving a hot, wet trail that led lower and lower.

Talia surrendered to the loving ministrations of her girlfriend, so much better and much more pleasant than the weird nightmare in that stark hospital, now slipping away into the back of her mind.

Talia sat cross-legged on the soft, cloud-like bed, with her head hung low, her tearstained face hidden by a curtain of dark curls. Her body shook with sobs of helplessness.

The door to their apartment closed and heels clicked over the hardwood floor. "Lia? I'm home, honey."

The sound of Eleanore's cheerful voice made Talia hide her face in her hands as she cried harder.

"Lia?" Eleanore said as she peeked through the bedroom door. "What's wrong?" She padded toward the bed and crawled closer to Talia, not bothering to change out of her work clothes - black business pants and a purple blouse hidden under a black blazer. She pulled Talia into her embrace and held her, crooning words of encouragement.

Once Talia's cries turned to sniffles, Eleanore reached for the box on the bedside table and handed Talia a tissue. The distressed young woman wiped the tears off her face and snot off her nose. She took a deep breath and let it out in a long sigh.

"What's wrong, babe?" Eleanore smoothed the hair away from Talia's face, witnessing the red-rimmed eyes with dark circles surrounding them. Talia gazed at her imploringly, a broken soul searching for salvation. "You didn't get any sleep again?" Talia shook her head. "Not even a nap?"

Talia blinked slowly and sucked the courage from thin air. "I tried... I really did. I managed to fall asleep but the dreams came again. I don't know how much longer I can take this!"

Eleanore bit her lip and nodded. She tugged Talia into her lap and circled her arms around Talia's shoulder. She spoke against the dark tresses, "What happened this time?"

"Same people, same story." Talia sniffed as she played with an antique-looking brooch of a golden spindle on Eleanore's blazer. "I woke up in a different room though, and I was strapped to a bed. Couldn't move my hands or legs; alone in a white room. The man came again, the father, and... and... this time I recognized him as my father. It was surreal - it was me but not me. That other me knew the man was her father, and when he realized that, he had me released and held me as I cried in his arms. Seems I've been crying a lot... here and there." She snorted.

Eleanore kissed her temple and squeezed her gently. "Go on."

"I felt like a five year old in his arms. I think I was more desperate and confused about everything."

"No wonder. This has been going on for far too long. It's been, what, two weeks now? I think we should seek help."

"I'm not crazy!" Talia pulled out of the embrace and looked at Eleanore, wide-eyed.

"I'm not saying that, honey," Eleanore said as she tucked a strand of hair behind Talia's ear and placed a soft kiss on her lips. "I just don't want you to suffer so. You haven't had a decent night of sleep since that first night. Maybe something is subconsciously bothering you and you need to deal with it. I'll help you."

"But I—"

Eleanore placed a finger on Talia's lips. "I can call Dee. He should be able to help, being a psychiatrist and all. I can ask his opinion. We can go from there, all right?" Talia nodded. "I bought some groceries on the way home. We can make cannelloni for dinner together, with music, dancing and all, and maybe it'll distract you from everything for a bit."

"I'd like that." Talia's mood brightened and the corners of her lips lifted up. She stopped Eleanore from getting off the bed by grasping her wrist. "Thank you."

Eleanore smiled softly and kissed Talia's forehead. "Because I love you."

"Love you too."

§

"Wake up, sweetie," a familiar male voice roused Talia. She yawned.

"That's it, my little princess. Wake up, time to eat."

"Papa?" Talia said as she struggled to open her eyes. The world was hazy and glowing again, hurting her eyes and making her squint. "The light." She croaked.

"Ah... yes. I forgot."

After some shuffling, and the sound of fabrics brushing, the light dimmed.

"Better?"

"Mmmmhmmm..." Talia's lids felt heavy again.

"Come on, baby girl. Stay with me. You've been doing so well lately."

"I have?" She slurred but her eyes fluttered open, focusing on the face of an exhausted man before her.

"Yes. You're even back home because we've been able to wake you up regularly. I think your episode might be coming to an end." Stefan took her hand and patted it gently.

Talia's gaze drifted about the room, unable to focus on anything.

"I'll let you clean up and come downstairs. Dinner's almost ready," the man said, and he stood up, placing a tender kiss on Talia's forehead.

"All right."

Once Stefan had left the room, Talia sat up and waited for the dizziness to disperse. When she was able to focus, she perused the unfamiliar room, still clouded in a soft haze, the lilac color of the walls giving off an unearthly glow. Stefan had left the door open, and next to it, right against the wall, rested a simple vanity table decorated with photographs, beads, news clippings, and some jewelry. None of it, though, looked familiar to her. She didn't care for any of it. Hollowness settled in her heart.

After tending to her needs, and changing into a clean pair of shorts and a university t-shirt, she made her way downstairs. She held on to the wall as she descended to the ground floor.

The den had a brown couch facing a TV, with a bunch of papers strewn all over the low table and the soft, cream carpet.

"Ah, work. Sorry for the mess," Stefan said from behind her.

Talia shrugged. "What do you do?"

"I work as a translator so that I can stay home and take care of you." Stefan placed his hand on her lower back and he led her to the kitchen. "I've also been looking into some medical research on your condition. There's a scientist, Dr. Philip - his work seems promising."

"Take a seat." He pointed to a chair, and walked behind the central counter to fetch the plates. Talia noticed more papers on the table. As she pushed them to the side to clear some space, a letter addressed to her caught her attention. She skimmed its contents.

We regret to inform you... missed three months of classes and finals... incomplete grades... aware of your condition... ability to re-enroll and re-take the classes—

"You shouldn't have seen that now," Stefan said with a sigh as he set the plates down.

Talia shrugged, not sure whether it mattered at all, whether it was all real in the end or not. She just wanted the confusion to be over, to be able to move on with her life. "I don't remember anything anyway."

"You never do remember what happens after an episode."

"No. I don't remember anything... or much from before. It's confusing. I don't know which memories are real."

Stefan frowned. "Must be because this episode has been so long and strong. It will all come back to you once you fully wake up. You probably won't even remember this conversation."

Talia nodded as she plopped herself on the chair and then scarfed down the food, even stealing extra from her father's plate. After the quiet dinner was over, she slumped in the chair, chin resting on her chest, and succumbed to the persistent call of slumber.

A day later, soft lips pressed against Talia's, tugging her out of a dreamless sleep. "Hey, babe, wake up. I got some news from Dee." Seeing Eleanore's happy, smiling face hovering above her brought a mirroring grin to Talia's. Eleanore pecked her lips again. "Good afternoon. Did you nap well?"

"Yeah." Talia stretched her arms above her head. "A short nap, but luckily the kind without dreams."

"Good." Eleanore settled onto the bed, leaning back against the headboard. "How was work today?"

"Exhausting, after getting practically no sleep. But Fay was great and let me do things at my own pace. She did warn me, though, that I should seek help if I want to keep the job. She can only tolerate so much," Talia said as she pushed herself up and leaned her head on her girlfriend's shoulder.

"Just what I wanted to talk about. I consulted Dee. He said you should come in and have a session with him. He also said something about projecting your worries and fears into your dreams, and he can help you figure out what those subconscious worries are and teach you how to deal with them." Eleanore rested her head against Talia's. "Basically, you have to face your fears in your dreams... face them and fight them off. It makes sense, don't you think?"

"It does. Did you tell him that the dreams repeat in a way... well... repeat differently each time, continuously but with the same person involved?"

"Yes, although he told me he was supposed to have that conversation with you. I guess that man in your dreams represents whatever is bothering you." Eleanore sighed and took Talia's hand in her own, playing with her fingers. "You know you can talk to me about everything, right Lia? No matter how bad you might think it is."

"I know, Elle." Talia nuzzled Eleanore's shoulder. "I really wish I could, but I don't know what the cause to all of this is. You know I tell you everything." She gazed up at Eleanore.

"I know." Eleanore graced her with a soft, sad smile.

"So, what do you suggest I do before I try the psych sessions?"

"Well, from what I understood, you need to... umm... fight him off. Not let him - them - control you. Do whatever you want, sleep as much as you want and get them to leave you alone. Maybe just walk out. Whatever it takes to slay those demons, you know?"

Talia sighed. "It sounds so easy. But when I'm there, it seems so real. I don't know how I'll be able to do it."

"But it's not real! You can't go on like this anymore. You're not sleeping at all. Either you try or we go straight to Dee tomorrow."

Talia cringed at Eleanore's raised voice. Eleanore then placed a few kisses against Talia's head and squeezed her hand gently. "I'm sorry, I didn't mean to—"

"I'll try," Talia conceded. The pressure was overwhelming, and she was just too tired to argue. If it meant finally having peace and living happily ever after with her Elle, she would do it, whatever it took. They shared a good and happy life, after all, and the sooner she dealt with it, the sooner they could continue living that life.

"Thank you," Eleanore said. "How about we go to the movies tonight? I heard that Perceforest is great."

"Sounds like a plan. I need to get out of here."

ॐ

Talia was forced to wakefulness as Stefan gently shook her by her shoulders.

"Dinner time," he said softly, and when Talia murmured her acknowledgment, he left the room.

Just as sleep called to her once more, Eleanore's voice echoed in her mind, "Get them to leave you alone... fight them off." Talia knew if she were to fall back asleep, Stefan would come back up to wake her again. She fought off the comforting blanket of slumber, slinging it away from her mind as she struggled to open her eyes.

Once the world came to the now-familiar hazy focus, she pondered how to do it, how to rid herself of the burden that had weighed down her spirit and heart the last couple of weeks.

Maybe just walk out, *Eleanore's words echoed again.* Right. I can do that. Walk out and never return. *Talia gave a decisive nod as she stood up and left the room.*

She walked by the den and went straight to the front door. As her hand grasped the handle, a voice spoke from behind.

"Where are you going, sweetie?" Stefan said as he stood by the couch, slinging a tea-towel over his shoulder.

"Just out." Talia shrugged.

"You can't go out now. It's not safe for you. Who knows where you might fall asleep. Let's just have dinner, and if you still want to go for a walk, we'll go together. How does that sound? Maybe you're finally waking up."

She shook her head. "No. I just need to get away for a bit."

Stefan sighed as he ran a hand through his hair. "You really want to go out now?"

"Yes. Now. I really need to leave." Talia's knuckles turned white around the handle.

"Fine. We can go now and I'll reheat the dinner later."

"No! I need to go alone."

"I can't let you out alone, Talia. You know that."

"I don't care... Just let me go! Why won't you let me go? Why won't you let me sleep? Who are you, really?"

"Talia," Stefan said in a soft, calm voice, his palms pointing down as he took a few tentative steps toward her. "Listen to me, my princess. It's dangerous for you outside. It'll be completely dark soon and you could get lost. You could—"

"Don't come any closer!" She stepped to the side and opened the door. "This is what I want to do. What I need to do. If you love me, you'll let me."

"Please, sweetie, I'm doing this exactly because I love you. Because—"

Talia jerked the door open all the way, not able to listen to him anymore, his words weighing her down, causing a head-aching struggle in her mind.

She took a first step, and strong arms wrapped around her own, pinning them to her body as she was pulled back into a muscular chest.

"Don't make me restrain you. Please don't make me do this to you, Talia," Stefan whispered in her ear, coaxing, encouraging.

"No!" Talia kicked her feet out as she struggled to shake off the chains holding her back from reaching freedom. "Let me go!" She thrashed her head, hoping to bang into Stefan's so his hold would loosen. Even though their heads connected briefly, and pain exploded in the back of Talia's, his strong hold on her body never wavered.

"I've got you. I'll protect you, even if it means protecting you from yourself! I'm not letting you go!"

Talia fought harder: thrashing, kicking, screaming, her teeth snapping, wishing she could sink them into his flesh. Stefan remained strong, enduring, as he pulled her back, further into the den, her weakened condition no match for his solid grip.

"Shh... Talia. Calm down. You're doing neither of us any good with this tantrum. Let's discuss this like adults."

Talia struggled a bit longer, desperation leading her actions before reason caught up. She slumped in Stefan's arms.

"That's my girl," Stefan praised, loosening his grip

only slightly.

"I'm sorry," Talia mumbled as they both sank to the floor, onto the creamy carpet. She glanced over her shoulder at Stefan's face. Her eyes widened at the sight of the crimson liquid trickling from his cut eyebrow, down the side of his face, dripping from his chin. It was not the blood that bothered her, or that she had hurt him, but the color of the blood: red instead of purple. Her heartbeat picked up speed and her breaths quickened. She wanted to comment on the wrongness of the color, but instead, she said, "Your eyebrow! Oh! I'm sorry, Papa! Let me take care of that. You stay here." She took his hand and placed it on the wound so he could stall the flow of blood.

Stefan reluctantly surrendered his hold on her, but his body remained rigid, ready to tackle her in case she went for the door again. Talia, though, disappeared into the kitchen. She paced in front of the counters.

"What do I do? What do I do?" She looked down at her hands smeared with red. It was wrong, everything was wrong when she dreamt, meaning that nothing here was real. Stefan wasn't real. He wasn't a person, but a projection of her suppressed emotions. Red, red, red... what does red mean? Anger? Hatred? Is it all about red after all? What is it? *Talia shook her head. She didn't have the answers but she wanted it all gone. She now realized she couldn't just walk away. They would catch her, they wouldn't let her go. She had to do it, she had to heed Eleanore's words: she had to do whatever it took to slay those demons.*

Slay...

Talia's gaze shifted toward the knife holder. Her feet carried her of their own volition, and she stopped in front of her weapon of choice. She wouldn't wash the red from her hands. The color grounded her, reminded her that nothing was real. She was not about to kill another human being - her own father nonetheless.

She took a deep breath and grasped the wooden handle, pulling a long knife out of the rack. With a long exhale, her mind left her body, and she watched herself, floating from above, as she grabbed a dish towel and calmly walked out.

The knife hidden in the folds of the towel, she approached Stefan.

"Close your eyes and tilt your head back," the words slipped past her lips as she crouched next to him.

Stefan studied Talia's serene features before obliging her gentle command.

Talia's mind panicked as her body raised the knife. She screamed at her hand to stop, that she couldn't do it after all. Couldn't take a life, even in her dreams. She couldn't kill Stefan because there was still a tiny chance that he might be real, especially when he looked at her with such tenderness and love, when his embrace felt so warm and safe.

Talia stopped breathing when the knife plunged into his chest, into his heart. She blinked, and found herself staring into his wide blue eyes. There was no anger, hate or resentment in his gaze, but love, sadness and defeat.

"I'm sorry," Stefan spluttered, blood coating his lips. "I failed you."

"No!" Talia's voice pierced the silence. "No, no, no!" She withdrew the knife and swallowed the bile burning her esophagus. "No," she screamed as she pressed her hands against Stefan's gushing wound. "I'm sorry, Papa!"

ℰ

Talia woke and burst into tears as her heart shattered to pieces, and the shrapnel pierced her lungs, leaving her gasping for air. She coughed, wailed and sniveled, her whole body shaking. Eleanore was quick to wrap her arms around Talia as the darkness kept them in its embrace. She had done it, but she didn't feel the expected relief and freedom. She was terrified and heartbroken, in denial, his blood still warm on her hands.

"It-it-it's done. I killed him. Oh my God, I killed him. It felt so real. Why did it feel so real?" Talia said through tears and hiccups.

"What happened?"

"I-I can't talk about it. I don't ever want to talk about it. Oh my God... I killed someone... I killed my father."

"No, no, no. Talia, that wasn't your father, it was just a dream and he was your fear... You beat him, I mean *it*. You won. It's all over now."

Talia shook her head. "I don't know... I don't know anymore. Is this life the real one? God, what if this is all a dream and the other life is real?"

Eleanore held Talia closer, running her palm up and down Talia's back. "This is real. I am real. You and I are real. You remember everything here. Why do you think you never remembered everything when you were there? It never existed."

"I don't ever want to go back. Please promise me I won't have to go back."

"Oh, honey. You never have to go back there. It's all over now. I promise." Eleanore held Talia in her embrace, praising and comforting. Talia never saw the wicked smile on her girlfriend's face. "I have you now. You're all mine," Eleanore whispered, her voice muffled under the sound of Talia's sobs.

෨

Maya Starling is a writer, a geek, an animal lover and a gamer. A native Croatian, she writes biographies of fictional characters, both short and long. Her four-legged, fury minions are rather useless because they always do as they please. She publishes most of her works for free on Wattpad under username Maya_2011. Her story, 'The Red Menace', is published on NOSF, a Croatian portal promoting SF&F. She hopes to one day find her novels on the shelves in the bookstores.

In the meantime you can read them on Wattpad and follow her on https://www.facebook.com/StarlingMaya.

Broken Souls

Adam Sigrist

ɛ3

I sit in the corner, back against the wall and chin against my chest. My thoughts remain stagnant and every bit of my flesh is itching with dirt and bugs.

"Ma'am," I hear a guard say, and heels click against the floor.

I listen to the rhythmic sound, letting myself be pulled back up from the sinking tar pit of my mind. The dim light around me seeps back into my vision. The blurry feet of a woman approach. I follow the line of her legs from ankle to knee to hip. The suit she wears is fine and pressed, a drastic contrast with the grungy styles I've become accustomed to.

She stops at the bars, shifting her weight to one leg and crossing her arms. "Well?"

"Well what?" I haven't used my voice in so long. Haven't wanted to before now. It's such an alien sound.

"Why'd you do it?"

I laugh and cough and cry. I shudder and slide to the floor, pulling my knees up under my chin.

"I want to help you, I do." She squats and I see her face, her silky-looking hair. "I just need you to talk to me."

I shake my head and cry some more, whispering the never-ending cycle of names which permeates my thoughts and dreams.

"What's that? Please, speak up."

I don't. I circle the names around and around. "Cyrus, Holly, Hatch. Cyrus, Holly, Hatch."

"Yes, your... friends."

"Friends?" I jump up. The room spins and I press my hand against my forehead. "They were my family."

The woman chews her lip and nods; a wisp of well-poised blonde breaks free. "Yes, of course. That was a sad day for us all. You know that, right?" I look away. "I think you're under the impression that none of us cared, but we did. When I heard what happened, when I realized it was too late to do anything about it... I was so mad."

"Word was, you ordered it."

"Is that what you think?" Eye contact for the first time in days. It's like fire down my spine. "I don't know who told you that, but it is not true."

"Who ordered it then?"

"The acts of one person can sometimes be just that, you know. Not everyone is following the orders of a higher power."

No. I can't accept it. It's not true. Someone cold and heartless must have made it happen.

"I want to hear about how you met them." She peers down at me through my bars and I feel like an animal on display.

I flash back to that miserable day when the world stopped working. "After... after the siege I - I was the only one willing to help."

"The only one? These people, your family, they had

none of their own?"

"They were alone, each of them, and terrified."

"So you brought them in, you shared your home with them, your food."

"What was left of it anyway." I twist the tips of my fingers, nervously twitching and shaking. "The Invaders - they didn't leave us with much, but what I had I used to make sure that my new family stayed alive."

"Until you couldn't anymore."

I look down at the ground. I pound my temple with my fist and scream, "I tried to stop it! I tried, I tried!"

"But you couldn't, could you?"

Another terrible day flashes to mind.

"He told me - he told me the other survivors thought my family were a waste."

"A waste of what?"

"Supplies, medicine, food." My jaw tightens. I imagine a hand on my shoulder and wonder whose it could be. *Is that you Holly? Or maybe Cy?*

"But all of you were willing to work, to earn your keep."

"There's only so much you can do to prove your worth to hate-mongers."

"I am so sorry."

"Yeah, well, that doesn't do much for me now."

"Tell me about them."

"Who?"

"Your family."

I see their faces again, clear as day. Each one is smiling at me. Or are they scowling? Do they think I failed them?

"Please," she says.

"Cyrus Falthom. Fifty-six years old. He liked to be called Cy and he told me that before the siege he liked bananas because they were yellow and easy to chew. When The Invaders came, he was living in a group home. I found him roaming around the broken streets crying, looking for his friends and family."

The woman puts her fingers to her lips and I see tears glisten in her eyes. She's refusing to let them spill, though. She's too important to cry.

"Holly Matthews. Thirteen years old. Her mom died when the Invaders came. Constable Garcia found her in-" I choke. I don't even want to say it. "- in a den."

The woman closes her eyes and I see the muscles in her neck grow tight.

"The things they did to that poor girl. She wouldn't speak when she came to me. I thought she couldn't. She tried to run away a couple of times, but eventually she started grunting, then smiling, then she asked me for things."

"What kind of things?"

"Her doll, her bed... her mother."

"What about the last one? Hatch?"

I think for a moment, wondering how much I should tell this woman. She urges me on with her eyes.

"William Hatch. He was the newest member of the family. Of course, I gave him that name. I never knew his real one."

"How old was he?"

"I don't know. Early thirties, maybe."

"What else can you tell me about him?"

My eyes slip out of focus as I think of Hatch.

"Hatch was... alone." I laugh just a little and wipe a tear with a dirty hand. "Not like the others though. He was living in isolation long before the siege."

"Why?"

"I don't know. I don't know who put him out in that

cabin. I don't know exactly how long he was there either but it was clear he was abandoned a long time ago."

"Why was it clear?"

"He hadn't bathed in years. There were these infections all over his skin. They smelled like death. He caught small animals and bugs for food. I could tell he used to speak, though his developmental disability would have restricted his vocabulary. When we met, however, there was nothing but grunts and moans and bird calls left."

"So. You took in these poor souls. That's very noble of you." The words don't belong to her - they are the words of a timid field mouse, soft and gentle.

"I'm not noble. Look at me!" My words lash out like a viper, and the field mouse cowers. "Look where I am! How could you possibly assume I'm a good person?"

"Because you went hungry to feed your family," she says. "You stayed up all night with them as they raged and fought against sleep, too terrified of what would be waiting for them in their dreams. You dedicated yourself to those people. They owed you their lives."

"Don't say that."

"It's true."

"It's not."

"Of course it is. As far as I'm concerned, you are one of the greatest survivors left on this crumbling planet, which is why I can't just let you fade away! We're dwindling. If I let the few of us who remain act on our primal instincts, we're going to go from tens of thousands to total extinction. I can't afford to lose people who keep us grounded in our humanity."

"If I'm so great, then where are they, huh? Where's Cy? Why doesn't Holly come running when I enter the room? If I'm such a fucking fantastic human being, then why couldn't I help Hatch?"

"Sometimes people are broken."

"That's not true."

"Yes, it is. I know it's hard to hear, but William Hatch was beyond help."

"Stop it."

"You knew it too, but you're so good you couldn't accept it. You were living in a dream then, and you're living in one now."

"That's not true. I saw Hatch's potential. I know he could have turned around. Before the incident he was beginning to sign with me. He was always so humble."

"He attacked three women in one night!"

I catch my first glimpse at the woman's true emotions. Her glasses slip down her nose, and she presses them back into place, taking a breath. "I'm sorry, but he was beyond any help. How much medicine did we waste trying to make him healthy again, only to... what? To have him go out there into MY streets and hurt people?"

"There's that word again," I chuckle. "'Waste'. In preserving life, nothing is wasted."

"What about the lives of Hatch's victims?" She tosses three photos into my cell and I look at the bruised faces of three women. "Melissa Haversack. She's thirty-four. She has night terrors now and her husband can't do anything to comfort her. Hariette Sylliboy is twenty-two, and before Hatch attacked her she was one of our most promising medical students. Now all she does is cry. Gabrielle Garcia is only eighteen. Eighteen! I'm sorry to dump this on you, but these are the faces of strong women who have been broken by a broken man."

"They can be fixed."

"Right, like Holly." A fourth photo falls at my feet. I bend over and pick up Holly's picture. She always smiled so big I could see her molars. "The things that were done to Holly were the same things Hatch did to these women. Would you try to fix the men from that den?"

Inner turmoil bubbles but I refuse to change my mind. *Everyone deserves a chance.*

"So, tell me about the night when Cyrus and Holly died." She sounds like she's about to settle in for a simple bedtime story.

"Why? You know about it already. Hell, I'd say damn-near every last person on this sad rock of a planet knows about that night."

"Indulge me."

"I'd been out trying to find some damn milk," I laugh. "What a cliché. A person goes out for some milk and never sees their family again. It was after Hatch was taken away. The day they... they murdered him."

"Executed. There is a difference."

"What did that miserable asshole do to Holly and Cy, then? Was that an execution? Was it in line with some pathetic, antiquated system of laws that no longer exists - except of course when *you* want something done?"

"What the constable did - that was murder. It was not execution."

I look at Holly's face again. I can almost hear her laugh.

"What happened when you got home?"

"I heard a gunshot and ran, even though I knew deep down it was too late. When I got inside there was so much blood. Holly was face down in it. I checked for a pulse even though I could see her brain through the hole in her skull. I just couldn't believe it was true. I couldn't believe she was dead."

"Then what?"

"I heard Cy screaming. I chased the sound, but my

mind refused to help. I struggled against my emotions but still they made the room shake. Everything was growing dark."

"Why was Cyrus screaming?"

I struggle to speak through raking sobs. I shake my head as tears and snot run to the floor. "He had a gun to Cy's head."

"Who?"

"Constable Garcia! You know that already!"

"What did you do?"

"I - I tried to get him to put the gun down. He said the council had decided, he said *you* had decided. After Hatch, my family couldn't be trusted. After so much medicine and food had gone into rehabilitating him, nobody wanted to take the chance that another 'broken soul' would steal our resources, only to hurt the people who helped them."

"And what did you say to him?"

"The same damn thing I've been telling you! It doesn't matter how 'broken' a person is, they deserve to be helped. Maybe Hatch was too far gone, but we didn't know that - couldn't have known it until we tried. Everyone deserves a chance."

"Obviously, that didn't sway the constable."

"I told him that the way a society treats their most vulnerable members says a lot about their humanity. I told him that his actions would destroy our foundations. When we play God, where are the lines drawn? Senior citizens, those women attacked by Hatch, orphans... once the killing starts, where does it stop? How do we decide who's a 'waste of resources'?"

"And what did Garcia do then?"

"He shot Cyrus right between the eyes." I lift my head against the weight of my words. I see the woman cross her arms, a tear finally trailing down her cheek. "It was like Cy's skull was paper. It just crumpled as soon as I heard that bang."

"So, then you killed Constable Garcia."

"No, not then. I cried and cried. Garcia just left. He said goodbye, as if his face and hands weren't splattered with blood, as if he'd just stopped by for a cup of tea. I put Holly and Cy together in one room and sat with them all night long, willing them to be alive again. When the sun came up - that's when I did it."

"How?"

"You know how."

"Indulge me." This time she doesn't sound quite as friendly.

"I had a gun. It was up in my room. Garcia had given it to me, ironically enough, but I refused to carry it. Until I had a good reason to, at least. I went outside. People were milling about, doing nothing in particular. I knew Garcia's rounds. I found him and called out his name. I wanted him to look at me. I wanted him to see the dried blood that still painted me. When he turned around... that was when I shot him."

The woman seems satisfied with my rendition of the events. She slowly turns and nods to my guards, who begin to escort her away. "Madame Prime Minister," I call out, "what happens to me now?"

She looks over her shoulder but doesn't turn around. Her eyes are narrow and she looks lost in thought. "You killed a representative of the law. Nobody can get away with that. What do you think I should do with you?"

"Execute me," I say without thinking.

"I told you, I need you."

"I'm not the person you think I am. I killed Constable Garcia. I'm a murderer."

"And so was he."

"Please. I can't keep living like this. Just... end it."

She turns back to my cage, approaches and places her slender fingers on the bars. "A great person once told me it doesn't matter how 'broken' someone is. Everyone deserves a chance."

My mind fights my fumbling tongue. A stuttering silence grows between us and she leaves.

૭

It's a long time before I see anyone after my visit with the Prime Minister. I don't know how long. There is no sense of time in my windowless cell. Eventually I'm released, and she's there for it.

"Congratulations," she says as I hide my eyes from the bright sun. "You'll be happy to hear I've got some new family members for you. I think first we'll give you some time to settle in, though. There are still some angry people out there, so we've got some guards posted at your house." She gestures to the desperate attempts at rebuilding. "How does it feel to finally be free? We've been working so hard to rebuild, I bet you barely even recognize the place."

I don't answer her. I'm outraged at the thought that my family can be replaced. One puppy dies, so you find another. It burns me worse than the unfamiliar sun.

I'm taken back to my home where guards stand by my doors. It's just another prison cell, but this one is drenched in bad memories. Everywhere I look I see their faces; in every expansive silence I hear their voices.

It's worse than prison.

Adam Sigrist

ↂ

Adam Sigrist has been writing all his life. After an exceptional moment in the Wattpad spotlight, his debut novel First Light, the beginning of The Zombie Prophecies series, was published by Fable Press in June of 2013. He is currently working on the sequel, as well as many other projects which are available to read on Wattpad.

You can find links to his work on his website at http://sigristadam.wix.com/writerscramp.

Lovers' Fugue

Charlotte Ashley

It had been twenty-two hours and six minutes since Evie Lancaster had gone off the Dimorphazine. So far, she hadn't noticed anything different.

"The symphony is over three hours long," Rochelle said, waving Evie's concerns away dismissively, "you'll peak sometime in the second movement. Relax, sweetie. Even if you are only half Awakened by then, you'll pick up the projections on display tonight. Believe me, this is gonna be *wild*."

Evie tried to affect an edgy, carefree grin and failed. She didn't really want *wild*. She was pretty sure she was too tightly-laced to appreciate *wild*. She was so terrified of not just the psychological, but the *legal* consequences of what might go on tonight, she wasn't sure she was going to enjoy herself at all.

Evie glanced nervously down the road. They couldn't enter the Opera House for another half-hour. She, Dex and Rochelle were slouched on a street corner, sticking out like a trio of lizards in an egg carton. Dex and Rochelle, veterans of the Opera House, were dressed to the nines in slick black corsets over neon blouses with pagoda sleeves and elaborately embroidered silk pantaloons, with brightly-dyed wigs sculpted precariously around Rococo headpieces featuring birds, fish, glass balls, and the guts of scavenged twenty-first century electronics.

Evie was, herself, dressed in a skin-tight, deep-purple dress studded with the remains of a shattered mirror, a flowing starscape over which her bare shoulders and blonde hair rose like the sun. She felt ridiculously exposed, but Rochelle assured her the best projections came when you gave the imagination something to work with. Maybe it was the Dimorphazine still in her system, but Evie had no idea what her ridiculous get up could possibly inspire in anyone.

What she did know was that if they were seen, they would be arrested. Nobody dressed like this unless they were planning on dreaming.

Dreaming. Despite her misgivings, Evie longed for it. She wanted to discover the secret things she knew and see something brighter than the dull, utilitarian greys and browns of New Rochester. Beyond her nerves and her skepticism and her fear, Evie was looking forward to the concert. She was going to dream for the first time.

"Oh my God," Evie breathed as they pushed through the crowds towards their box. A smokey blue mist drifted through the crowds on the ground floor, rolling gently past heels, boots and canes towards the orchestra pit. "Who is projecting that? Is that a collective projection?" she asked Rochelle.

"Oh, darling," the other woman laughed, taking her hand and squeezing, "you're like a baby bird that has fallen out of her nest. That's not a projection. It's dry ice – a special effect." Evie startled. Nothing about this place looked real to her – how was she going to know a projection when she saw one?

They were deep underground, in a secret space recovered from an ancient aqueduct. Structured like a 19th century opera house, the decor was salvaged from the ruins of centuries' worth of churches, government buildings and classy skyrises. Stone faces were affixed to every balcony, aisle and doorframe, repainted to match the Opera House's neon colour scheme. Tricks of the ancient stonemasons made the beasts leer and wink from every angle as if they were alive. The carpeting and upholstery were woven with Baroque, neon-embroidered patterns that hid still more faces if one looked the right way.

The whole place could only have been designed by a broken dreamer, one of those outcasts who refused to take their Dimorphazine and live with civilized society. For the most part, broken dreamers were exiled, voluntarily or not, to the ruined and macabre spaces of the badlands. Reality had no hold out there, where the streets were built and haunted by anything and everything you could imagine. After the chaos that ensued in the wake of the Awakening, when everybody's dreams came to life and destroyed so much, broken dreamers just couldn't be permitted in Real spaces. The Opera House, hidden beneath the Real streets of New Rochester, was illegal – and so dangerous.

Evie, born in a Real City, couldn't imagine why anyone would trade the stability and safety of reality for the chance to dream, but people did. Musicians, artists, addicts and madmen. The garish design of this strange concert hall was doing nothing to convince her it was a worthwhile trade.

"Evie, baby, are you going to sit down?" Dex called to her, interrupting her thoughts. They'd reached their private box, a balconied space big enough for six, though they were only three. Evie scuttled into her seat beside Rochelle.

Bodies flowed through the doors and took their seats, each person more elaborately dressed than the next. Most wore masks, like characters in a pantomime, and almost all seemed to be under the influence of drugs or alcohol of some kind. They laughed and shrieked and sang songs she'd never heard of; danced and kissed and climbed over rows of chairs.

I don't belong here, Evie thought. The entire world of underground dreaming was on display tonight. Artists and hedonists and students and revolutionaries. Evie was just – *well, what am I?* she wondered. Her heart skipped a beat, betraying her hopes.

I just want to know what it's like, she thought, but that wasn't entirely true. *I'm here with my friends*, she allowed, but she wasn't here for their sake either.

She could hardly bear to admit it, but she was here for Duncan. Evie just wanted to meet him.

He had always been with her, ever since high school. Maybe longer. At first it was a vague awareness of his presence, the sense of sharing a space with someone in comfortable silence. Then it was moments when she was sure she wasn't alone. She sensed someone sitting at the foot of her cot when she'd had her wisdom teeth out at fifteen. Holding her hand on the way to her grandmother's funeral at twenty-two. At thirty, his body next to her in bed, warm beneath the sheets – and once she opened her eyes, nothing.

Evie had been on Dimorphazine her whole life, same as everybody. She never dreamed, and she had no idea what it was to imagine something. And yet she was sure he was there, barely suppressed, just beneath the surface of her consciousness. Even knowing he wasn't real, he was her foundation. When she'd finally guessed Rochelle had a finger in the dreaming underground, she insisted on being brought along. She needed to unlock the door to the part of her mind that was keeping him in. She needed to imagine him and dream him. She had never longed for anything so badly in her whole life.

When the overhead lights dimmed, Evie was grateful. The visual cacophony filling the chamber was giving her a headache, and with the darkness came relief. She sat back and closed her eyes, trying to ignore the continued chatter and titter of the audience. Already she was starting to experience a strange sinking feeling, as if she had internal eyes which could rove about the inside of her skull at will. She recognized the sleepy feeling of looking at the inside of her eyelids, but as the first sounds from the orchestra pit rose up towards her like an enormous sigh, she sensed a trapdoor to another kind of blackness, another kind of mental space. *Is this what it feels like to be Awakened?* Evie wondered.

Picture a tree, she remembered one of her earliest teachers asking her first-grade class. Unable to imagine anything, every one of them had drawn a child's facsimile of the little sugar maple from the school's front yard. It was a test - if they'd drawn anything else, they'd have been removed from the school. But Evie tried it now, using the new black space visible to her mind's eye as a slate. *Picture a tree*, she tried.

Immediately, a more mature version of that same maple appeared for her, naked and grey like in the deepest months of winter. The tree floated, grey on black, as the people around her finally stopped whispering and the first quiet bars of the symphony began. A creeping baseline, joined by an eerie tune hinting at melodies to come, augmented her tree, each whistle of the flute drawing out a winding branch of a complex root system that balanced the tangled half-moon of the maple's top branches. The tree and its root-reflection spread and grew in two great arcs as a second flute joined the first, the two wrapping around each other to form a simple, but mounting, harmony. The circular explosion of twig and branch in her mind was like nothing Evie had ever seen, glistening with frost to the beat of the music. Evie opened her eyes and sat up in surprise. That was not a tree. That was an *idea*.

"Rochelle," she hissed, "I just *imagined* something!"

"You're not the only one, baby," Rochelle laughed. Evie followed her gaze up towards the vaulted stone ceiling of the Opera House.

The ceiling was gone. The oval walls of the auditorium now stretched into a starry sky, crenelated like the walls of a fairy tale castle and flying flags and banners of every colour. The moon was a glistening egg-yolk in the sky, shrouded artfully with mist.

"How can that be?" Evie asked as a cool breeze tickled her bare shoulders. She imagined the roof had been rolled back like a pool-covering, or the dome had been lifted off. "Won't somebody hear the music? They'll find us!" But Rochelle and Dex were making out and didn't hear her. Evie took a deep breath and tried to relax. Nobody else seemed concerned. She leaned over the edge of the balcony and scanned the crowd. Several of what she had taken to be candle-flames suddenly launched themselves into the air, circling towards the freedom of the sky. *Fireflies*, Evie realized, but she had seen weirder pets in the last half hour alone.

Evie listened to the music instead. The tune which had begun so simply had been repeated over and over again, building with added instruments and new themes. It was beautiful, she thought, though she had little enough to compare it to. Music was banned, and pointless when you're on Dimorphazine. She understood why, now. Each controlled swell of the musical theme caused a similar swell in her chest, a bubble of love or excitement or joy that begged to be released. She closed her eyes again and found herself swaying, a movement that was deeply satisfying. Why should the simple act of shifting position with each thrum of a bass feel so good? *Is this why people dance?* She wanted to add the instrument of her body to the piece.

No sooner had the idea occurred to her than Evie flushed with self-consciousness and irrational shame. She forced herself to stop swaying and opened her eyes, suddenly sure she was being watched. Despite the dark, she squinted across the yawning space where mist drifted and fireflies flickered, to the opposing box. There was a man staring brazenly back at her.

Evie didn't recognize him at all, yet for a few seconds he held her gaze as if she should have. He was dark-haired and dark-eyed, roughly her age, and dressed simply in a black dress shirt and slacks. She combed her memories for a hint – maybe they worked together? Or he was one of her many cousins? *Oh my God, what if I'm recognized here?* Evie suddenly wished she'd worn a mask like so many others. Now she understood what they were for.

Before she could place him, the man abruptly stood up and turned his back to her, exiting his box with a flare of the velvet curtain. Evie slouched back in her seat, mortified. Obviously the man was embarrassed, too. She felt exposed and very, very silly, dancing in her seat like some *drunk*. She wanted to close her eyes and imagine she was somewhere else, anywhere else, except she was afraid she was Awakened enough to actually project the fantasy onto her surroundings. *I wonder if I can imagine that never happened*, she thought sardonically, but she was pretty sure it didn't work like that.

So far, the only thing about the concert that didn't make Evie uneasy was the music itself. The music was exquisite. They had reached a kind of interlude, the repetitive building of the original melody making way for a lighter, tinkling composition that made Evie think of icicles melting on a blindingly bright winter day. She shivered, drawing her knees up to her chest and wishing she'd brought a shawl of some kind. She let the music play over her like tiny footsteps, and soon enough she had forgotten about having made a fool of herself.

She shouldn't have been surprised when it started snowing. After all, they'd taken the roof off. Snowflakes fell like tiny stars all around her, vying for atmosphere with the mist and insects. The audience was delighted, and a wave of polite applause washed over the room. Evie watched moonlit squalls form up and blow away as her mind started to drift again, retreating to the blank slate of her imagination. She tried to conjure her Duncan, the whole reason she was even here, but she had never been able to clearly imagine him before. What did he even look like? The pitter-patter of notes gave her other ideas, evoking intangible landscapes of lighthearted beauty. Evie wondered when she would peak enough to see some real projections, real dreams.

"Evie!" Rochelle's voice was right in her ear. Evie sat up with such violence that she almost fell out of her chair, heart pounding. Her friend laughed throatily and took her by the elbow. "Don't fall asleep, darling! Sleeping dreams are a menace, trust me. Keep your eyes open, your mind open. Come on. I have something I want to show you!" Evie scowled, embarrassed, again, to have been caught unawares, but she let Rochelle lead her back down the stairs to the mezzanine, then down the central aisle towards the stage.

From her vantage point in the box, Evie had been able to see right into the orchestra pit with its forest of bobbing bows and glinting brass, but she couldn't see far onto the stage, which she'd assumed to be deserted. Looking now, Evie couldn't fathom how she'd missed it before. The deep stage was flooded with coloured light and packed with people in pairs, whirling and dipping to the music.

"Dancing!" Evie breathed, enchanted. The dancers were all dressed in matching outfits adorned with flowing sleeves, tails and skirts that traced their whorling paths like many-coloured shadows. They skipped and sighed, spun and stepped as one, caught in eddies on the stirred-up stage. Evie felt herself lurch towards them involuntarily, aching to join.

"Come on!" Rochelle urged, tugging her towards the ring, "We'll find you a partner. They'll be lining up for you, darling!"

"What?" Evie planted her heels and tugged back. "I can't dance! I'm not a part of -"

"You will be once we're up there. Come on, Evie baby, trust me!" Rochelle squawked as Dex took her by the waist and spun her towards the stage, laughing. Several of the birds in her wig startled and took off.

"No, please, I can't!" Evie panicked, despite the protest of her limbs. It was too much all at once. She stepped back and let Dex carry Rochelle away from her. "Maybe - maybe another time!" she called apologetically, though the pair were too far to hear her. She watched as they ran happily up the curving steps of the stage and launched themselves, spinning, into the waltz. Evie saw now that their outfits matched those of the dancers on stage, and within seconds her friends were part of the faceless churn. Each dancer matched the next, right down to the ecstasy on their faces. Evie shivered with cold and nursed her jealousy. *Next time*, she promised herself.

"Here," a deep voice reverberated next to her, "take this." Evie turned as a body-warmed cloak was set around her bare shoulders. She froze when she recognized the man in black from the other balcony. Up close, she recognized him even less than she had from afar. *Surely I'd remember a guy like this.* He was tall and broad-shouldered, with strong features and dark eyes. The only hint that he belonged here was the chain of silver rings piercing the tops of his ears, almost hidden beneath his black hair. Evie blushed.

"Thanks," she offered faintly, now wishing she had gone with Rochelle and Dex after all. The man watched her with a troubled look on his face, as if he was trying to remember something, or decide what to say.

"It's Evie, right?" he finally asked. Evie's cheeks burned even redder.

"That's right," she stuttered. She considered bluffing for a moment, pretending she remembered him, but it was just too impossible. She smiled apologetically instead. "I'm sorry, I don't remember you at all. I'm usually so good with faces – but here, you know..." She gestured generally at their chaotic surroundings. The man nodded.

"This place is pretty mind-blowing, that's for sure. I wouldn't have thought this was your scene." He fixed her with that troubled frown again, working out some puzzle. Evie could only shrug.

"It really isn't. But my friends," she pointed at the stage, "anyway, this is my first time here. I'm not even sure it's working on me, honestly." She looked at the revellers around her, dancing, swaying, chatting and laughing, playing with elaborate props and bizarre animals. They all seemed to be in on some joke she couldn't quite grasp.

"Then why are you still here?" the man asked, taking a step closer and lowering his voice.

"I... I..." Evie stuttered, grasping for an excuse. The stage's coloured lights had gone black with the end of the musical movement, and a hush had fallen over the Opera House. She thought about Duncan; tried again to conjure him on her mind's slate, with no luck. The music was more real, more immediate. Evie's ears prickled, anxious for the next movement to begin. "For the music," she finally whispered, barely audible, as one long, reedy note floated up out of the orchestra pit like a cock at dawn.

From a slow, teasing start that drew out maddening anticipation, the music shot out of the pit like a racehorse. The lights in the room exploded at the same moment and Evie staggered back, blinded. When the pain subsided enough for her to open her eyes, sparks had replaced the snow trickling to the ground.

This movement of the symphony was relentless, a

violent contest between brass and strings for speed, each keeping up with the other just enough to maintain harmony. All around her, Evie could hear people gasping and releasing strangled cries of shock and awe. Crashing percussion set off further explosions in the hall's wiring and a strobe light started up on the stage, illuminating the dancers, who had somehow found the time to execute a costume change to white, all white. Evie snuck a glance at the man next to her, who quickly looked away.

Evie's heart raced with the music. Several people pushed past them, shuffling up the aisle towards the doors. She ignored them, and the next few, but by the time it looked as if the entire front row had left the hall, Evie and others around her started to look about, confused.

"Where are they going?" she whispered at the man in black, noticing the frightened look on the face of the latest woman to pass her. "Did someone project something awful?" Her eyes were involuntarily drawn to the darkest shadows near the foot of the stage. She tried not to imagine what might be lurking in there, lest she inadvertently bring those horrors into being.

"I don't know." The man craned his neck looking down the hall, concerned.

The dancers didn't seem to have noticed anything. Like a flock of white swans, they still soared around the stage, in some cases, literally. Nor had the orchestra slowed its breakneck pace.

"Do you want to leave?" the man asked her. Evie thought about it, then shook her head. The fireworks, improbable dancers and savage ferocity of the music were not enough to trouble her. The company of the stranger was soothing, and she found herself unwilling to leave the music so long as it lasted.

"I couldn't. This... I need this," she tried to explain, "and my friends are up there. I can't leave without them." The man looked around skeptically.

"Do you mind if I stay with you? I'd feel better knowing you weren't alone."

Evie looked the man full in the face and smiled. The corner of his mouth twitched, returning a nervous half-smile. *I bet we were at school together*, Evie thought. Something about his demeanour told her he was used to watching her from afar. "I'd appreciate that," she replied simply, feeling more calm and focused than she had all evening.

The piece thundered towards its crashing end with no further interruption. Evie had settled into a space of her own, finally able to ignore the distractions of the rollicking crowd and aggravating special effects. She breathed deep, letting the music run through her like a ghostly stampede. Remembering Rochelle's advice not to close her eyes, she snuck another glance at the man in black instead. He was leaning forward, elbows on his knees, listening with the same rapt attention she was. Evie smiled again, privately.

The room went black with the stroke of the last note. A moment of complete silence hung in the air before the audience erupted in applause, hooting and whistling and crying out for more. Evie leapt to her feet, clapping and cheering instinctively. Warm candlelight slowly rekindled as they stood, and Evie looked excitedly at the man next to her. He smiled back at her with a full, unrestrained grin. Evie stopped clapping and bouncing, immediately embarrassed.

"Um," she said, and his laughter was lost in the din.

"Don't," he said, his voice deep enough to be heard

despite everything. "I know exactly how you feel. There's no reason to be ashamed."

"I don't know anything about music," Evie explained. "I don't know why it touches me like this. Is it the Awakening?"

"No, Evie," he shook his head, "that's just what music is like. It stirs everything in us that is good. It will reach into you and pull your insides out. It speaks directly to the most personal part of you – your heart, your soul, your spirit – whatever you want to call it. It always has."

"You come to these a lot," Evie realized.

"No, this is my first time."

Evie frowned. "Then how do you know-"

A discordant noise from the orchestra pit interrupted her, suggesting there was more music to come. The man looked at her expectantly. What was she going to say? Could he be a broken dreamer? Where else but in the badlands could he have heard music, if not here?

"Evie," he leaned towards her to be heard over the renewed chatter, punctuated now by a distant thumping noise, "I know you don't remember, but-" The thumping suddenly seemed to be right over their heads, at the back of the second-floor seating. Evie looked up, startled. The man's head snapped towards the sound, suddenly animal-alert.

"The orchestra has stopped playing," he said in a low voice, reaching for Evie's hand. "That's not right. Come on."

"What?" Evie said, confused. How was this any different than any of the other interruptions they'd experienced this evening? She looked around and realized the stage was empty, just a gaping black maw.

Lined with teeth.

"We need to go." The man herded her up the aisle

and led her by the shoulders. "There's an exit under the balcony-"

"Wait!" Evie pulled away and turned back towards the stage. The curtains trembled like jowls, and a rumbling snarl entered, stage left. Audience members were scrambling out of their seats, bolting for the exits, fleeing the jaws that seemed to be slowly realizing their purpose. "Rochelle and Dex! They were dancing, they were up there!"

"They've probably been swallowed. Or they've fled. Please, Evie, I can get you out of here safe if you just-" But Evie pulled away, fighting the flow of bodies towards the stage. She could see shadows of people in the orchestra pit darting back and forth, fish below the water's surface. There was no reason Rochelle and Dex couldn't have leapt down there when they realized they were dancing inside the mouth of an enormous monster. Evie knew she couldn't just leave without them. "Evie!" the man in black called in frustration, and took off after her.

Evie didn't answer, but was glad to see the man at her heels. She ran for the edge of the orchestra pit and looked in. A foot of water covered the ground and instruments flitted beneath the surface, abandoned. She leaned over the railing, her attention drawn to a splashing deep under the stage. She could feel the hot, yeasty breath of the stage tousling her hair, and a sharp coldness around her ankles.

"Rochelle!" she called into the dark space, "Dexter! Any-"

Behind her, something exploded with the force of an artillery barrage. Evie surged into the rail, holding tight despite being winded by the shove. Ears ringing, she turned to see a wall of dust and debris where the back wall of the auditorium used to be.

"Police," the man in black shouted into her ear, barely audible. "We have to get out of here!" Evie watched as a green fog started to fill the ruined upper balcony. Then all hell broke loose.

The stage roared, leonine, as gunfire erupted from the balcony. Pink, orange and blue bolts of light pierced the air and vanished into the green fog. Evie heard screams and roars from inside the cloud, and the shadow of something huge and winged eclipsed the moon.

"What's going on?" she had to yell to be heard over the noise.

"Get down!" the man called, taking her by the shoulders and pulling her to a crouch. "People are panicking. Their minds are fighting back with projections - watch out!" His arm darted out and encircled her protectively. The ground was shaking and cracking as something enormous broke apart the foundation of the ancient building. Evie curled into as small a ball as she could. She peeked over his arm and saw a huge, prehensile tongue rolling across the stage, searching for something to grab hold of.

"We'll have to get to the cops," the man decided grimly, placing one hand on her back. "They're flooding the place with polyasinazine. It will knock the projections flat."

"Projections?" Evie asked, puzzled, even as the first leathern talons of something enormous gripped the crenelated walls. *That isn't real*, she realized stupidly, but she couldn't understand why it wouldn't be, any more than the fog or the chairs or the silk of her own dress might be. *Maybe I'm not even here*, she thought. But the pain slicing up her legs felt real enough. Evie looked down.

The shadows were pooled at her feet, coating her legs with a sticky, black ichor. More was welling up by the second.

The man in black followed her gaze downward, then snapped back up to her face in alarm. "No!" he yelled just as Evie felt the floor vanish beneath her, and she plunged into cold nothingness.

"Help!" Evie screamed as she fell, slipping from the man's grasp. The last thing she saw before she went under was the outright panic on his face.

Over and around she tumbled, thrashing in panic and trying to cry out for help with a voice that would not respond. She lost track of which way was down, then realized it didn't matter. *I'm drowning*, Evie thought as darkness took her. But beneath the surface, the shadow was less liquid and more empty. She reached out in all directions with her arms and legs, flailing for something to hold.

Her fingers tickled something briefly, and she snaked both her arms over her head in desperate panic. After an eternity of falling, she brushed something warm and soft again, and took hold. It was a hand.

The hand clasped her wrist and pulled, hauling her up with inhuman strength. She grasped the forearm and broke through the surface, greeted by the deafening rattle of automatic weaponry, blinding flashes of lasers, and the ichor-soaked form of her man in black, panting and shaking as he lifted her from the well.

"Oh God," he breathed, pulling her close without letting go of her wrist. Evie gasped for air, coughing when the dust and debris of the ruined theatre caught in her throat. She clung to him like driftwood. "We have to go. Now. Please!" Evie pulled away and looked into the man's face. He was as white as snow. Evie nodded her assent.

It was dark as they crept, low to the ground, down an empty row of seats towards the wall. The open-sky ceiling was gone, and the hall's regular domed ceiling had been replaced. Flashes of neon light sliced the air just above their heads, fired from unseen weapons at unseen enemies. The green fog drifted down towards the hall's floor ominously. Evie stepped on her dress and tore it, tripping, but the man had her tight by the hand and reacted to her every misstep instantly. She was slow, but he didn't make her hurry. All around them, battles raged. The last stragglers of the concert ran and hid or fought with stranger things: beasts and soldiers and worse. Evie couldn't tell who has supposed to be fighting who. She kept her head low and trusted her guide.

They paused at the end of the row of chairs and watched the aisle. Other people were huddled here and there and a few bodies lay on the ground, motionless. Evie glanced at her companion, who looked resolute.

"We could just make for the exit. Turn ourselves over," Evie suggested. She watched one of the men sprawled across the aisle. He was dressed in some kind of military uniform and had started to twitch. The man in black touched her cheek, forcing her to look away, at him.

"No, I can get you out clear. We just have to wait."

"For what?"

"Him." The man pointed up at the opposing balcony. Whoever it was was half-buried in weapons like an avenging robot, firing energy bolts and missiles into the smoke. Only maroon dress pants suggested a human under all the machinery. "He's projecting half of this warzone right now," the man growled. "When the polyasinazine gas reaches him, this place will get a lot safer." Evie couldn't believe it. She stared at the box where she'd sat not long ago. "Just watch," the man bid her. She did.

A canister flew through the air with a muffled pop, smacking into the youth's metal exoskeleton and bouncing off ineffectually. Green smoke started to swirl about his legs, then seeped up under the metal suit. He was all but obscured by the fog when the gunfire stopped abruptly. Two of the bodies on the ground nearby vanished. Evie startled and looked around her.

"What else isn't real?" she asked. The man shrugged.

"None of it is real. It's all real. *It doesn't matter.* It will eat you or hurt you or kill you all the same."

Evie just stared. "How do you know that? Who are you?"

"Right now, I'm the guy who is going to save you," he said, paused, and looked at her for a moment, then another, without saying anything. Evie kept waiting for him to explain himself, but it didn't come. The man took her hand and ran for the bank of green fog that concealed the back wall.

Evie scrambled to keep up. They leapt over bodies and ducked away from the grasping talons of loose raptors, and finally plunged into the thick green cloud of polyasinazine. Evie held her breath instinctively. The man in black kept tugging her ahead, not giving her a chance to lag behind. They slowed as the fog started to thin out, revealing a circular crater in the wall where the double doors to the mezzanine used to be. The man let go of her hand and gestured for her to stand back.

He approached the opening like a prowling tiger. Then with one darting twist, he disappeared around the corner and Evie heard shouts, thuds, and then slightly muffled coughs of gunfire. She drew a corner of the man's cloak over her face to cover her mouth before taking a desperate breath and chancing a few hesitant steps forward. She wanted to call his name and know if he was alright, but, absurdly, she couldn't.

He was back a few second later, rounding the corner again with a pronounced limp.

"Now we run. Can you run?" he asked her through heaving breaths. Evie looked him over, eyes wide.

"Can *you* run?" she asked. "Your leg!" A thin spike protruded from his calf where his torn black pants were wet with viscous fluid. The man pulled her so close to him that she couldn't see anything but his chest and face.

"It's a dart. I'll be fine," he panted, forcing a pained smile. "It doesn't matter. We have to go."

And he ran. He ran with a limp, but he ran, and Evie ran with him. Dead or unconscious police officers in unmarked black uniforms lay just outside the door, and the maze of tunnels that led to the underground Opera House reached out ahead of them offering potential escape.

The air was clearer here but the tunnel was pitch black. The man ran as if he could see in the dark, keeping her so close to him that she had to mirror his steps. They crashed out the concealed trapdoor on James Street, tumbling into the deserted June night. The man took her by both shoulders and spoke urgently.

"We won't have long. You have to keep running-"

Evie heard a shout in the distance. "There they are. Ready! Shoot-"

"No!" The man turned to them and held out a hand, tugging Evie behind the broad protection of his frame. "Don't shoot!" He was cut off by toy-like bangs that caused him to recoil and stagger, but he still stood tall.

"Stop!" Evie shrieked, terrified. The man turned his

back to the officers on the road to face her. Guilt, concern, fear and pain were all marked in his expression, and another spike-like dart was lodged near his collarbone. Evie gasped and touched it, pulling back fingertips stained with red blood. "We surrender!" she yelled, locking her eyes with the man's.

"No," he whispered, "you have to stay free. Whatever happens."

"I don't understand!" Evie hissed, a lump stuck in her throat. "How can freedom be worth – this?" She gestured at the man's bloody chest. She heard the footsteps of the police jogging in their direction, along with the shouted instructions to lie on the ground.

"They'll drug you up worse than before. You'll never dream again. You'll lose the music. You'll lose *everything you ever dreamed.*" He looked at her meaningfully, then spun around, launching himself with unreal speed at one of the approaching men. There were four of them, and they got off five, eight, two dozen shots, though Evie was screaming too fiercely to count or care. The man braced himself with the impacts and barreled full-body into the first cop, knocking him to the ground and crushing his gun wrist with the boot of one foot. The he ducked and spun, turning on the second officer with nothing but determination on his drained, white face. They fired two more darts at him, each connecting with his chest with sick thuds.

"No! Stop!" Evie screamed. The third officer seemed to notice her for the first time, turning his weapon on her. The man in black changed his trajectory mid-punch, taking an extra skipping step through one man and ploughing his fist into the next. The cop dropped to the ground like a bag of rags.

With moves as quick and deadly as lightning, the man

danced through three more roundhouse kicks, absorbing even more shots of the guns as he dropped the last two police officers. Evie had exhausted her voice with her screams for peace, and could only watch with tears drenching her face as the man in black finally staggered back towards her and collapsed to his knees at her feet. Whatever drug the darts carried was irrelevant now. He was pierced and shot in so many places, he would bleed to death before the drug mattered.

Evie sank to her knees in front of him and covered her face with her hands, wrung out. "Why?" she whispered. "Why would you do this?"

"Stay free, Evie," the man whispered back to her, exhausted. "Stay free and we can be together. My beautiful, beautiful Evie." He lifted a bruised and blood-soaked hand to her cheek and cupped it devotedly.

"I don't even know you," Evie said, though her heart ached and told her something different. "Who are you?"

"I'm Duncan," he smiled, and leaned into her. His lips touched hers, warm and soft, and for endless moments Evie couldn't think of anything else. She pressed against him and drank deep, knowing the flavour of him as if she'd tasted it every day. She closed her eyes and remembered every touch and every smell.

Then he was gone. She knelt on the grey road alone but for the bodies of four police officers. Even the cloak around her shoulders had gone. Evie's strangled sob of grief echoed down the empty streets.

When she lifted her hands to her cheeks to wipe away the tears, she saw the blood on her fingers. Red blood, real blood. Though she couldn't see him or imagine him anymore, she knew he was there. Just below the surface. In her dreams.

ଔ

Charlotte Ashley collects the works of Alexandre Dumas, and owns 19 editions of The Three Musketeers, *one of which is a purse. Her family tolerates her book obsessions because they pay the bills: she is also a writer, editor and independent bookseller in Toronto, Canada. Her story 'Fold' appears in* Lucky or Unlucky? 13 Stories of Fate, *and her story 'Aisthesis' will appear in Crossed Genres' upcoming anthology,* Fierce Family. *She chronicles her literary musings at* http://charlotteashley.wordpress.com.

Christmas Epiphany

Alexandra Owen

❦

I sighed as I sat down at the dinner table. It was Christmas break. I grabbed an egg roll and couldn't help but notice the disappointment in my father's eyes when he looked at me. I took a small, tentative bite of my salty fried rice and glanced at my father again. His eyes were two slits and his lips were pursed. My body shook as I braced myself for the lecture about my failing grades at Northwestern State. I began to wonder what would have happened to me if I had followed my heart and pursued a different degree. If Mom hadn't died three years ago, would I have had some support?

"Sophia Arthur!" he said with force. "Why didn't you tell me about the email NSU sent you?"

"I'm sorry I didn't mention —"

"You failed half your classes and you have no chance of getting into the College of Business. What good is that for your future? It was your *responsibility* to mention that email to me!"

I took a deep breath. I had let myself go my second semester at NSU. I hated being an accounting major. I didn't enjoy it at all. How could I tell my father that? He was an accountant himself.

"I'm sorry, Dad," I whimpered, looking at the floor. "I promise I'll do better."

Even though he had high expectations for me, I knew he didn't think much of me as a student.

"Just *hearing* that isn't enough for me. You have a D-minus average. There's no way you're getting off this easily. Sign an appeal. If you don't, you've failed in my eyes." The look on my father's face sent chills up my spine. His fists trembled and he looked as if he was ready to split the table in half.

I knew I had failed. I knew I hadn't tried my best, but I wasn't happy. My father didn't really know who I was. If he really did care about me, he would have seen the fact that I was miserable as an accounting major. It wasn't a good match for me and my college buddies knew that. I didn't even want to be in school anymore.

"What are you going to do now, Sophia?" Dad asked me.

"I'm looking into other departments," I lied. I was afraid of how he'd react if I told him I was planning on taking a semester off. I would lose all my financial aid but I didn't care about the money. I hated being in school.

I dared not look at him when I said, "I don't want to sign an appeal." If I'd looked at him straight in the eyes he would have seen that I was lying.

"What?" my father asked, leaning in to look at me closer. His brown eyes were filled with skepticism and worry.

"I don't want to sign an appeal," I said, my voice trembling like a leaf. My heart was beating too fast. I really didn't want to go back. "I thought I'd take an acting class, maybe?" There was an acting studio not too far away from my home that I could join. It seemed reasonable. My throat was parched after asking the question. It was the first time I had exposed myself in front of him like that.

My face fell when I saw the flash of fury that flickered in his eyes. I should have known it was a bad idea to tell him that. My sister, Charlotte, was an actress, and my father hadn't spoken to her in years.

"I won't allow you to do that. Anything but an acting class, Sophia."

"But Charlotte—"

He pounded his fists on the table, making the plates rattle with a high pitched ringing. With a dark calmness he said, "*Never* mention your sister again."

"I'm sorry. I won't."

"Finish your dinner."

After dinner my dad made me wash the dishes as punishment for failing the semester. I stood at the sink and let the water run down my hands. Scrubbing away at the residue made me feel better about myself. All the emotion I felt bottled deep within me resurfaced. The vivid images of my mother's grave and my sister leaving the family behind eleven years ago played on a loop in my mind.

ॐ

The day my sister left had stuck with me my whole life. It was the look of pain in her eyes as she stood in the driveway with two suitcases in her hand. I remember hearing the sound of my mother's racking sobs coming from inside the house, and Dad was outside staring hard at my sister with revilement. I remember the way my sister cried in front of my father, but his stoic look was unchanging. He didn't seem to care about the fact that Charlotte was in distress. I remember her getting down on both knees, looking at me earnestly, with a frown on her face.

"What's going on, Charlie?" I asked.

"I'm leaving, Sophie. I'm leaving forever."

"But why?" I remember screaming as I dropped my doll.

"Daddy doesn't want me to live here anymore. You'll never see me again. I'm so sorry, Soph." I remember the way her lips trembled, and the tears as they flowed down her cheeks. "Goodbye."

She walked slowly away, the two suitcases in her hands. Her head drooped down. I thought she looked like an angel. But I furrowed my eyebrows as she waited at the foot of the driveway until a red Corvette stopped to pick her up. She dashed inside, as if embarrassed to be seen.

That was the last time I saw my sister and that was the reason my family was so dysfunctional. Dad told me some high school kid had knocked her up, but I found that hard to believe. I knew he was hiding something from me.

I remember the pain I felt when I found out my late mother had died of alcohol poisoning. After Charlotte left, she limited her activity to going into the kitchen to grab a bottle of wine, then returning to her bedroom. When she was done with the bottle, she would go back and grab another. She did this for nine years, until it killed her.

As I lay on my bed, staring at the expanse of nothingness above me, I understood that my father felt responsible for her demise. Though Dad tried hard to hide it behind his strong facade, I didn't see it as a strength, but rather an extreme weakness.

I shot up when I heard three knocks on my door. "Yeah?"

"Come out."

I cautiously opened the door, not knowing what to expect from Dad.

He stared at me. "We have something we need to talk about. Come downstairs."

I dreaded these kinds of conversations with my father. They were usually in the study, and he always wanted to say something about how unsuccessful I was.

"You need to make a decision and soon." He shook his head, as if he had lost hope in me. "Your future depends on the choices you make now. I've got other departments in mind for you. I think you'd be fine with a degree that doesn't require too much thinking. You're not especially bright. Your poor grades are a reflection of that."

That was a knife to my heart. "Dad, I have something to say about—"

"Let me finish!" he said, glaring daggers at me. "Don't be rude."

I bit my lip. More than anything I hated being called 'rude'. I was only trying to tell him something. I was trying to have some kind of conversation with him.

"Why don't you try a language degree?" he asked, calming himself.

"Dad," I said. "I'm ready to tell you. You're not going to like it."

"What is it?"

"I'm taking a semester off."

He stood up from his desk and looked at me with wide, fearful eyes. "Damn it, Sophia. Why do you have to throw your education away?"

"I just need some time off to figure out what I want to do with my life," I pleaded.

"You're going to be a college dropout. Do you know what happens to dropouts? They end up standing in the unemployment lines, *begging* for jobs. You know how I know this, Sophia? *I* was there. I'm speaking purely from experience. You want to drop out like I did? Fine. You want to learn the hard way?" he asked, raising his voice. "Then fine, but don't come to me for help when the going gets rough. You're going to have to start from the bottom up. I had to practically beg the college to let me in their Accounting department."

"Dad, why do you hate me?"

Dad threw his arms in the air, sighing as he looked up at the ceiling.

"Sophia, I don't hate you. Did I ever say I hated you? I just think at your age, you need to learn what life is really like."

"What is life *really* like, Dad?" I asked, putting my hands on my hips. I made no attempt to hide my sarcasm.

"I'm not answering that question. You're going to have to figure that out for yourself."

"So, I can drop next semester?"

My father sighed. "Do whatever you want, Sophia. Just don't take acting classes. Can you do that for me?"

As I left the study I was for certain of one thing. I didn't care what my father said. I was going to take acting classes, and I was going to the acting studio to enroll.

There was something charming about the prospect. After all, I had been in a few stage productions before. I was Maria in *Twelfth Night*, a mime in a production my drama teacher had written while I was in high school, and I performed the part of Miriam Kirby, a strange spiritualist in *You Can't Take it With You.* I actually loved miming and I thought I was good enough at it. The stage was my passion, my fire and my reason for being alive. It coursed through my veins, harassed me like a bug. I knew I wouldn't be satisfied until I actually stood on that glorious stage, performing for people. Deep down, I knew the person I wanted to perform for the most was my father.

ॐ

On the sly, I signed up for acting lessons. It was an easy thing to do, since I had a bit of money saved up from Christmas and birthdays.

I don't know why I decided to wander onto the stage in the auditorium. I suppose it just happened that way. As I walked on the stage I was overcome by a fit of passion. That giddy rush of excitement that made me feel happy to be alive, to be a part of something grand. I closed my eyes, and when I opened them, I saw the stage transformed around me into a Victorian home. I heard the sound of people walking in the street outside, of petticoats rustling like paper in the wind. I smelled the scent of Cornish hens roasting in the kitchen downstairs. There, in the center of the foyer, was a Christmas tree, bedecked with golden spheres and a glittery garland. Candlelight glittered off glass icicles like glowing diamonds, warming me and making me feel alive inside.

I approached the tree and noticed a small lark sleeping inside an iron cage. I smiled as I opened it and let the sleeping bird sit on my hand. When I touched it, the lark's wings fluttered with vitality. As I walked to the window, I said to the bird, "I'll set you free."

I opened the window and smiled as the sun's warm rays kissed my face. I held out my hand and the beautiful lark spread her wings and soared higher than the clouds, her feathers ruffling with the wind. The bird sounded beautiful as she sang her melody of sweet freedom, finally set free from her prison.

When I opened my eyes, I collapsed onto both knees as my heart raced wildly. It was an experience I had never had before in my life. Still high from the euphoric rush that was coursing through my veins, I didn't know what to think. I only *felt*, knowing then that this must be what actors experienced when they were on stage.

I jumped when I heard the words "Great performance!" coming from the back of the auditorium. It scared me out of my skin.

"Thanks!" I shouted back, not expecting anyone to be in the room. Was I going to get in trouble for this?

I started to leave the stage out of complete embarrassment, but by the time I had clambered to my feet, the person from the tech booth had already reached the ground floor.

"Hello," he said with a smile, raking a hand through his wavy brown hair. He looked at me and his blue eyes twinkled. "I'm Greg Barnes. I own the studio. I was doing some light testing just now. Have you done pantomime before?"

"A little," I said with wide eyes, hoping he wasn't going to berate me for a poor performance.

"You did a good job, but you should put more *emotion* into it."

"Thank you for the advice, Mr. Barnes," I said with a happy smile.

"Excellent, excellent. You have potential. Would you like to be a part of The Actor's Studio? We have some openings. We also have great teachers, ones you could learn a great deal from. You have talent and with some work you could be a good actress."

I couldn't believe my ears. Was he actually telling me that I had talent? I was someone who could be a successful actress? "Really?" I asked as my smile reached my eyes. I couldn't help but wonder what Dad would have thought of that.

"Your beautiful face belongs on that stage. I don't have very many openings, but I'd be willing to teach you myself."

"I'll have to think about it sir, if that's all right with you. I do want to act very badly, but it's my father. I need his permission."

"And your father is against you acting?"

"Very much so. I'm not sure why, but he is. Let me convince him and then I'll consider lessons."

❧

I ended up leaving The Actor's Studio with a smile that reached both of my ears. I knew then I had made the right decision. It seemed like everything was coming together. I was going to become an actress. I could forget about what Dad said about finding the meaning of life. Being an actress was the definition of life itself, and I couldn't have been happier.

My bliss came crashing down on me when my dad called me to his study the next day. My face was on fire as his menacing gaze sent chills up my spine. He leaned towards me as he said, "What do you think you were doing at that acting studio last night?"

My heart lurched. How much more of this could I endure from him? It was getting more difficult to be a daughter, a person who was supposed to be loved, in front of him. He said he didn't hate me, but my father had *never* said he loved me.

"You saw me?"

"I was on my way home from work and I saw you walking into the studio. Are you taking acting classes behind *my* back?"

"N-no, Dad. I was going to ask for your permission. I wanted to know if you'll let me take acting lessons at the studio. I'll pay for it myself, I promise. I have lots of Christmas money saved up from over the years. This is something I want *so* badly, Dad!"

My father sunk in his chair and I could see a look of complete sorrow in his eyes. It was the first time he had ever shown this side of himself to me. He buried his face in his hands and shook his head.

"Sophia, sit down. This is something you need to know. It's about your sister."

I sat down and watched my father. In that moment, I saw a different man. He was a human being. He had sorrows and concerns just like everyone else, and wasn't a cruel person at all. I was a fool ever to have thought of him like that.

"Your mother and I told you that a high school boy got your sister pregnant," he explained, "but that was something we told you so you wouldn't ask too many questions. It was eleven years ago and she was involved in an acting studio. Sophia, she was seduced by her theatre instructor. I don't know where she lives now or if she's even married to the man. We didn't disown her, Sophia. She left us because we didn't approve of her relationship with him. Just be careful, okay? If you want to be an actress, that's up to you. You're my daughter, but I realize you're growing up. Just act because *you* want to act. Not because someone else tells you you're good. There are charmers out there. Evil people. I was only trying to protect your from your sister's fate. I suppose it's a blood thing, but you can't hide your blood. You're so much like Charlotte. In so many ways, Sophia."

It obviously took a lot of effort for him to tell me the truth about Charlotte, but I didn't really understand what it had to do with me. I was still going to stick to my guns and pursue my lessons, regardless of what Dad said.

"I'm sure my prospective acting teacher is safe, Dad," I said. "He gave me solid advice. He'll teach me a lot."

"Sophia. Are you sure he's kind? Are you sure he's not trying to seduce you?"

"No, Dad. He's not seducing me. You don't have to worry about that. I promise."

My first lesson was on Epiphany Day. My hands were clammy and my heart raced as I knocked on Mr. Barnes's door.

"Come in!" he said from the other side.

I walked in and instantly something in my heart told me to go back. I didn't pay it any attention.

"Why don't you sit down for a moment? I've got to take care of some business."

I sat down on the chair in front of his desk and looked at the photos arrayed along it. Within a second, I saw *her*. Here she was, right before me, after years of not seeing her. The woman who was smiling and holding a young child in her arms was my sister. There was no mistaking it. She looked the same as I remembered, but older. She had grown even more beautiful with age and her eyes were so deep, but as I looked closer into them,

I noticed how plaintive they were. She was suffering and it made me angry. Why didn't she come back to us if she was *that* unhappy? Dad would have helped her. I felt hurt.

"Who is that?" I asked Mr. Barnes.

"Oh," he said, waving his mind dismissively. "Just my wife. No one special."

"She's very beautiful, sir."

"Not as beautiful as you," he said with a wink and a smile.

I didn't know what to think. Was this man *coming on to me?* I quickly glanced at the picture of Charlotte. Her eyes changed. They looked desperate, as if they were begging me to leave the room and never to return. I didn't know what to say, or even what to do. I had already signed up for an acting lesson. Maybe it wouldn't have been all that bad – maybe I was imagining things.

"Uh, thanks," I said, chuckling nervously.

"Are you ready to start your lesson?"

I nodded and he led me to the sofa. My lips trembled and my heart raced. My sister's steely blue eyes burned into my mind.

He sat next to me, talking about the plans he had for me and my *talent.* There was an intense energy in the way he talked to me, but all I could see was the man who had married my sister. Before I knew it, his hands weren't on his lap anymore. They were on my thighs.

"Come on, why don't we get out of here?" he said with a smile, looking at me as if he was ready to eat me alive.

"No, I'm sorry. I can't do this." I said quickly.

"Are you sure? You seem like you really want to."

"What kind of person do you think I am?" I shouted, backing away.

"Come on, Sophia. Lighten up a little. I'll give you the lead role in the next production."

"I *don't want it!*" I shoved his hands away from my lap.

He sneered at me and moved closer to me. "You're never going to be an actress anyway. You're terrible. Wooden. All of this was so that I could..." He didn't even finish what he was going to say. His hands were on my face, my back—all over me. The lusty fire in his eyes filled me with disgust. My father was *right.* I had been duped.

I tried to leave his office, but he placed himself in front of the door and grabbed hold of me. Memories of my father's eyes burned into my mind. I should have listened to him. The thought of him gave me strength. I shoved Mr. Barnes away and left his studio. There was no chance I would ever return.

What was I if I wanted to act, but had no talent? Those were the thoughts racing through my mind as I drove my car. I didn't care where I was going; I just needed to get out and away from everything that was holding me back. I thought of my father at home, and Charlotte with the way her eyes looked so sad in Barnes's office. As the silvery moonlight shone through the window, I immediately knew the mistakes I had made helped to form who I was going to be. Life was all about choices and consequences. My choice was simple. I wasn't going to let people control me. I was going to define myself.

ଓଃ

Alexandra Owen had dreams of singing on the stage of the Metropolitan Opera, but when she realized her true passion, writing, she changed her degree path. Her passion for writing historical fiction is evident to everyone who meets her. Alexandra loves sharing her stories with others.

You can find her on Wattpad as Davrielle - http://www.wattpad.com/user/Davrielle.

Mina's Sanctuary

Tim McFarlane

 C3

"You should smile more," my mother said, looking at me in the rear view mirror. "How do you expect to make friends if you don't smile?"

I let the question remain unanswered as I stared down at my hands. I had friends back home. Moving to the other side of the country made it difficult to continue those friendships. I wanted to say something, but the look in my mother's eyes made me keep my mouth shut. If I said anything I would get the long guilt trip about how this is 'best for us'. Which I'm sure it was, in some way.

"I love you, Philomina," my mother continued. I hid a cringe at my name. "Try to have a good day."

I muttered an 'I love you' back as I climbed out of the car. We'd moved because my mother got a new job. She worked as an accountant for some company that made cars and when they opened a new plant on the other side of the country, my mother took the promotion to become head of the department. She was very happy, but it meant the family had to move to some town we knew nothing about.

Once I was inside the building, panic rose up in me. There was no way I was going to survive the day. Students were already racing back on forth down the halls. I could feel everyone staring at me and I instantly regretted wearing a sweater. It was still too warm to be wearing one, but puberty had left with a chest that attracts both creepy looks from the guys and looks of hate from the girls. Sweaters were my best friend.

A loud crash drew my attention as I reached the office. A skinny, tall guy was down on the ground, his books were scattered everywhere, and a larger guy towered over him.

"Watch where you're going, nerd!" the bully said. The skinny guy didn't even look up as he started to pick up his books. "Nice jewfro, loser." The bully kicked one of the kid's books further away before high-fiving his friends and leaving.

The guy continued to pick up his belongings quietly while everyone else went about their business. I wanted to go over and help him, but I stood frozen in place. What could I say to him?

When he finished cleaning up, I disappeared into the office before he could see that I had been watching him. The opportunity to help him had passed and maybe it was for the best that I hadn't gone over there. He wouldn't have wanted to talk to me anyhow.

The office was slow moving, and by the time I got my schedule, I was late for my first class. I quickly sat down in the nearest seat and counted the seconds until the class was over.

The day passed by in a blur and when the final bell rang, I left quickly. School hadn't been as bad as I thought. The rest of the semester should be easy if I keep up this pattern.

It took me twenty minutes to get home and I used the time to reread my favourite parts of *Through the Looking Glass,* looking for inspiration for my next painting. When I got there, I immediately headed up to my room to begin. I threw my back pack towards the closet, got changed into some more comfortable clothes and grabbed my easel.

The fresh canvas started back at me. I grabbed my sketching pencil and started doodling. A creature started to take shape, with long, lanky arms and legs shooting out from a humanoid torso, a large mouth and four beady eyes. It looked like a twisted version of a spider and not at all what I had wanted to draw, but my hand worked like it had a mind of its own. I forced myself to drop the pencil and turned the canvas around so I wouldn't have to look at it.

"What the hell?" I muttered, staring at the back of the canvas.

I sat quietly for a second until I heard Dad call me down to dinner. I fled my room as fast as I could, the image of the creature still in my head. I would have to destroy it or I would never be able to get sleep tonight.

After dinner, I took the canvas, put it into an empty moving box and sealed it up, planning to throw it out with the others on trash day. Then I went to my movie collection and looked through for something to watch. My mind kept straying back to the box until I finally picked it up and placed it in the hall.

I settled on Spirited Away for the millionth time. I spent the evening trapped in one of my favourite worlds, and for the millionth time I wished that the real world could be more like a fantasy world. It would be the only place where I would feel like I fit in, and I would finally be happy.

Tomorrow would be Day Two of our new life in a new town and it already felt exactly like the old life. I sighed as I lay down in my bed. All I could do was hope that something new would come my way eventually and things would finally change for me.

The feeling of warmth on my skin made me sigh and I stretched out on the hard ground...

My eyes snapped open and I stared, confused, at the tall grass towering over me. It wasn't exactly how I remembered my bedroom. I sat up slowly to survey the area around me. I was in an open meadow surrounded by a forest.

In the tall grass, taller flowers with interchanging blue and red petals rotated as they stared up at the high sun. The sky itself was a bright violet and the sun shone down on the world, brightly lighting everything with the fake light of a stage.

I rose to my feet and the strange flowers turned their attention to me. The sunflower-like black centres seemed to be staring at me. A couple slowly reached closer to me and made a sound like they were sucking in air.

"Are you sniffing me?" I asked.

The flowers backed away, shocked by my voice, then slowly returned to continue sniffing me. They seemed harmless and a giggle escaped me as I pictured them as dogs, curious about my presence. I studied the field again, hoping to find some answer as to how I got here.

The flowers in the meadow suddenly stopped and all faced the same direction. I turned to see what had caught their attention but could only make out what looked like a lake in the distance. I looked back to the flower closest to me and I thought I saw it trembling.

"What's going on?" I asked it, feeling a bit silly talking to a plant.

All the flowers suddenly closed up their petals and dropped below the grass, leaving me standing in the bare meadow by myself. In the distance, I saw the slow rise and fall of long, lanky black arms. All my instincts shouted at me to run. I quickly chose the direction of the surrounding forest, and broke out into a full run.

A piercing scream tore through the silence behind me. Stealing a glance, I saw the arms speed up and the grass start shaking as the beast started running. I screamed in terror and pushed myself to run faster, breaking into the forest and looking for something to climb. I picked a sturdy-looking tree and frantically pulled myself up the branches, breathing heavily with panicked squeaks escaping me involuntarily.

The heavy grunt of a beast made me pause. I latched myself to a branch and hugged it close, covering my mouth with my free hand in case it could smell my breath. I waited for the beast to pass by, but it slowed instead, the grunting replaced by clicking.

I frantically searched the ground for the beast. I clamped my hand tighter around my mouth as the sight of a long, lanky, spider-like leg almost made me gasp. My whole body felt frozen as the realization that I would not be able to escape sunk in.

Tears started to run down my cheeks when a loud thud in the distance caught my attention. The beast also clicked quickly as another thud followed shortly afterwards. It screamed in its inhuman, high-pitched tone and skittered off towards the sound.

I released my mouth but I continued to hug the branch and cry. I didn't know where I was but I didn't want to be here. As a big fan of Carroll's novels, I was ashamed that I was acting just like a stereotypical crying heroine - but to read the books and to live them were two very different things. I wasn't strong enough to handle whatever this was.

"There is no reason to cry," a tiny, male voice said. "They are easy to trick and he shouldn't come back for a long time."

I wiped away the tears and looked around, but didn't see anyone. "Hello?" I tried.

A hummingbird flew in front of me. "Helloooo," he said pleasantly.

I almost lost my balance. The tiny creature wasn't exactly like a hummingbird - there was some butterfly in there too - and it stared at me with bright, happy eyes waiting for me to speak. I remained quiet, not trusting my voice to sound right.

"I know you are capable of talking," he said. "I heard you talking to the Sunlilies. They don't have the ability to speak, though. They're plants."

I smirked and forced myself into a sitting position on the branch. "I'm sorry, I just... what are you?"

The bird lowered itself to the branch and morphed into a cross between a chipmunk and a guinea pig. He chuckled dryly. "That's... hard to answer. As for my name? I'm a little ashamed of it."

I smiled. "I know what you mean. I'm ashamed of my name too."

"What is it?" he asked.

"Philomina," I answered.

"What's wrong with that name?" he asked.

"It's just... old-sounding," I answered. "It sounds like the name of a grandma, not a teenager."

The little shape-shifting creature nodded. "At least it sounds pretty."

I shrugged. "Not when it gets shortened to Phil. What's your name?"

The creature looked down at the branch. "Doncifence."

"Don-ci-fence?" I asked.

He nodded. "It's stupid, I know but... that's what I'm called."

"Well," I started, thinking of a way to be helpful. "Donci sounds cute. Could I just call you that?"

He looked up at me for a second and nodded thoughtfully. "Ok. Could I call you Mina in return?"

I shrugged. "Sure."

"Better than Phil," he pointed out.

I nodded and chuckled. "So, Donci... what is this place and what was that thing chasing me?"

He looked at me, confused. "You don't know?"

"No, I'm not from here, I-" I hesitated, trying to figure out how to say it, "-just woke up here."

Donci morphed back into the bird and flew up to look directly into my eyes with a shocked look on his little face. "You're-" he started, "-we have a prophecy that an outsider will come here and save us from the evil witch. Are you really an outsider?"

I studied him for a second. "Save you from an evil witch? Did I wake up in a fairy tale?"

"I should start from the beginning," he said.

"Please," I replied. "No, 'Once upon a times'."

He shook his head and returned to the branch, turning back into the chipmunk thing. "You are in Sanctuarium," he started. "Once... a long time ago -" I rolled my eyes. "- things were quiet and peaceful here. It was, as the name suggests, a sanctuary for creatures like me. Until *she* showed up. Her name is Fledsoubt. She killed the old king," he paused, "... banished the old prince, and seized control. That thing that chased you is an Eraf, a soldier of Fledsoubt used to keep the locals living in fear so they can't rise against her."

"There are more people like you?" I asked.

"At one point, yes, but not so much anymore," he said. "There are few creatures left that haven't been turned in Erafs."

"That's terrible," I said sympathetically.

"The prophecy states that an outsider will come to the land and overthrow Fledsoubt, returning Sanctuarium to the old ways but-" he continued. "let's just say hope was the first thing to die here."

"And I'm that outsider?" I asked, dreading the answer I already knew.

"Yes," Donci answered happily. "We have waited a long time for your arrival."

"I can't," I stuttered, "I... how?"

"You have to confront Fledsoubt in her lair and vanquish her," Donci answered matter-of-factly. Like it was a trip to the corner store for some milk.

"Is that all the prophecy says?" I asked. "Do I not get any more details?"

Donci shook his head. "I'm sorry, I do not know the prophecy as well as I should. It's been a long time since I last heard it."

"Ok then. Where is the witch?" I asked.

"In her castle, at the top of the mountain," Donci said, motioning out of the forest. "On the other side of the lake. So, you are going to help?"

I looked at Donci glumly and he just stared up at me. "I can't. I need to get out of here."

"We need you," he pleaded. "Besides, the only way out is through her castle."

"How do you know that?" I asked.

"Well...maybe it is, I don't know," he answered, his desperation clear. "But why else would you be here?"

I shrugged. "I don't know."

"Please, come with me to meet my friend," he said, changing into the bird. "Maybe seeing her will help you understand why we need you."

I chuckled dryly. "'Need me'. You sure know how to make a girl feel wanted."

"We just have to get to the lake," Donci said, getting excited. "Come on."

Despite my fear of being discovered by the Erafs, the lake had a peaceful, serene presence. It reminded me of a similar lake I used to camp at with my family - until my parents' careers occupied most of their free time. I would always cherish the memories of the lake. Being here filled me with a welcomed sense of calm and gave me time to think on what Donci had told me.

If he was really thought I was a saviour, he was in for a tragic reality check. I could barely save myself, let alone anyone else. He would be better off turning me over to this witch for a reward.

Donci, sensing my mood, did his best to boost my confidence and we quickly fell into an easy friendship. According to him, my simple presence was going to cause the witch to melt into a puddle of stinky water and cause rainbows to shoot of the castle while creatures paraded in happiness. I wanted to correct him, but the mental image was making me laugh too hard to ruin the moment.

Donci stopped flying next to a large, hollow, partially-submerged tree trunk. I stopped behind him and listened as he whistled a catchy little tune. From the tree trunk, a large creature that looked like a salamander emerged and smiled up at Donci.

"You've returned!" the amphibian exclaimed in a female voice. "Why did you leave in such a hurry? Don't you know that you could get hurt out there?"

"Mina, I want you to meet Anorapai, my, uh, mother," Donci introduced us.

"Your mother?" I asked, unable to picture the shape-shifter coming from a salamander. Unless she was also a shifter.

"Well, she adopted me after Fledsoubt ravaged the land," he explained.

"Ah," I said, turning my attention to the salamander. "It's nice to meet you."

She didn't respond. She just stared at me in horror.

"I won't hurt you," I said reassuringly.

"You are an outsider," she breathed. "Doncifence, you brought an outsider here. The Erafs are running around like crazy and you brought an outsider HERE?"

"She needs to understand why we need her help," Donci pleaded. "You have to help her."

"No, no, no, no," Anorapai stammered, backing up into the tree trunk. "She's going to get you killed. Get her out of here before Fledsoubt punishes everyone."

"She might be right, Donci," I agreed, "Maybe I should just get out of here."

"But look at how the fear has forced us to live," Donci countered angrily, looking me square in the eyes.

"Would you really leave us like this, even if you could escape?"

I opened my mouth to answer but nothing was going to come out. I felt ashamed, but it was quickly replaced by fear as a familiar scream cut through the air.

"Oh, creator, no," Anorapai said, tears starting down her face. "This is it. I told you they would come for her. Quickly, Doncifence, into the trunk. Leave her for the beasts."

I was appalled she would suggest that but before I could speak Donci rose to my defense. "No, Mother. She is my friend and I would rather die out here with her than turn her over."

"You would die for me?" I asked, shock spread all over my face. "We barely know each other. What makes you think I'm worth it?"

"I just know," he answered. "We can talk more after we've escaped. Quickly, where can we go?"

My mind raced and I got an idea. "Does the trunk still float?"

"That's how it got here," Anorapai answered. "Why?"

"You might want to get on top of it, then," I said, running over to it and pushing it into the lake.

"Good thinking, Mina!" Donci exclaimed, morphing into the chipmunk and helping his mom up onto the log.

When we were waist-deep in the water, I grabbed the trunk and struggled to pull myself up with the help of Donci. On the shore, a large group of Eraf were rushing to the water.

Getting a better look at them, I almost screamed. They looked exactly like the creatures I had painted this very evening. They let out a screech and Anorapai hid her head as we slowly drifted away.

Donci continued to look up at me and maintained eye contact. He seemed pleased with our escape and I was happy that we were safe, only... "I didn't think this through," I said. "We're stranded out here. Assuming the Erafs don't swim."

"They can't swim and tend to avoid the lake," Donci explained. "It's the last peaceful place we have left."

"It's beautiful out here, but now what?" I asked.

"We continue with our plan," Donci answered. "We have to cross the lake to reach the gatekeeper at the base of the mountain. He can get you to the top."

"It's not going to work," Anorapai said. "He's going to just turn her away and feed her to the Erafs."

"Ignore her," Donci said."Her paranoia has grown out of control recently."

"It's not paranoia to understand our fate," Anorapai snapped.

"Our fate has changed with Mina's arrival," Donci countered.

"How?" I asked. "Where does this confidence in me come from?"

Donci sighed. "Because I see a lot of me in you. We are almost the same person. The more time I spend with you, the more I know it. We see things that we want to change, but feel powerless to do it. Seeing you here has given me some strength back. I know we can do this, Mina. Don't ask me how, because I just do. I want you to see and feel the same thing. Together, we are going to turn this place back in the sanctuary it once was. Together, we can defeat Fledsoubt."

The conviction in his voice made me pause. I didn't know if I could feel the same way as he did, but for him, I would try. The thought of him being crushed by defeat broke my heart.

I reached down and scooped him up into my two hands. I brought him up close to my face so I could look into his eyes. "I will do my best to help you, Donci," I promised.

He smiled, reached up and hugged my face. "Thank you, Mina." He broke away from the hug and looked up at me with new respect. "A quick warning about the gatekeeper. He can be difficult, so you must be firm."

"I will be like a strict parent," I said, lowering him to the trunk. "Now, which way?"

❧

The gatekeeper's hut lay at the bottom of the mountain next to the path. Half way up the mountain, I could see the castle. Its ominous appearance wasn't the most welcoming of sights, but I had been to scarier places. Like my grandma's nursing home. If I could survive that trip, the castle should be a cake walk. I hoped.

Donci flew ahead to the modest, wooden hut while I scooped up the reluctant Anorapai and followed. Donci signalled for me to knock on the door and after a couple seconds, a short creature resembling a sloth or a bear on two legs answered the door.

"Are you Vinz, the keymaster?" the sloth asked.

"What?" I answered.

"Never mind," he said, and shut the door.

I stared at the door for a second before knocking again. The door remained shut and no sounds could be heard from the other side.

"Redip, this is serious!" Donci called out. "Open the door."

Donci flew in through the open window and a moment later the door opened. I walked into the dirty hut. "What do you want, Prince?" the creature asked.

I narrowed my eyes at Redip. "Prince?" I asked.

"He must have told you the history," Redip answered. "Evil witch descends upon the castle, kills the King and the little Prince flees into the forest."

"That's not what happened," Donci countered.

Redip snorted. "'Course not."

"You're the prince?" I asked Donci.

He sighed. "Yes."

"Why didn't you tell me?" I cried.

"Because it meant admitting that I had failed and everyone's suffering is on my hands," he answered. "You already seemed shaky with everything. How would have this have affected you? Would you have still joined me if you thought I was using you?"

"I need a moment to think about this," I said.

"Oh, Prince, you've done it now," Redip chuckled. "Not only did you find the outsider of the prophecy but you've also driven her away. She'll never help you now."

"What makes you think that?" I asked.

"Look at you," he answered. "You don't want to do this. Whatever confidence you had when you walked in here is gone. Give up, and accept the world around you. Things are fine the way they are."

I looked to Donci, but he was looking at the ground. My anger melted at the sight of him. I'm sure the lie hurt him more than it did me and I understood I had been difficult to deal with since the start.

"Hey," I said softly. He looked up at me slowly. "I promised to help if I could. I won't break my promise."

"You didn't lose your faith in me?" he asked.

"I can understand not wanting to overload me with information, but I'm not a child," I said sternly. "Be up front with me."

"Deal," Donci said happily.

"You," I said, pointing to Redip. "Open the gate. We are going to talk to this witch."

"No," Redip replied.

"Yes."

"No," he persisted. "You don't understand what's happening."

"Yes, I do," I said, getting frustrated.

"Ok," he smiled. "How are you going to defeat her?"

I stared at him for a second while I thought. "I'll think of a way."

He laughed, shaking his head. "Nice plan. But highly ineffective. How about you hear the tasks to defeat her first? Then you can decide to quit this foolish task and just move on."

"Fine," I shrugged. "Lay it on me."

"One," he started, "face her army and expose them for what they are. Two. Test your mind against hers and prove she isn't as clever as she believes. Three. Destroy her anchor to this world, and banish her."

"Ok, expose her army for what they are," I said. "Well, what are they?"

"The soldiers of fear," Anorapai said with a shudder.

"The soldiers of fear," I said thoughtfully. "This whole thing almost sounds like a riddle."

"Are you any good at them?" Anorapai asked.

"I have a soft spot for them," I answered. I continued to think about the riddle and remembered all that hogwash parents and teachers say about facing your fears. I wondered: if we faced the Erafs and showed no fear, would they be able to harm us? Was it really that simple?

"Ok, if the Erafs are just fear and we have to expose them," I started, "then standing up to them should do the trick. Show no fear and fear can't harm you - or whatever the saying is."

"Would you really be willing to test it?" Redip asked, skeptical.

"Has anyone else tried it?" I asked.

'No, because they were too afraid to," Anorapai said.

"Exactly," I said.

"If you believe it will work, then we have to try it," Donci said. "I'll be right behind you, Mina."

"Thank you, Donci," I said. "Take us to the castle, Gatekeeper. Let's see if the witch's fearsome army is all it's cracked up to be."

"Very well, Mina," Redip said. "Allow me a moment to channel my magic into teleporting us up the mountain."

His hand started to glow purple and he waved it in a circle above his head. With a flash of white, I felt my body tugged upward before dropping back onto solid ground. We had been teleported right in front of the giant castle on the mountain. It took a second for the disoriented feeling to pass and I stumbled a step before I regained my footing.

The castle looked as if it were straight out of a fairy tale. Stone walls circled the large stone structure with three tall towers started from the top and stretching up as to see which could touch the sky first. Beside the castle was a large waterfall that fed the moat around the castle. The entire scene would be perfect if the water wasn't blood red.

"That wasn't like that when I lived here," Donci said.

A scream cut through the air and twenty Erafs bounded out the castle towards us. The big moment was upon us. We'd soon see if I was right.

Redip's hand glowed purple as he stared down at the Erafs in fear. "I only have enough magic for me to get out of here. If this doesn't work - I told you so."

I looked at him, ready to kick him off the mountain, but decided to save my strength. As the Erafs continued towards us, Donci landed on my shoulder and morphed into his chipmunk form. Anorapai grabbed my fingers and pulled them around her body so my hand protected her. I focused on breathing steadily and tried not to think of them as spiders.

The Erafs stopped two meters in front of me, clicking, but wouldn't come any closer. I stared at them, willing them to do something, but they just stood still, staring and clicking menacingly. Without the threat of danger, their attempts at intimidation were almost laughable. They *were* nothing to fear at all. We were completely safe.

Redip lowered his hand and the purple disappeared. "Well, I'll be."

"I told you so," I smirked.

"Looks like I owe you some respect," Redip said.

"Would your pride allow that?" I asked.

He laughed once. "I said *some* respect."

I started towards the castle. The Erafs backed up, but still stood in front of me trying to scare me. Half way to the castle it was getting pathetic.

"Come on, guys," I said. "Move on."

"Be careful," Anorapai said. "They could just be luring you into a trap."

"We'll be fine, Anora," I said to her, shortening her name instead of trying to pronounce it.

"Anora?" she smiled. "So pretty."

At the door, the Erafs ran away, aware that they had failed at their task. We were free to confront the witch and claim the throne for its rightful King.

We crossed the bridge over the moat and pulled open the castle door. Redip walked in first and gave me a nod of 'all clear'. I entered the main hall where a bright white orb stood on a pedestal. Redip motioned towards it and mouthed "anchor". I stared in shock. Why would she leave it up front in the open like that? She must have believed no one would make it this far.

"She didn't have the option to hide it," Donci said, reading my thoughts. "It's my father's Orb of Perception. He used it to see everywhere in the kingdom so he could help those that needed it. We don't know how it had been corrupted, but when it was, the witch was created. Only by destroying it can we remove her from this land."

"Ok," I nodded, checking out the orb. "How?"

"Oh, don't worry about that, child," a female voice said, amused. "So, the little prince finally returns."

A very tall woman strolled causally towards us. The robe she wore was a deep purple that covered her from her neck to the floor. Her sharp facial features were heavily covered in make up to create the illusion of beauty, but it was lie. She could never be beautiful.

I searched her hands for a staff or anything that could be used as a weapon but she was essentially just a head floating on top of the robe.

"You're Fledsoubt?" I asked.

"Of course, Outsider," she answered. "And I see that you were quickly scooped up and brought here to banish me."

"That's right," I said proudly. "We defeated your army by exposing them for the wimps they were."

Fledsoubt chuckled. "And now you've come to 'test your mind against mine' to prove I'm not as clever as I believe?" She took a moment to laugh dramatically. "You have chosen poorly, child, putting your faith in these pitiful creatures. But I shouldn't be too surprised; you look just as pitiful as they. Do you really want to embarrass yourself by testing my vast knowledge?"

"You can't be that clever," I said, trying to act tough. "You hope to make me doubt myself by childishly insulting me. It doesn't seem like you have enough confidence in yourself to beat me in a battle of smarts."

She hissed and I felt Donci close to my ear. "Good work," he whispered. "Keep believing in yourself and she won't have any power over you."

Easier said than done, I thought, taking a deep breath.

Fledsoubt composed herself and smiled. "If you wish to carry on with your humiliation, I will not stop you. Just know that when you lose, I will destroy your little friends. Their deaths will be caused by you and your failure."

I took another deep breath, trying to ignore the mental image of Donci and Anora dying. Oddly, Redip being hurt didn't worry me as much.

"We're here for you," Anora whispered.

"You can do this," Donci whispered.

I gathered my courage. "Begin your test or get out. I don't have all day."

The expression on Fledsoubt's face changed to one of anger again before she composed herself. "Very well, child, the game will be riddles. Solve my riddles and prove you are at least as clever as I am."

I chuckled, to hide my uncertainty. "Ok. I like riddles. I can do this."

"Poor people have it, rich people need it. If you eat it, you die. What is it?" Fledsoubt asked.

I mulled it over in my brain. I looked down to Anora and Redip to see if they could be any help, and Redip just shrugged.

"I got nothing," he said.

My eyes grew wide and I looked up to the witch. "Nothing," I answered.

She gritted her teeth. "Correct. If I have it, I don't share it. If I share it, I don't have it. What is it?"

I thought for a second before smiling. "A secret," I answered. "I've heard that one before."

"Correct," Fledsoubt said, getting irritated. "It has mountains but no land, oceans but no water and cities but no people. What is it?"

"Oh, that one is actually pretty clever," I smiled. "But easy. A map. Are you actually going to give me a hard one or are we going to break into the children's puzzles next?"

"I destroy your dreams!" she shouted, her rage growing. "I am the reason you fail at something before starting it! The reason why you can't maintain friends and the reason I am here is because you put me here! WHAT! AM! I?"

I looked at her in confusion before realization took control. A smile stretched across my face as everything about this place began to make sense. It was my mind, and the creatures around me were parts of me. The witch standing in front of me was also a part of me that was allowed to take control and ravage my mind. Like the army of fear, it was time for me to face her and banish her forever.

Donci nudged me and whispered, "Do it. I'll always be here for you."

"WHAT AM I?" the witch screamed.

"You are my self-doubt!" I shouted. "And you are no longer welcome here!"

Fledsoubt shrieked and her robe opened up to reveal a blackened and diseased body. A green wave of power exploded outward from her, covering the entire room like water and knocking me off my feet. Anora and Donci jumped off of me. Anora morphed in a kimono dragon and Donci morphed into a tiger. Even Redip surprised me by morphing into a grizzly bear. All three of them charged at Fledsoubt and I scrambled to my feet.

"Destroy the orb!" Donci called out.

The witch shrieked again and a purple beam of power shot from her eyes into Anora. She cried out and was launched backwards. Landing hard, she lay motionless on the ground. The witch tried to push past them and focus on me, but Redip got in the way and bought me enough time to get to the orb.

Freeing the orb was difficult, but with both hands I lifted it up over my head and slammed it into the ground with all my might. Another shriek escaped Fledsoubt as a vortex of wind and power swirled around the castle, knocking Donci and Redip back. A white light opened under Fledsoubt and she was sucked into it, disappearing from the land, hopefully, forever.

I immediately ran over to the body of Anora, who was still breathing, though weakly. "You did it," she breathed.

Donci rushed over to join me, still in his tiger form, and nuzzled Anora. "Anorapai, no," he said, tears streaking down his face. "Please don't die."

"I'm so proud of you, Doncifence," she said dreamily, slowing slipping away from us. "Never forget that."

Anora slowly morphed back into the salamander and Donci pulled her body to him so he could cuddle into her. His body shook with his sobbing and I scooted closer to him and covered his body with mine.

"I'm so sorry," I said.

He sniffed and turned so he could look at me in my face. "Don't apologize. You've done so much for us. Never in a million years did I think this would ever happen."

"I should have been able to save her, though," I said.

Donci shook his head. "You did everything you could. We knew what we were getting into when we decided to fight the witch." He sighed. "She wouldn't want us crying for her."

Out of the corner of my eye, I saw Redip join us, back in his original form. I stood up and faced him. "I was shocked to see you join the battle."

He nodded. "Couldn't let you get all the credit." I shook my head and smirked. He smiled. "You did good, kid."

I turned back to Donci. He nuzzled Anora's body once more before standing up to face me. "I wish you could stay here forever, but I suspect our time is growing short," he said.

"Will I be able to come back?" I asked.

"Of course!" Donci said. "Sanctuarium will always welcome you."

"Then I will return soon," I said, "for Anora's memorial."

Donci smiled. "I would like that." He took a deep breath. "I promise you that I will rule this place properly and never let a witch like that take over again."

"Same." I smiled back. I bent over to hug him. "Thank you for helping me through this."

"You're a wonderful person, Mina," he said. "If you ever doubt yourself, I will be here to help you."

"Thank you," I said, hugging him tighter before pulling away. "Ok. How do I get home?"

"Crouch down in front of me," Redip said.

I crouched down in front of him and his hand started to glow purple. He closed his eyes and reached out to smack me in the forehead.

❧

My eyes flew open as my alarm went off. I quickly sat up and looked around my room. It looked exactly the same as it had last night. I lay back down and stared at the ceiling for a moment, memories of the dream still swirling in my head.

I had never experienced a dream that felt so... real before. Either I have been reading too many books or I had had an actual spirit journey into my mind.

The buzzing of the alarm began to annoy me and I reached over and shut it off. I pulled away my blanket and stare down at the mess between my legs. The blood-red waterfall made a little more sense now.

"MOM!" I called out.

I'm going to need a shower, I thought.

ॐ

The second day of school was less scary than the first. I knew the layout a little better and was able to get to my classes on time. People even seemed to pay less attention to me as they did yesterday - though I still wore a sweater. I had debated whether or not to bring it before finally grabbing it at the last second.

After the first class, there was a commotion in the hallway. The bullies were circled around a tall, skinny guy with curly hair on the ground, picking up his fallen books. I recognized the boy from yesterday. It seems he had unwittingly fallen on their radar yesterday and was going to be target number one for a while.

The bullies left the kid and everyone went back to what they were doing except me. I watched him for a moment, feeling the same desire to help him pick up his things but feeling the same fear of what to say to him.

Only this time, it felt a little bit silly to be afraid to speak to him.

I've faced down creatures of pure fear and bested an evil witch at riddles, I thought. I should be able to help a boy pick up his books.

I forced my feet forward. I knelt next to boy and gathered some of the stray papers. He looked at me with confusion as I handed them to him.

"It looked like you needed some help," I said shakily.

He took the papers and mumbled "thank you," still watching me like I was about to prank him or something.

I picked up one of the books and smiled at the title. "*Through the Looking Glass?*" I asked. "I'm reading this. Well, reading it for the millionth time, I should say. It's always been one of my favourites. I've always had a thing for the surreal and fantasy. I own, like, every Studio Ghibli movie possible. I even paint creatures that could be in those movies." I stopped myself because I was rambling nervously and he was just watching me with a slight smile. "Please say something," I said, feeling a blush creeping on my face.

He chuckled. "Sorry. I just... didn't think there were girls that liked that stuff."

I laughed. "I could say the same about boys."

All his belongings were back in his bag and we stood up to face each other.

"I recognize you from Art class," he said.

"Yes, I'm, uh, Philomina," I said. "Please, just call me Mina."

"I'm Donald," the boy said. "Just call me Don. We should, uh, probably get to our next class before the bell rings, though."

"Yeah," I said sadly. "I'll see you in Art?"

"Yeah, I'll bring my sketch pad," he said, scratching the back of his head. "Maybe we could, uh, compare work."

I smiled, feeling my face warming with a blush. "That would be great. I'll see you then."

I hurried away as he muttered "bye". I couldn't wipe the stupid grin off my face. I had no doubt I said something stupid or made myself look like some sort of freak, but it didn't matter. I had talked to him and he seemed to want to continue talking to me.

So why did it feel like defeating a witch and her army was easier?

Ↄ

Tim McFarlane is the author of the sometimes-funny fantasy series The Legend of Kairu *and the forthcoming science fiction series* The Galactic Council Chronicles. *He currently lives in Cambridge, Ontario, Canada.*

For more short stories and previews of his book, visit him on Wattpad at http://www.wattpad.com/user/TimMcFarlane.

The Ribbon Chasers

Len Webster

It was a dream he had every night, a dream that made his heart pump, his sweat drip and his head hurt. The same damn dream every night. He remembered the squeal and then the gunshot. He watched those brown eyes flash before he heard her final scream, and then silence.

He tried. As much as he tried to change the outcome of his dream, it was always the same. He couldn't fix the ending. It was set, though he tried desperately to save her. He remembered the day he took the case. Sometimes he wished he hadn't. Maybe another agent could have saved her.

"Why did you name the case 'Ribbon'?" he asked as he looked at the folder. The report had 'classified' stamped across the face of a young brunette.

"This is Sadie Harris, seventeen, from Melbourne. Witnessed her father get gunned down by one of Melbourne's underbelly gangs. The AFP has her under

225

protection until the trial. You're the leading agent, Bale. You've got Agent Dawson as your case partner. You've worked together a few times. This is a high-priority case. Her testimony will send a couple of the gang leaders to prison. You need to keep the Ribbon alive." Patrick Bale looked up at his team leader, Frank Riley, and composed himself. The young girl's file photo was drawing him in.

"You didn't answer my question, Frank. We don't code name our assignments. We're not Special Ops."

"She's an exception. She wears a ribbon necklace that her father gave to her for her sixteenth birthday. When you talk about this case, you reference her as the Ribbon. Got it? No one outside of us knows about the necklace. It has a small GPS tracking device in it. We can't let them get her. You can't let her die. We need to keep her alive and get her on that stand. Dawson will be joining us in the next hour for a briefing. She knows about the Ribbon codename but not the tracker. You need to gain this girl's trust. The last trial her father handled was the prosecution of some AFP agents tied with the Melbourne ganglands. She doesn't trust anyone with a badge, Bale. Protect her and make sure she comes out alive." Frank opened the top drawer of his desk and put his gun in it with a sigh.

"Understood. Why isn't Dawson filled in on the GPS?"

"The more people know, the more at risk she is. The girl's testimony could clean up the streets of Melbourne for good. Take her out to the safe house and have her monitored." Frank explained before turning his attention to another file on his desk. "She won't live a normal life once this trial finishes. The moment it ends, Sadie Harris disappears. She will become *Rachel Sims.*"

Patrick nodded and skimmed her file. Sadie Harris, grades that put her in the top 5% in the state, a popular and active member of the social scene. It would be hard for her to disappear.

❧

Patrick walked with Agent Miranda Dawson towards the unmarked black SUV. Dawson's short heels clicked as she read through Sadie Harris's file. There was no hint of emotion on her face. She was composed, her ashy blonde hair tied up in a low ponytail and her black suit impeccable, without a foreign fibre on it. Patrick walked over towards the driver's side door and opened it. He slipped in and adjusted the rearview mirror until a pair of lost and faded brown eyes met his.

"Hi." Her small voice was barely a whisper. Patrick observed Sadie as she sat there. Her body tensed as she looked at him and then at Dawson.

"You must be Sadie," Patrick smiled. He knew the only way to gain her trust was to be kind. She would need it after what she'd been through. "I'm Agent Patrick Bale. This is my partner, Agent Miranda Dawson." Sadie smiled up at Patrick before the smile faded at the sight of Dawson.

"You shouldn't be sitting out in the open, Miss Harris. You need to be careful. Next time, you don't leave without any officers or agents by your side. What are you even doing in an unsecured location?" Dawson turned in her seat and glared at Sadie. Patrick guessed that she didn't like Sadie's surprise appearance. It wasn't procedure.

Sadie squinted her eyes and breathed out heavily.

"I snuck away from my complimentary tour of this

prison. They pointed out that my bags were packed in this car and it didn't take much to just walk off. You lot don't run a tight shift around here, do you? Cars unlocked, witnesses running away. To think, my life is in your hands." Sadie let out a short laugh as she shook her head. "Do you really think those gangsters are going to assassinate me in the parking lot of the Australian Federal Police headquarters? Do your research, Agent Dawson. If they wanted me dead, they would do it in public. They would want a public execution. It sends a message." Sadie smirked at Dawson before she leaned back into the car seat, completely satisfied with herself. The girl had done *her* research. Patrick was impressed.

"You'd make a great AFP agent," Patrick chuckled as he started the car. He noticed the irritation on Dawson's face as he pulled out of the car park and exited towards the safe house.

Patrick parked the SUV on the dirt path that led to the beat up wooden cottage. The planks were worn with time and the Australian climate, and the tin on the veranda was as rusty as the nails that held the wooden planks in place. The grass resembled the rest of town: dried up.

When Patrick removed the keys and got out of the car, the blistering summer heat hit his skin instantly. He heard the sound of both doors open and shut behind him as he looked over the property. The drive from Canberra should have taken them an hour, but it had taken them three. Patrick didn't want to take any risks. He had gone through every small town and down every lonely road he could to ensure they weren't followed.

"Wow, the AFP really splashed out for me. Royal treatment. I am so lucky," Sadie sassed. Patrick turned to see a teasing smile on her face before she winked. He let out a laugh and noted the necklace twinkling in the sunlight. *The Ribbon had to live.* He felt himself tense and reminded himself of the mission. Sadie Harris had to live.

Patrick heard his partner's phone ring and he turned to find her giving him a cold stare. He heard a 'yes, sir' and a 'copy that' before Dawson hung up.

"Perimeter's been checked and the house has been swept. We have two agents stationed in Gudgenby who are able to get here in three and a half minutes if we need them," Dawson said. He watched her return her phone to her jacket pocket as she, too, inspected the cottage before returning to the car to remove the supplies. Dawson was the type of agent who followed the rules. Her father had been the Deputy Commissioner of National Security. Being a federal agent ran through their bloodline.

"Home, sweet home," Sadie sighed.

"It's only for a little while, Sadie. We'll get you to Melbourne safely, I promise," Patrick said. Sadie bit her bottom lip as she inspected Dawson.

"I trust you," she said as she hoisted her bag on to her shoulder. Patrick could tell Sadie didn't trust Dawson, and he wouldn't push her to, either.

Patrick led the way up the unpaved path, dust and dirt sticking on to his black suit pants with every step he took. The wooden steps creaked under his weight as he walked towards the front door. The fly screen resembled the rest of the house: old and worn.

Patrick waited until Sadie caught up. He wiped his sweaty forehead with the back of his hand and hoped that retreating into the cottage would bring them some relief from the harsh sun.

"Of all the towns in this country. There's more wildlife than people, and more tumbleweeds than I can count. When did the AFP get all Western?" Sadie raised an eyebrow. If Patrick had had a sister, he imagined she'd be the image of Sadie Harris.

"For a girl in these circumstances, you sure like to joke around," Dawson said coldly as she walked up the creaky steps. The smile on Sadie's face vanished and Patrick noticed the flare in her nostrils.

"Would you rather I cry, Agent Dawson?" Sadie asked. He could see Dawson's body stiffen. "I didn't ask for my father to be gunned down in front of me. I've had enough of crying, and being seen as weak. Don't try to deny it! You see me as inferior because I'm not some sort of agent. Well, you know what? I'll laugh. I'll live whatever normal life I can get. At least I'll die without a stick up my ass!" Patrick stifled the laugh that rumbled in his chest. He cleared his throat.

"Pull in the claws, Dawson." The warning tone in his voice was met with a nod. Sadie grinned and Patrick let out a sigh before taking out the key. After a short struggle, he finally unlocked the door. Inside the cottage, the furniture was covered by large, dust-coated sheets of plastic. Cobwebs lined the frames of the windows and the air smelt stale.

"Sadie, why don't you go choose a room? Agent Dawson and I will get this place secured." Patrick asked kindly. Sadie nodded.

Patrick waited until he heard a door shut before glancing over at Dawson. She looked pissed off, but Patrick didn't like her attitude towards Sadie either. After reading the case and knowing what was to come for

Sadie, Patrick felt a paternal need to save her. His wife, Trudy, recently learned she was pregnant and the thought of losing his own child to a gang made him sick. In all his years in the witness protection service, he had never come across a young woman like Sadie. He had met smaller children, but they still had their mothers or fathers. Sadie had no family left.

"Don't look at me like that, Patrick," Dawson scolded. His shoulders fell and he removed his jacket. He pulled the plastic covering off an old armchair and placed his jacket over the arm.

"Cut the kid a break," he said. Dawson apparently didn't like his answer.

"Why should I?"

"Because I said so, Miranda. She had her father gunned down in front of her. She's a teenager. She should be in school, not hiding from gangsters."

"Dying is a part of life," she retorted.

"Your father is still alive, hers isn't. She has no family and she is putting her life in our hands. Don't be so by-the-book with her. Be compassionate, for Christ sakes, Miranda." He knew she didn't like him using her first name. Dawson believed her name was too feminine for the work they did. With a surname like Dawson, she felt like she had the respect she deserved.

"She's going to get herself killed with that mouth of hers, Patrick. This case is a joke. She's a joke." Patrick's jaw clenched. Dawson had crossed the line.

"You know what's a joke? Your attitude. You're an agent. You take whatever case you are assigned. What are you even doing in the AFP? Every case is important. You don't decide what case is worthy of your time and what case isn't. If I hear you even criticising this case, your job, your superiors or Sadie, I will report you to

Internal Affairs for misconduct! I won't hesitate, Miranda. I've been in this business far longer than you have and you have a duty of care to that girl. You hear me?" Patrick threatened.

Dawson flinched and took a step back. She straightened her jacket and her posture. It was a nervous tick she had when she felt threatened by a higher authority. Deep down, Patrick knew she had only joined the AFP to acquire her father's love.

"Fine. If this goes downhill, Patrick, it's your ass on the line."

The sound of crickets filled the night. The still air was as dry as it had been during the hot day. Nights were the loneliest moments of Patrick's job. He missed his wife, being able to hold her as she slept, having his hand on her stomach, and sometimes, when he was restless, he missed speaking to the baby that grew inside. Patrick looked over towards the old armchair to see Dawson reading over Sadie's file.

Patrick stood and knocked on the door of Sadie's room. Only silence answered him. He knocked again. His instincts told him to reach for the gun in his holster, but reasoning made him reach for the door handle instead.

Unlike the rest of the cottage, her bedroom door did not creak. Patrick peered into her room to find it empty. He drew his gun slowly and carefully tiptoed towards the open window. Adrenalin coursed through Patrick's veins, making him feel fearless and composed. Patrick reached the window and pointed his gun out as he scanned the horizon. There were no cars out on the open land. His heart pounded until he looked down.

Relief flooded his system when he saw Sadie sitting on a blanket looking out in the distance. He returned his gun to its holster and climbed out the window. He landed on his feet right near Sadie. She didn't seem startled.

"Took you a while to find me," she said without turning to meet his concerned face.

"You should have told me if you wanted to sit outside, Sadie."

"Not gonna tell the fuzz, are you?" she joked, and Patrick let out a laugh.

"Technically, I am the fuzz." Patrick shifted slightly on the blanket. They sat there in silence and looked up at the stars. Patrick thought of his wife and frowned at the thought of her going through the pregnancy alone. Soon he'd have a child and he wanted to make sure his little son or daughter had a father he or she could depend on.

"You're frowning, Agent Bale," Sadie said.

"I'm not. I'm just thinking," he replied.

"Thinking about your wife?" Patrick turned and watched Sadie draw up her legs, wrapping her arms around them and resting her chin on her knees. "Tell me about her?" Sadie asked sweetly. Patrick let out a hum and rested his hands on either side of him.

"Her name's Trudy. Met her in high school, we fell in love, and I married her after I graduated from the AFP college. She'd been right there even when people told her not to stay with me. I told her to give up that white picket fence dream, but she stayed with me and I've tried my best to be a good husband. She's pregnant with our first child." Sadie didn't lift her head off her knees but he could see her smile in the light the moon offered.

"Are you telling me this much because you think you owe it to me?" Sadie unwrapped her arms and shifted to face him. She had a soft smile and played with the ribbon necklace that was around her neck. He was tempted to tell her to be careful but he had been assured that the GPS chip was resistant to shock and water.

"Actually, none of my cases have ever asked me about my life. Guess it's just nice." Sadie offered a smile and he smiled right back. He liked her. There was a light in her that drew him in. "Before it all happened, what did you want to do with your life, Sadie?" He watched her go still before a sad smile touched her face.

"I wanted to be a psychologist. Be an expert in facial expression and body language, like Paul Ekman. I liked noticing the faults in people's body language. My dad's a..." Sadie paused and her head dropped before she looked back and smiled. Patrick saw her eyes water. "Was... my dad *was* a crown prosecutor. He was a damn good one too. He could always tell who was a liar and who wasn't." Patrick froze for a moment.

"You're talking like you're not going to do these things," Patrick said. He could see it all for her. He could see her in university and he saw her living her life. He had to make sure she lived. "Sadie, they aren't going to get you. Dawson and I will make sure you get to the trial safely and become Rachel Sims. You will become a psychologist, and even if you don't want to be one after all of this, you can be whatever you want. You will live a long and happy life, Sadie." Silent tears fell down her cheeks and she gave him a tight smile.

"You weren't there," she whispered. Patrick kept quiet and his silence gave her the cue to continue.

"Dad and I, we were talking about my upcoming final exams. We were out for lunch and I already had an early acceptance into Melbourne University. I hadn't told him because I thought I'd save the good news for when he was down. But I never got the chance, because the moment we hit the corner a car stopped in front of us. I felt Dad try to push me back, but then shots were fired and I felt blood hit my hand. He was shot five times. Five. Dad fell backwards on the concrete and I just stood there. That gangster pointed the gun at me and smiled. Told me that he'd get me when he was good and ready. For being the daughter of the crown prosecutor, I had to die as well. My death would be slow and torturous because I was pretty and innocent-looking. He'd enjoy killing me. Bring me back to life if he had to, until I got to the edge of death again. He promised I'd be begging him to kill me."

Patrick held the grip of his gun tightly. This information wasn't in Sadie's case file. She must never have told anyone.

Sadie shrugged her shoulders and stood up, then looked down and reached her hand out to him.

"I've accepted my fate, Patrick." He took her hand and she helped him up. "Want to play cards?" she asked before he could tell her she was wrong. He nodded and let go of her hand. He frowned before faking a smile. Securing his gun properly in its holster, he rested his hand on Sadie's shoulder. She was going to come out alive, he'd make sure of it.

ço

In the three days that they waited for the trial, they played cards and listened to the small battery-operated radio they had. No phones and no Internet access meant it was impossible for them to be traced.

Dawson had said little during those three days but in the last twenty-four hours she had seemed nervous. She spent more time cleaning her gun than she did reading Sadie's file. There was something in the air that left a sour taste in Patrick's mouth.

The trip to Melbourne would take eight hours of nonstop driving. Patrick opened Sadie's passenger door and she looked up from the book she was reading. She rested it on her lap and tilted her head up at him. "Agent Bale?"

Patrick looked down to see the ribbon necklace fastened around her neck and he breathed out in relief. If anything should happen, he'd be able to find her. He closed the door before slipping into the front seat.

Patrick looked over at Dawson. Beads of sweat were forming on her forehead, so he turned on the air conditioner. He adjusted the mirror until Sadie's eyes looked back at his. He could see she sensed something wrong. Her eyebrows met and she looked over at Dawson. Patrick tensed before he put the car into reverse. They travelled out from the outskirts of town until they turned on to the main street.

When they went over the bridge that signalled that they had exited Gudgenby, Patrick looked in the rear view mirror and noticed a black sedan with Victorian plates behind them. He swallowed hard and memorised the plate numbers. Patrick turned to tell Dawson to run the plates, but she was sound asleep.

Patrick reached for his phone on the dash, when he heard the car behind him rev up and slam into the back of the SUV at an excessive speed. Patrick saw Sadie's eyes open and she held on to the door handle tight as he tried to get the car back under control.

The force of the impact pinned Patrick against the car

door as he tried and struggled to control the vehicle. The SUV skidded across the empty highway until it hit a small post on the side of the road. Patrick reached up to touch a warm wetness on his forehead. When he looked down he saw blurry red on his fingers and he could hear a ringing in his ears.

He unbuckled his seat belt, his head feeling light and his body in heated pain. He heard the sound of the back door opening and then a muffled scream.

"Sadie? Sadie!" Patrick turned and winced, finding the back seat empty.

He looked in the rear view mirror to see two men carrying Sadie towards the black car. She looked to be fighting but they were too strong for her. Patrick heard the sound of a click and he turned to his right.

"Dawson," he said into the barrel of her gun. She had blood running down the side of her face but she had a look of determination and rage in her eyes. Patrick watched as she removed her seatbelt.

"Shouldn't have gotten close to her, Patrick," she said. He swore he saw two Dawsons and two guns pointed at him. He swallowed and blinked hard in an attempt to clear his vision.

"You follow us, she's dead. I know how much you want her to live. Even if you tried, you wouldn't find where he takes her." There was so much anger and resentment in Dawson's eyes that he didn't understand.

"Why are you doing this, Miranda?" Patrick breathed out in utter disbelief.

She let out a short laugh, "You want to know why I hate that little brat you want to save? Those agents her father convicted, I loved one of them! My father told me I was a dishonour to my badge and the Commonwealth for not turning in a dirty agent. Even though he's retired

237

he thinks he can still dictate my career!" Dawson's hand squeezed her gun as she breathed in sharply.

"I've done nothing but be in my father's shadow in the AFP. Salvatore offered me a chance to show my worth and show my father what real dishonour is about. I don't care about the money. All I want is my father's face in the media trying to explain what happened to his little girl!" Dawson yelled.

The black car pulled up beside them and the window rolled down. Patrick recognised a man with silver eyes and tattooed arms from the case file. Vincent Salvatore, Mark Harris's murderer. Dawson exited the car without lowering her gun. She wiped the blood off her face, walked over to the black car and opened the door. Patrick didn't see it coming and neither did Dawson. A loud gunshot erupted in the air and Patrick watched Miranda Dawson get shot, point blank, in the chest. Blood poured out of Dawson's wound.

Patrick's hand automatically reached for his gun as his eyes met Salvatore's. The gang leader winked before running his index finger along his throat. Patrick's breathing tightened, and he forced himself to leave the gun where it was.

The black car sped off. The ringing in his ear started to silence and his head slowly stopped spinning. He went around to the boot of the car and lifted it open. He found the first aid kit, rummaging through until he found the bottle of painkillers he needed.

He swallowed them dry and looked down to see Dawson's lifeless body on the ground. Patrick felt disgust and betrayed as he looked into her wide eyes. He'd call it in, but he was in no rush. She was dirty. Her father was all about anti-corruption within the AFP, but his own daughter was the dirtiest of them all.

Patrick hovered over her body before he searched through her pockets and retrieved her badge. No matter how dirty she was, her badge had to be returned to her father out of respect.

Patrick felt numbness take hold of his body. He walked back around the car and slipped inside, finding his phone sitting in the corner of the dash virtually unharmed. He unlocked it and clicked on the GPS tracker. He waited those slow seconds until the GPS stopped searching and pinpointed Sadie's location. They had her near the banks of the river just ten minutes away. That's all they had - a ten-minute lead. If what Sadie had told him all those nights ago was true, then Salvatore wanted to slowly torture her. He had time to save her.

He turned the key in the ignition and he heard the car struggle for a second before it came to life. He mentally thanked God and slammed his foot down on the accelerator.

Everything ahead of and beside him blurred as he sped down the highway. He kept glancing at his phone to see that the red dot had not changed location. He felt doubt in the pit of his stomach, but he had to believe that Salvatore would deliver on his promise.

Patrick slowed down when he was only meters from Sadie's location. He sat there for a moment and thought of Trudy. He tried to remember the last time he told her he loved her, thanked her for their marriage and for her love. He mentally told Trudy he loved her and that he would come home to his family. He took his gun from its holster, readying it. With a deep breath, his hand found the door handle and he opened it. He was determined to fire the first shot undetected. From the metal railing of the small bridge that blocked the river from the road, he spotted two men near the edge of the river. He jumped over the railing and slowly stepped down the incline until he was on levelled ground.

Salvatore was holding Sadie's face in the river. Patrick could see her struggling to lift her head up as her nails scratched at the gangster's arms. Patrick wanted to pull on the trigger and wipe the smile from his face. He gripped his gun tighter. He had to be careful. Salvatore was too close to Sadie for Patrick to fire a clear shot. She coughed and choked when the bastard pulled her up by the hair, then threw up whatever she could. As Patrick slowly approached them, he could see the tears streaming from her eyes as her ribbon necklace glistened from the water.

"Do it! Go on. Shoot me! There isn't anything I want more in this damned world than for you to kill me. But just know my blood will forever stain your conscience. Can you live with that?" Sadie tried to provoke the man. Salvatore just cackled as he bent down and ran the tip of his pistol along Sadie's face.

"Oh, you thought I was joking? Princess, I'm going to enjoy killing you. Your Daddy cost me some good men. He could have joined me, but he was against me. Had to be honourable, didn't he? Thought you were safe? With the fucking AFP? I run the AFP! I have dirty agents in the heart of every operation. Dawson wanted to show her Daddy what a big girl she was. Her daddy issues got her killed. Oh, to see her face when she was shot - priceless. But you... oh, princess, I'm going to enjoy every minute we share together." Salvatore tucked his gun into his waistband before pulling Sadie's hair back.

Before Patrick even had time to breathe, Salvatore pulled out a knife and plunged it deep into Sadie's shoulder. She let out a squeal as he carefully twisted it.

Sadie's high-pitched screams filled the air as Salvatore pulled it out slowly before driving it back into her flesh.

"Just kill me!" Sadie begged. Patrick looked over her body. She was covered in small knife wounds on her arms and on her legs. He felt violently sick. His nose flared, anger coursing through him. He needed to pull the trigger and kill this twisted son of a bitch.

Patrick didn't duck or hide. He walked forward, drawing his gun up higher. Without a hint of hesitation, he fired two shots that entered the back of Salvatore's accomplice. Patrick watched him drop dead as Salvatore laughed.

"I needed him dead anyway, thank you, Agent. Nice shootin' by the way. I need men like you," Salvatore stated as he faced Patrick. His grip on Sadie's hair tightened. "Vincent Salvatore," he introduced himself with a wicked smile.

"I know who you are, let her go!" Patrick demanded. He looked over to see the knife still stuck in Sadie's shoulder. Her face was turning white as she bit down on her lip.

"Oh, now why would I go and do that? I'm having too much fun, Agent." Salvatore's hands returned to the handle of the knife and he twisted it again. Sadie let out a strangled scream as the sadist took out the knife with a satisfied smile. His tongue licked the length of the blooded blade.

"I said, let her go!" Patrick gave out his final warning. Salvatore let go of Sadie's hair, threw the knife into the river and took his gun out.

"Come and take her from me!" Salvatore challenged him with a smirk. Patrick looked over at Sadie. Her eyelids were starting to slowly close.

"Sadie!" he yelled. Her eyes opened wide in shock

and Salvatore whipped his head towards her.

This was his chance. Patrick pulled the trigger, the bullet entering Salvatore's chest.

Salvatore let out a loud laugh. "Silly agent." Salvatore fired a shot into Sadie's stomach.

"Sadie!" Patrick yelled, but he could see the shock in her eyes. She had already lost a lot of blood. The bullet in her stomach just limited her chances of surviving her injuries.

Before Patrick had time to react, Salvatore fired another bullet into Sadie's stomach, just centimetres from the first one.

The impact of the shot made Sadie fall on to her back, her eyes closing as the blood poured out. Patrick fired three more shots in disbelief and anger. Salvatore wouldn't move with four bullets in him. He fell to the ground.

Patrick kicked Salvatore's gun away and rushed over to Sadie, crouching over her. Her clothes were drenched in blood and her skin was pale. He could sense he was losing her. He had never made a friend on a case before. He had wanted Sadie to be one of his success stories. She deserved a life outside the underbelly.

"Sadie," he cried out as he applied pressure on the gunshot wounds in her stomach. He heard her groan at the pressure he was putting and felt relief. He pulled out his phone and dialed the first number programmed in it. It didn't take long for the agent on the other side to pick up.

"Sadie's shot. Dawson's dead. Twenty-five minutes from Gudgenby, she's dying! Send help!" Patrick shouted before he hung up. He felt his own tears fall. He couldn't stop the blood pouring out from her. He was so concerned with her gunshot wounds that he forgot her knife wounds. Patrick lifted his hands up and saw they were stained with her blood. He felt his own body shake.

"Come on, Sadie. Stay with me, help is coming. Don't die, Sadie. Don't die!" he cried as he returned his hands to her stomach. He felt her breathing stop and he shook her, screaming out her name until she opened her eyes.

"Stay with me, Sadie. Please, think about being a psychologist and meeting my kid. You've got to live, Sadie. Keep your eyes open! Stay with me!" She lifted her hand and held on to his forearm.

"I'll stay, Patrick, but only for a little while... Just for a little while," she said softly before she slowly closed her eyes.

"Paddy! Paddy, wake up!" Trudy nudged Patrick awake. It had been a year since Sadie Harris's case. A year of nightmares, a year of dreams that consisted of Sadie's blood on his hands.

The nights since her case had closed had been the worst of his life. That was, until his baby girl was born four months ago. He never spoke about his cases to Trudy but Sadie's case had removed him from the world. Her case was the first and only one Patrick had spoken so openly about to his wife.

He was ordered to appear and testify at an anti-corruption tribunal after Dawson's betrayal of the AFP.

"Paddy, you promised you'd go today. You need to," Trudy said as she kissed his forehead. He lifted himself on to his elbows and looked at the date on his phone. It was the one-year anniversary.

❧

Patrick walked along the grass until he reached it. He took a deep breath and looked at the flowers in his hand. He had been here exactly a year ago. He read the words that would always pain him.

In loving memory of Sadie Felicity Harris.
27 June 1995 – 14 November 2012.
Forever free.

Under the shade of the large oak tree, he crouched down and rested the flowers on her headstone. He looked at either side of Sadie's grave to see her mother's and father's graves. A whole family, killed. He looked at his watch and stood up straight. Patrick heard footsteps behind him and he reached for his gun. Turning, he saw a blonde woman in a blue jacket holding flowers before him. She gave him a smile and he stepped aside.

"Did you know her?" she asked softly as she placed her bouquet with Patrick's.

"Enough to name my child after her," Patrick explained. The blonde turned around with a look of shock on her face before a proud smile appeared. "Amelia Sadie Bale," he finished. Her brown eyes watered.

"Well, Sadie would have been very honoured by that name. It's lovely."

They both stood there for a second looking at Sadie's grave.

"If she were alive, what do you think she would be doing with her life right now?" Patrick asked. He turned to see a bright smile on the blonde's face.

"Me and Sadie were close. We were practically the same person. If she were alive, Sadie would have joined me in the psychology department at Cambridge in the UK. You know, studying body language and facial expressions." Patrick let out a laugh as she winked at him.

"Agent Patrick Bale, Australian Federal Police." He said as he held out his hand towards the blonde.

"Rachel Sims." She took his hand and shook it with a grin. Patrick looked down to see a ribbon necklace fastened around Rachel's neck. He felt the peace in him settle. It was time to stop pretending.

The Ribbon was alive.

❧

The truth is, Len Webster is a romance-loving Melburnian with dreams of finding her own chance at love. She calls Australia home, but secretly wishes a man with a beautiful accent would whisk her away. She's been called a hopeless romantic and a firm believer of happily ever afters, which she doesn't object to. When Len isn't acting as the voice of her characters, you can find her drowning in business textbooks as she slaves over her Bachelor degree. You can follow Len's writing at https://www.facebook.com/lennwebster.

About LitWorld

The *Library of Dreams* is published in support of LitWorld, a 501(c)3 non-profit literacy organization fostering resilience, hope, and joy through the power of story. All profits from the sale of the *Library of Dreams* will be donated to support projects like LitCamp, World Read Aloud Day, and Stand Up for Girls, a campaign which mobilizes girls and boys, men and women, to advocate for every girl's right to tell her story to change the world. By learning to read, write and share their stories, girls understand that their words have the power to create monumental change.

For more information on LitWorld, please visit http://litworld.org/.

www.ingramcontent.com/pod-product-compliance
Lightning Source LLC
Chambersburg PA
CBHW021028130626
46552CB00005B/1729